Alfred Duggan was bo
American descent: his
Hinds, was born in Illi
grandmother (born in A
appointed Consul Gene......................aggan was taken to
England at the age of two. After his education at Eton
College and Balliol College, Oxford, he worked for the
British Natural History Museum, collecting specimens. At
the age of twenty-one he sailed in the 600-ton barquentine,
St George, from England via Madeira, Trinidad and Panama
to the Galapagos Islands, pursuing his job for the museum.
In later years he travelled extensively in Greece and
Turkey, studying Byzantine monuments, and in 1935
helped to excavate Constantine's Palace, Istanbul, under the
auspices of the University of St Andrews. From 1938 to
1941, when he was discharged as medically unfit, he served
in the London Irish Rifles (TA) and saw active service in
Norway. For the rest of World War II he worked in an
aircraft factory.

A prolific writer, Duggan turned out more than one book
a year. His first was *Knight with Armour*, written in 1946
and published in 1950. Next came his novels *Conscience
of the King* and *The Little Emperors*, the latter dealing in
lively fashion with the decline and fall of the western
Roman Empire as it impinged upon the life of a British civil
servant. 'As one novel follows another in pleasant succession', wrote Thomas Caldecot Chubb in the *New York
Times*, 'it dawns upon this constant reader of historical
fiction that in Alfred Duggan he has found an extremely
gifted writer who can move into an unknown period and
give it life and immediacy.' 'A specialist in decline and fall',
in *The Lady for Ransom* he dealt with one of the great crises
of Byzantine politics. 'Mr Duggan's characters are sharply
drawn', wrote Chubb, 'and, as always, he keeps his eye on
the flow of history'. His 'cheerful cynicism' and satirical
view of men and politics 'have introduced a refreshing new
element into current historical fiction'. Orville Prescott
wrote in the *New York Times*, 'Mr Duggan looks upon the
past with a connoisseur's relish of villainy and violence'.

Alfred Duggan died in 1964.

FAMILY FAVOURITES

Alfred Duggan

PHOENIX

A PHOENIX PAPERBACK

First published in Great Britain in 1960
by Peter Davies Ltd
This paperback edition published in 2007
by Phoenix,
an imprint of Orion Books Ltd,
Orion House, 5 Upper St Martin's Lane,
London WC2H 9EA

1 3 5 7 9 10 8 6 4 2

A CIP catalogue record for this book
is available from the British Library.

ISBN-13 978-0-7538-1825-1

Typeset by Deltatype Ltd, Birkenhead, Merseyside

Printed and bound in Great Britain by
Clays Ltd, St Ives plc

The Orion Publishing Group's policy is to use papers
that are natural, renewable and recyclable products and
made from wood grown in sustainable forests. The logging
and manufacturing processes are expected to conform to
the environmental regulations of the country of origin.

www.orionbooks.co.uk

CONTENTS

PROLOGUE

It is really most extraordinary that I am alive, and as far as I can see reasonably safe, at the age of forty-five. All the same, a few years ago I had to make a fresh start, in a land where my past would be unknown. I have settled down here, in northern Britain, just fifteen miles within the Wall. The climate is horrible, but in other respects the situation suits me. I live in the province, but four hours' walking will get me outside it; and if the police should try to follow me, well, the auxiliaries in the forward blockhouses stand in some awe of a veteran from the regular army; with any luck they would cover my tracks.

So here I am, a genuine time-expired Praetorian with an honourable discharge. That entitled me to a grant of a few acres of ploughland. My fields do not produce very much; how should they, when I don't know the first thing about farming? But the holding carries grazing-rights on the hill, and I do know something about animals. The oxen and pack-horses I breed for the army bring in quite a decent income, provided I watch for the right moment to sell them. The art is to send them into camp when you know the quartermaster has money; because of course soldiers need transport all the year round, and requisition the beasts if the pay-chest happens to be empty. To make money out of dealing with the army needs good contacts; I have them.

Soon after I settled here I married a local girl, whose family acquired citizenship only under Caracalla. But she can trace her descent from landowners who were gentry when the Brigantes were free, before the Empire had been extended into Britain. If you look only at the Celtic side, her family is as good as mine. Now I have two sons. I am writing this account of my ancestry and my own adventures so that when they are grown up they will know they come of good stock.

CHAPTER ONE

Early Days

Y ou may think it odd that a mere Praetorian can write easily
enough to compose his memoirs; in general we are a rough
lot. But then, though I am proud of my standing as a veteran,
there can be no denying that it was a come-down when I
enlisted; though at the time it seemed to be the only sensible
course. So I must tell about my family.

My father was a citizen and landowner in a backwater of
provincial Gaul, the canton of the Pictones. To real Romans
from Italy I suppose we would have seemed very rustic and
barbarous; but in our own district we were respected. It may
surprise an Italian to learn that we could trace our ancestors for
more than three hundred years, but many of the surrounding
landowners could do the same. Our pedigree was quite genuine,
and if necessary could have been proved in a court of law; Gauls
take pride in good Gallic descent, even those who are Latin-
speaking citizens. Our ancestry was the most important thing
about us; for as landowners we were poor, only just above the
peasants who plough their own land.

It is more than 250 years since the Divine Julius brought
Gaul within the Empire; and at the same time founded the
mediocrity (I cannot call it greatness) of the Julii Duratii. At that
time a certain Duratius was chief of the Pictones; you will find
his name in the continuation of Caesar's *Commentaries* written
by Aulus Hirtius. This Duratius took oath to Caesar, and served
his lord loyally through all the Gallic Wars. As a result he kept
his estates under the Empire; and transmitted his chieftaincy, by

3

this time merely a social distinction, to his elder son. For more than a century the Duratii Pictones were very great men; in fact too great, for they came to the notice of the government. In the terrible Year of the Three Emperors the chief was not quite quick enough in changing sides. Otho took his head; and when Vespasianus had beaten Otho the family estate remained in the imperial fisc.

But the Duratius who followed Julius Caesar had also a younger son, who served as an auxiliary in the Roman forces and received the citizenship at his discharge. This Julius Duratius (for of course he joined the gens of his patron) inherited a little portion of his father's land, just enough to allow him to live without working. He was a citizen, in days when that was still a distinction; and his elder brother, though a mere provincial, was a man of great influence among the restless Gallic tribesmen. The police and the tax-gatherers dared not disturb him. When he died of old age his son succeeded him. Since then no member of my family has earned a living by working with his hands.

The common people respected us because we were descended from the ancient Gallic nobility; even Romans respected us a little because though we were not rich we were truly independent. Very few real Romans are genuinely independent, for they must seek the protection of some powerful patron. We had no patron save the Emperor.

I was the only son of my father, though I had an elder sister. At the time I was born inland Gaul, away from the German frontier, was more prosperous and peaceful than it had ever been. There were no bandits, no foreign raiders, no garrisons; we seldom saw a soldier, and though the taxes were heavy everyone had grown used to them. Our land was farmed by three competent tenants, who paid their rent punctually. The estate would come to me one day; to enjoy it, all I had to do was to live longer than my father. Best of all, in the eyes of the government we were country folk. Some of our neighbours had been persuaded to become town councillors, and found that the honour let them in for a number of expensive duties. Our way of life was very quiet, but it seemed utterly secure.

I suppose that if my father had been compelled to defend a lawsuit, the magistrate would have ranked him at the very bottom of the *honestiores*, the upper class; we held no official rank, but we paid our tax direct to the government, not to an intermediary. That is the real mark of an *honestioris*; though some civil servants hold that every mere taxpayer, who does not directly serve the state with head or hand, should be reckoned among the *humiliores*, the lower orders. But the question never arose, for we kept out of the law courts.

When I was a child we had only one worry: our income did not go as far as it used to. Prices were rising, and we could not raise our rents; in that countryside everyone knows the worth of a farm. Its value was decided when the Divine Augustus fixed the tribute of Gaul, and no one will pay more. My father kept going by cutting his expenditure, but there was nothing left over for emergencies; in particular there would be nothing to pay for all the renovations and new household gear when I grew up and brought home a bride. Reluctantly it was agreed that one day little Gaius would need to earn a salary, in addition to the ancestral rents.

That meant that I must have a proper education. But where I should go to school was a very tricky question. There were good schools in several neighbouring towns, but my father was afraid of them. Town councillors were now being held responsible for all arrears of tax from their cities, and the existing councillors were looking round for new recruits to share the burden. So far my father had escaped, though he was just the type of man who was being roped in; if he took a town house, or even sent his son to lodge regularly in a town, he would wake up one morning to find himself an unwilling decurion.

In the end I managed to get a sound education without leaving home. In our valley there happened to be a small government endowment for a free school; for the last fifty years it had been quietly embezzled by the local burial club, but when my father threatened to make trouble the peasants agreed that it should be used as the Divine Hadrianus had intended. A few other local landowners clubbed together to add to the income, and that made just enough to hire a rather seedy schoolmaster. Eutropius was a learned man, and he knew all the tricks of teaching; he boasted that at one time he had been head of a fine school at Lugdunum, and I think he was telling the truth. He was obviously anxious to live in obscurity; no friends came to see him and he never received a letter. We pupils discussed romantic theories about unsuccessful conspiracies against the Emperor; nowadays I suppose he had stolen some money somewhere.

Anyway, I learned from him to read Greek at sight, and to speak it well enough to be understood; though later, when I was in the east, I was always known for a Gaul as soon as I opened my mouth. I learned also to write correct Latin, and to make a speech in proper rhetorical form; though that was not very difficult, since in our part of Gaul we speak an old-fashioned Latin. An Italian, full of up-to-date Roman slang, finds it far harder to write the true language of Cicero. Even our tenant farmers spoke Latin of a kind, though in other parts of Gaul the ploughmen still jabber in Celtic.

It would be easy for an educated man of my standing to get a minor post in the civil service. The government would not pay me a living wage, and every few years there was a drive against corruption in the civil service, with very unpleasant punishment for those found guilty; but my rents and my salary combined would give me enough to marry on, and the work would not be exacting. When I was ten years old my sister married a clerk in the imperial fisc, and he more or less promised to get me a desk in his office when I was old enough. My future seemed assured.

In the winter of that same year the Emperor Commodus was murdered, and the long peace came to an end. It seemed at first that Pertinax would succeed him peacefully; or that any trouble would be confined to Rome, where they enjoy proclaiming and deposing Emperors. But in the spring we heard with horror and shame that Pertinax had been murdered in his turn and that the Praetorians had put up the Purple to auction, offering their swords to the highest bidder.

Didius Julianus did not last long. He had nothing to recommend him but money, and as soon as that was spent the Praetorians threw him over. The commander of the Danube, Severus, assumed the Purple at the head of twelve legions, and the commander in Syria, Niger, marched against him with nine. Albinus, the commander in Britain, stood neutral, and after the army of Lower Germany had joined him his support was worth buying. On my eleventh birthday, which falls on the 12th of June, news came that Severus, marching east to fight Niger, had recognised Albinus as Caesar; that is, as his adopted heir and second in command.

All these high politics afforded an interesting subject of conversation, but they did not promise to affect us personally in the middle of peaceful Gaul. The taxes increased, of course, to pay for all the fighting; and no luxuries came from the east. But my father screwed most of the extra tax out of his tenants, and our family did not buy eastern luxuries even in peace-time. The first sign of serious trouble did not appear until midwinter. A detachment of British soldiers suddenly descended into our valley. They loaded on to wagons all the corn they could find, and seized the plough-oxen to draw them. Of course they did not pay for what they took; soldiers never do. Instead they gave our tenants drafts on the military treasury at Eboracum. Then they withdrew northward. The boldest of our tenants set out to cash the drafts on the British treasury; but he bumped into a patrol of Severan horse, who beat him within an inch of his life for the grave crime of trading with the enemy. Albinus was still the lawful Caesar under Severus. That was why the peasant was only beaten when found in possession of drafts on the British treasury, instead of being hanged for treason.

Ours is an old-fashioned part of Gaul. Though we had enjoyed unbroken peace for more than a century the peasants

7

still remembered the old hiding-places of their ancestors; a stray patrol of dismounted legionaries could not find all the corn and cattle in our valley. We had a hungry year, and I still remember that there was no feast for my twelfth birthday; but we got through somehow until harvest.

Formal war broke out in the following winter. The British army advanced south to Lugdunum; of course as they marched they lived on the country. Again foragers visited us, and this time they were more experienced. In the next summer things were really bad. But though our tenants could pay no rent they still cultivated their familiar fields. Everyone lent a hand to save what could be saved; even my father used a hoe, and I was sent out to hunt hares and snare birds.

For fourteen months we endured war without fighting, which for the countryside is more destructive than the bloodiest campaign. The British in Lugdunum behaved like conquerors in hostile territory, and Severus was still marching back from Syria after his destruction of Niger. It was not until the February of my fifteenth year that the two armies clashed outside Lugdunum. Ten days later I came back from a day on the hill, where I had been hunting hares, to find that a gang of defeated British legionaries had pillaged our valley and killed every human being in it.

The scoundrels had already vanished, which was lucky for me; since in my then mood I might have attacked them with my hunting javelins. In fact I was just beginning to follow their trail when a section of Severan horse appeared. The horsemen were German barbarians; only their leader could speak Latin. But they had taken as guide a neighbouring landowner who knew me and could vouch that I was not a belated British straggler.

I was a better guide than the frightened elderly gentleman who had identified me. The Germans put me on a horse, and made me lead them at a gallop. My hounds were too tired to keep up, and I never saw them again. Oddly enough, at the time that distressed me more than all my other losses, I suppose because it seemed so wanton when the soldiers could easily have kept them safe for me. But then soldiers never consider the happiness of civilians when they are on campaign.

In those days, when I had been kept busy hunting to stock the family larder, I was a good horseman and quick at following tracks. Before darkness fell I had the satisfaction of seeing the plunderers punished. The Germans did not offer them quarter. They killed them one by one by casting javelins from a safe distance; until the last surviving legionary threw down his shield and knelt to beg for mercy. He would have done better to die on his feet. The Germans hung him by one hand from a tree, set him swinging, and used him as a target. Then of course they searched the corpses, and shared out all the plunder they could find. They would not give me even my mother's ear-rings, though I described them before they were found. Their leader explained that a soldier is entitled to take as booty anything found on the body of a foe he has slain; granted that the British legionaries had stolen my mother's jewels in the first place, I had seen them punished as they deserved. If I wanted compensation as well, my proper course was to bring a civil action against the treasury in Rome. He said that in my own interest I must bring the action in Rome; any complaint to the quartermaster of the Severan army would bring down on me the enmity of a number of armed and loyal troopers, an enmity which could be very dangerous to a mere civilian. Furthermore, for all he knew my parents might have been traitors, supporters of the usurper Albinus, who had willingly given their valuables to the rebel army before the stragglers murdered them.

As I discovered later, it was only by luck that the murderers had been punished at all. The Emperor's policy, as always after victory in civil war, was to grant pardon to rebel soldiers and incorporate them in his army; and this had actually been published in orders after the battle of Lugdunum. If legionaries had caught these fellow-soldiers they would have taken their booty and welcomed them into the ranks. By pure accident they had been overtaken by German auxiliaries who had lost comrades in the battle and who shared the hatred and jealousy felt by all barbarian auxiliaries for regular Roman soldiers. These men were glad of the chance to kill Romans lawfully, even though the Romans were really Britons.

The victorious army, I gathered, was short of food and especially short of draught-oxen. What army isn't, at the crisis of a campaign? So the few sheep and oxen we had found with the rest of the plunder must go straight to imperial head-quarters. It was too late to ride back to camp that night. The troopers butchered the fattest ox, and roasted it on a great fire. They gave me a generous helping of my own beef, for there was more than they could eat at a sitting; and of course they would not trouble to carry a little cold meat back to camp. The greater the need of food in the main army the more do casual foragers guzzle by themselves; unless indeed they are under stricter discipline than you can expect to find in German auxiliaries.

So that night, for the last time in my life, I derived some benefit from my ancestral patrimony. Since then I have earned, or at any rate acquired by my own efforts, every morsel of food I have eaten.

In the morning the Germans rode back to camp. Naturally they took the horse they had lent me. But by this time I was thinking of them as the last friends I had in the world, and for lack of any other object I walked after them.

I have never again seen the valley where I spent my childhood, or the ruins of the villa where I was born. Perhaps I ought to have made sure that my parents were properly buried; but they were well known and respected figures, and the neighbours would see to that as soon as the district was quiet. Besides, my ancestry is rather Gallic than Roman, as I have explained. We Gauls do not feel so strongly about the rite of burial as do the Italians and Greeks; only Jupiter-Zeus demands that his worshippers be properly buried before they can be happy in the World Below. I was brought up to worship the Three Ladies (I know their names, but I scruple to write them). The Ladies have a special affection for warriors killed in battle; and if the warriors have been killed in defence of their own hearths that gives them a stronger claim on Divine Justice. While he lived my father was no warrior; but he met an honourable death. From time to time I placate the ancestral shades, but I feel sure that all is now well with my murdered parents.

I had another sound reason for avoiding my ancestral valley. My father had died owing nearly two years' taxes, and if I tried to claim his land, there would be inheritance tax in addition. I had of course no money; the tax-gatherers would be within their rights if they sold me into slavery.

Soldiers, on the other hand, seldom bother to enslave free citizens, unless slave-dealers are jingling ready cash before them. No soldier particularly wants to be waited on by a slave, whom he may have to support when there is no work for him to do; they find it much less trouble to press free men into unpaid service, and turn them adrift when they are no longer needed. After victory the soldiers of Severus would probably have plenty of money; they would be glad to hire boys to water their horses and clean their armour.

Everyone else in central Gaul would be poor and frightened. This is how the world goes; when soldiers are rich civilians will be starving.

I was in Rome for my fifteenth birthday, as muleteer to a *principalis*, a senior non-commissioned officer in one of the Danube legions. My master had followed Severus from the start, when he first assumed the Purple; naturally, he had done very well for himself. We had three mules to carry our baggage, and could have done with a fourth. But in the autumn, when the Emperor marched east to carry on the unending war against the Parthians, we went back to our garrison on the Danube. After that we had no further need of mules, since our legion never left the camp which had been built for it by the Divine Trajanus. But while my master was selling them (a lengthy negotiation) he was transferred from his cohort to employed duty in the quartermaster's office, as a reward for long and loyal service.

His work was to check and file receipts for requisitioned transport; which he would have found a pleasant and easy job if he had not been practically illiterate. Somewhere in the regimental records he was marked as able to read and write, and that may have been true when he enlisted; but for thirty years he had never had occasion to handle a pen. It was all he could do to sign his name in large letters, sticking out his tongue as he did it. When he discovered that his muleteer was a scholar he kept me on to do the work for which he drew pay.

He was a kind and considerate master, and an experienced old soldier. He dodged his duty, but his papers and his kit were always ready for inspection and he never told a direct lie to a commissioned officer. He could sift camp rumour so that he always knew what would happen tomorrow; he took bribes if they were big enough but it was impossible to cheat him.

After three years in the office my master, who was not a greedy man, was ready to retire. I was then eighteen years old, and he offered to find me a clerkship at headquarters. These clerkships are real plums; you cannot help making money when you are ordered to requisition one ox-cart and ten peasants are anxious to pay you not to take theirs. I knew the ropes already, and in fact I had done the work. As a citizen, with some claim to the rank of *honestioris*, I was better qualified than most of the other applicants for the post; and with my master's backing I was certain to get it. I myself was rather surprised when I refused his kindly offer.

I suppose it was because I am a Gaul. Every Gaul is at the mercy of unexpected quirks of honour. What it really came down to was a feeling that it is degrading for a grown man of eighteen to push a pen for a living; if I could not own land I ought to be cutting throats. You may ask in that case why I had allowed my father to educate me for the civil service. But if all had gone well with my family I would have become a country landowner who supplemented his rent by part-time work in the governing of his native district. I would have been far above the kind of imitation soldier who carries an inkwell in his scabbard instead of a sword. That was the aspect of it that stuck in my throat: to be in the army, and to be a non-combatant.

I explained that since I was of full military age, and since my master had no further need of my services, I intended to enlist as a legionary.

That was what my master had done, all of thirty years ago. Nevertheless he considered my plan most eccentric. The army has changed during the last generation. In the old days only Latin-speaking citizens were accepted in the legions; provincials, and of course barbarian foreigners, might serve only as auxiliaries. Nowadays most recruits are the sons of old soldiers; but their fathers have settled on farms just outside the camp and married barbarian girls. Half the recruits learn Latin after they have joined the Eagles.

The law still lays down that every legionary must be a Roman citizen; but town-bred citizens won't face the life, and the recruiting officers don't welcome them. In practice any able-bodied man who looks fit enough to march will be accepted into a legion, even though he happens to have been born on the wrong side of the Danube and so is technically not even a provincial but a foreigner. In fact a sensible legate is glad to see the ranks of his legion filled by Germans, provided they are not tribal nobles whose touchy honour makes them unwilling to obey orders. Germans of the lower class are habituated to obedience; and they take the oath of allegiance seriously, since oaths of that kind are the foundation of German society. A legion of German swordsmen, officered by Romans and with a stiffening of Latin-speaking provincials as centurions and N.C.O.s, is a very fine military machine.

That was the kind of machine I joined, soon after my eighteenth birthday. I had decided, on my master's advice, to move right away from the Army of the Danube, where I might any day meet a soldier who remembered me as a clerk. The nearest place where I could make a fresh start was the Army of Upper Germany, where I took the oath to the Emperor Severus and was mustered into Legio XIV Gemina Martia. It was a first-class corps with a fine record, which had been stationed on the Rhine since the days of the Divine Tiberius.

I quickly settled down and made myself at home, even though most of my comrades regarded me as a freak. In my maniple I was the only ranker who spoke grammatical Latin as my mother-tongue, the only ranker who could read and write without effort. At first our tribune tried to push me into the quartermaster's office, and the legionaries could not understand why I should prefer marching in full armour to sitting on a padded stool under a weatherproof roof. But the ranks of any long-service corps are full of eccentrics, who must be tolerated if life in a barrack-room is to be peaceful; when I had refused not only soft employment but also promotion I was allowed to exist in peace after my own fashion.

I was left in peace partly because I was a good legionary. I may say that without boasting; bad soldiers are not chosen for the Praetorians. I was strong enough to do my share of the work and lend an occasional hand to a sick comrade; I dodged fatigues if I could, but when I had been detailed I put my weight into the digging; I kept my equipment spotless, because in those days I was vain of my appearance; I stacked all my kit in my own bedplace and never borrowed anything from a comrade without asking him first; I did not get drunk, except on the Emperor's accession day and the anniversary of the legion's founding, days on which I would have been considered mad if I had gone to bed sober.

When they tried to make me a *principalis*, the first step to becoming a centurion, I refused without thinking about it. The idea repelled me, and that was enough. Plenty of good soldiers refuse to 'go for promotion', as the saying is, because they dread responsibility, and my tribune was quickly persuaded to take No for an answer. Later, when I had thought it over for myself, I realised that I for one did not dread responsibility; when I found myself senior legionary in charge of a party I enjoyed it. Presently I understood that I had refused because my loyalty to the Emperor (it is safe to write this now) was qualified.

Severus was the darling of the army, chiefly because his first act as Emperor had been to raise our pay; he also reserved the best jobs in the civil service for retired officers and centurions, and in general favoured the soldiers in all his dealings. There was no one else whom I wanted to see Emperor in his place; and obviously for the chief task of an Emperor, which is to defend the frontiers of Rome, there was no better candidate. All the same, I was by upbringing a civilian landowner. I could not but regret the end of the Antonine Peace. I could not forget that civil war had brought death to my parents and ruin to myself, only because Severus wished to preserve the succession for his son instead of recognising Albinus of Britain as his adoptive heir.

While I stayed in the ranks I could follow orders blindly. If I took promotion I might one day have to choose between loyalty and treason, a choice I wished to avoid.

When I had served on the Rhine for eight years I was drafted in a vexillation from the XIVth to join the Emperor's army in Britain. That was serious campaigning, but under such a leader never dangerous. The Caledonian barbarians cannot face a real Roman army; our only trouble was to bring them to battle. I did my duty, and received the military decorations normally given to legionaries: bracelets, necklets, and medals to be worn on the cuirass. When the Emperor died I was among the troops who proclaimed Caracalla as his successor, and the handsome donative I then received was the beginning of my private savings. But it is not a sound plan that soldiers should be more richly rewarded at the opening of a new reign than at any other time; it makes them hope for frequent successions.

When the Emperor campaigned against the Alemanni I was transferred back to my original legion. In Germany the fighting is always stiffer than in Britain, and the Alemanni gave us plenty of hard work. For two days, after we had suffered heavy casualties, I was senior soldier of my century. After that I found it more difficult than ever to dodge promotion, but once again I stood up for my right to continue in the army as a simple legionary.

After a single campaign the Emperor left Germany and marched east to continue that everlasting Parthian War. On the Rhine we went back to our peacetime routine. I was in my thirty-fourth year, and had served fifteen years with the Eagles. The normal term of enlistment is sixteen years, and I must begin to decide my future. I could take my discharge, and settle down to farm on my allotment near the camp. Or I could sign on for another sixteen years, since I was still young and fit.

It seemed to me that in my middle thirties I would soon grow bored with the life of a veteran smallholder. It would be pleasant to lie in bed while the trumpet blew for reveille, but that kind of pleasure very quickly wears off. I would be free to spend every evening in the regimental canteen, whereas guards and duties keep a serving soldier busy two nights out of three. But my pension would not cover steady drinking thirty nights in the month, and after a couple of years all my cronies would have left the Eagles; I had seen plenty of veterans sitting about the canteen, cadging drinks from recruits, avoided as bores by every experienced soldier. I did not want to dwindle into that kind of nuisance.

On the other hand, if I took the oath for another sixteen years I would have to accept promotion. *Principales* dislike old soldiers who remain in the ranks and give advice while dodging responsibility, and if I stood on my right to remain a legionary one of them would presently charge me with disaffection. While Caracalla was Emperor we soldiers had the best of everything, but in his day no one ever wriggled out of a charge of disaffection. Yet if I accepted promotion they might detach me from the legion and post me to the interior on internal security duties. In other words I would be a policeman, arresting decent farmers because they were slow to pay their taxes; worse still, I might be made into a loathed and loathsome tax-gatherer.

I made up my mind that I would get right away from the army. I would sell my veteran's allotment (that was illegal, but done every day), and leave the frontier. Somewhere in central Gaul a steady man with a good military discharge could get a job as night-watchman to a merchant or private bodyguard to some grandee. It would be a dull life, and I did not look forward to it; but there seemed to be nothing better.

Suddenly I was offered a way out, and one that had never occurred to me. The *primus pilus*, the senior centurion of the whole legion, ordered me to report to his quarters. As soon as I got there he told me his plans.

'Duratius,' he said, as I stood at attention before him (every soldier is a good deal more respectful to a *primus pilus* than to a legate), 'within less than a year you can take your pension and go. I won't stop you. But they tell me you are thinking of signing on again, and that I won't allow. When you apply to re-enlist, someone will ask for a confidential report, and I shall advise against you. I'll tell you why, since the regulations don't permit you to ask me questions. I have no complaint against you so far. You are smart on parade, sober, willing when there is digging to be done, and never the first to run from a tight place. You have never been first in the charge either, but that only proves you are a well-trained soldier. In fact you would be a model legionary, but for one serious fault. We have followed the same Eagle for twelve years and more, and I am still not certain that you are on our side. There's no zeal in you, either for the cause of Eternal Rome or for our glorious Emperor Caracalla. The next time we charge the Germans I don't want you behind me. So now you know the worst. In a few months you leave the army – for ever.'

'Very good, sir,' I said, standing stiffer than ever. If he felt like that about me he could have me flogged to death as a malcontent; when he offered to get rid of me peacefully he was being very lenient.

'That was the right answer,' he said in a more friendly tone. 'I don't like legionaries who argue. I wish I knew what lies at the back of your mind. You are an educated man and a citizen; in the roll they have you down as doubtfully an *honestioris*. Yet you carry a sword as though you were a labourer digging a ditch at so much a foot. Everyday you earn your daily pay, and never try to do more ... And yet you want to stay in the army. I shall offer one more chance. I have been told to pick a draft for the Praetorians. I have put down your name, though of course you may refuse the honour. Take it or leave it. In either case I shall be rid of you. Either you start for Syria within three days, or at the end of the year you are mustered out of the army, with your discharge marked "no readmission". Which shall it be?'

'The Praetorians, of course, sir. And thank you for the opportunity.'

'Very well. Tomorrow you will report to the paymaster, for your papers to be brought up to date. Then take a day's leave, to put your kit and baggage in order. On the third day you will parade in full marching order, with your baggage packed and your paybook signed and balanced. You are not entitled to a government baggage-mule, but if you have a mule of your own the government muleteers will look after it. The legate will inspect the parade, so take pains with your turnout. But you always look well on parade, so that will not bother you. I wish I knew why you are content to be a parade-ground soldier. You have never done that little bit extra that would earn commissioned rank for a man of your stamp. That's all. Dismiss, and never let me see your face again.'

CHAPTER TWO

Marching to Antioch

The draft I joined on the third day was about 800 strong, the equivalent of two cohorts; for it was made up of that year's recruits to the Praetorians from the two armies of Upper and Lower Germany. Nevertheless we were commanded by a centurion, with two other centurions to help him. Of course we were to march through the peaceful interior of the Empire, and only legionaries of good character are chosen for the Praetorians. All the same, the Praetorian Praefect would have done better to send an officer of higher rank. Our three centurions were splendid soldierly figures, men in vigorous middle age who filled out their cuirasses most martially; and those cuirasses were hung all over with decorations won by valour in the field. But they regarded this peaceful march as a holiday. During their long journey from Syria to Gaul there had been no soldiers under their command, and they had got out of the habit of doing duty. So long as we answered our names in the morning, and reached our appointed billets some time before dawn, we were left very much to our own devices. Any one of us could have deserted without trouble; but then no legionary would desert while on his way to join the glorious and highly-paid Praetorians.

I had a mule to carry my baggage, and once we had got through the final ceremonial parade I hung my armour on him as well. But I slung my baldric over my handsome linen tunic, to show the world that I was a soldier on active service, a man not to be bothered by inquisitive civilian police. The whole draft together must have had nearly a thousand mules, but they were no trouble to us. I was amused to see that there was only one official muleteer from the military train; others had indeed set out from the Praetorian camp in Syria, but they had been left behind to enjoy themselves in the cities of Asia while requisitioned peasants did their work for them. We would pick them up again on our journey. Meanwhile the chief muleteer from time to time requisitioned more peasants, and sent the first lot back to their homes. It was an excellent arrangement. Muleteers of the train never bother to fit a pack-saddle properly, because they know that when they gall a beast the quartermaster will produce another. These peasants took care of our animals, for fear that if they displeased the soldiery they would be made to walk all the way to Syria.

I had a little Gallic pony to ride on the journey; most of my companions were afoot, but there were enough of us mounted to make up a small detachment of horse. It was pleasant to avoid the dusty high road by day, and yet be sure of reaching our billet by midnight. Altogether the first few days of our long march were most enjoyable.

Then as we approached Italy we left the military zone, and saw something of the civilian life of the Empire I had been defending for the last fifteen years. When I marched to Britain and back I had been in the midst of the imperial field army, which was so numerous that I had never come into contact with civilians. My military career had begun at the age of fourteen when I took service with a *principalis*; now I was thirty-four. The manner of life in the peaceful provinces seemed to have changed greatly in the last twenty years.

When I was a boy at home we hardly ever saw soldiers. But if a few of them passed through our valley my father would go out to greet them. The peasants would deliver rations in exchange for tickets which could be offset against the land-tax; and the local gentry would display their loyalty by providing free wine and cakes.

Now, as we climbed the foothills of the Alps, the peasants

were reaping the early harvest of those parts; but we saw only the half-reaped fields. Watchers on high ground shouted that soldiers were coming – we could hear their eerie calls echoing down the pass – and the rustics fled.

To me this seemed strange, though my companions saw nothing odd in it. They were all sons of soldiers, reared on the outskirts of the camp; Alpine Gaul was to them as foreign as Syria, and they were not interested in the habits of the natives. But I wanted to find out whether this fear of the army was something new. At a post-house on the road I inquired of an official courier who happened to be changing horses.

He was an elderly man, a retired trooper (Numidian horse, I should think, though he spoke passable Latin). My question interested him, and he thought a bit before answering.

'They have done this for some years now, but all the same I can remember the beginning. I have ridden this road since the days of the Divine Commodus. When I first came here the peasants were always glad to gossip with passing soldiers. Every village had a young man in the army, and they liked to hear about the wars. That's all changed now, of course. You don't take the sons of peaceful villagers into the army. Then later, when the Divine Severus marched against Albinus, his patrols foraged round here . . . Still, that was civil war, and the soldiers were hungry. The ill-feeling wore off after a year or two. The real trouble began when our present Emperor marched back to Italy after the Alemannic War. His troops were victorious, and laden with plunder, and on their way to enjoy themselves in Rome. There was really no excuse for the way they behaved. That was only three years ago, and the peasants remember it. That reminds me, a word of advice. Don't ride alone in these hills – a stone might fall on your head. Round here any sort of nag is very precious.'

'You are just setting off to ride alone, and on a much better horse than mine,' I objected.

'Ah, but the imperial post pays cash. I bought my horse in

that village over there, and they look forward to selling me another. Soldiers take animals by force, what they call *annona*.'

'But when a quartermaster levies *annona* he gives tickets, which the tax-gatherer must accept at face value. At least, that's how we do it on the frontier. I know. Once I worked in the quartermaster's office.'

'And now you are only a Praetorian. What happened? Did they change the lock of the strong-box?'

'Never mind that. I'm a soldier now, not a clerk. But I don't understand how *annona* for the transport of the imperial field army could harm these villagers. The tickets they get in exchange would pay their land-tax for years to come. At a pinch you can sell those tickets, though you lose money by it.'

'Indeed you don't understand. This wasn't the quartermaster's *annona*, with tickets given in exchange. This was private plunder. The soldiers wanted ox-carts to carry their booty, and mules to carry the German girls they were going to sell in Rome. They took every animal. Next spring I saw peasants pulling their own ploughs. That's how some of them kept alive. Others didn't.'

'Of course soldiers steal an odd mule if they can. I have never heard of them sweeping a whole village bare. Anyway, if you complain to the legate you generally get your beast back, though somehow it always seems to be impossible to identify the thief.'

'That may be true on the Rhine, where every ploughman is an old soldier or has a son in the army. In these parts they keep away from legates. Every officer is on the lookout for able-bodied men to repair the roads. A peasant who complained against a soldier would soon find himself swinging a pick, unpaid and in fetters.'

'Well, thank you for explaining. I see there won't be any dalliance with village maidens on this march.'

'Village maidens! You won't find a virgin in this countryside, and if you did she wouldn't be allowed to meet a soldier. Ride together, and keep your swords handy. If a boulder should roll down the hill on top of you, it would be very hard to fix the blame. Any messages for Lugdunum?'

A boy led out his horse and he picked up his letter-bag.

We rode carefully through the mountains, and met with no trouble. It was disappointing to travel through empty, hostile country, especially when we had been looking forward to the delights of civilisation. But Italy would be more rewarding. Unfortunately we were not routed through Rome; drafts seldom enter the City while the Emperor is absent. But we saw a number of fine towns, from Taurinium to Brundisium, and while we waited for shipping at that port they held their annual festival in honour of the Divine Trajanus.

There is no garrison of real soldiers at Brundisium, but the Emperor's ships in the harbour are commanded by a praefect of commissioned rank, who carries a sword and apes the manners of the military as much as a sailor can. He persuaded our centurions to furnish a guard of honour for the sacrifice to the Divinity of the Emperor (I suppose the centurions got a present, but they did not share it with us and I don't know how much it was). After we had done our part in the religious ceremonies we were given reserved seats in the amphitheatre; they were bad seats, right at the top, but then there were so many of us that we took up a lot of room. Some of my comrades grumbled, but I realised that the local magistrates were doing their best.

On the frontier we watch wild beast hunts, and occasionally some military offender is sentenced to fight until he is killed. But this was the first time I had seen gladiators on a big scale. From our distant seats the many duels going on at once made a fine spectacle, but of course we missed the finer points. I could not follow the details of the fencing, or see the expression on a swordsman's face as he meets death, which the experts tell me is the thing to watch for.

All the same, I was a little disappointed in the gladiators. I suppose a civilian is thrilled to see a man die by violence; but in Britain and German I had killed men, and seen others die in the ranks at my side. Besides, a soldier can very easily work up a feeling of sympathy for an over-matched swordsman; in the next battle he may himself meet a better man.

The wild beast hunt was much more interesting. The magistrates had provided a dozen bears. First these smashed up some naked criminals; then hunters carrying boarspears fought the bears. That was a most thrilling spectacle. One big brown bear killed three hunters, and fought so fiercely that the crowd begged for his life. The magistrates agreed, so the hunters caught him in a net and put him in a big cage on wheels. I envied the citizens of Brundisium, who would see him fight again while I was trudging across Asia.

Next morning we sailed for Dyrrhachium, and though it was now the beginning of winter we had a smooth and easy passage. From Dyrrhachium through Thessalonica to Byzantium we would follow the Via Egnatia, the great highway to Asia. It is a good road; beside it stand taverns and post-houses, and there are depots of provisions for the troops who pass along it daily all the year round. On such an easy journey I would as soon walk as ride, and it would have been expensive to ship my pony over the Adriatic. I sold him in Dyrrhachium, though I lost on the deal.

The Via Egnatia is always so thronged with soldiers that it is as much a part of the frontier as the Rhineland. All the civilians we met earned their living by catering for soldiers, and they were pleased to see us. In Italy we had seen the peaceful provinces, and we should march through more of them in Asia; for the present we were back in our familiar military world.

Of course we discussed what we had seen. I had been especially impressed by the gracious beauty of Brundisium, its fine amphitheatre, and the splendid imperial arch that marks the terminus of the great road. I thought how pleasant it would be to live always in such a gracious city, to see the gods and the Divine Emperor worthily honoured, to meet learned travellers and hear the gossip of all the world. The citizens, well fed, in clean tunics, appeared to me the happiest of men. I was proud to know that for sixteen years I had toiled to protect such gracious living from the rough hands of grubby barbarians.

My fellow-Praetorians did not see things in the same light. Marching beside me was a fellow named Flaccus, who had served his time in one of the Rhine legions. For three generations his family had served in the same legion, as he told every stranger within ten minutes of meeting him. He was a real professional, who could see no good in anything done by civilians.

'It's all very well,' he answered, when I had praised the Games at Brundisium. 'You may say if you like that those magistrates were generous; but they didn't really do anything. The bears fought well; bears always do. The criminals squealed most comically; that's why criminals are killed in public. The hunters were brave, because otherwise the bears would have killed them. As for the gladiators, they were too far off for me to see them properly; but I'm sure they could not face legionaries. The point is that all these people, and the bears too, were doing what they are fitted to do. The magistrates just stood about and watched, and at the end we were ordered to give three cheers for their generosity. I would have liked to belch instead of cheering; but somehow when you are lined up on parade you can't disobey a command.'

'We thanked them because they had spent a lot of money. There would have been no Games if they had not paid for the bears and the gladiators.'

'I know that, of course. But where do they get their money? Why is it that everyone who lives in a city is rich, and you never meet a peasant who has a second pair of boots? What do they do in their city that is any use to the rest of the world? They eat flour milled in the country, from grain grown in the country. The linen and wool of their clothes came from the country. The marble for their temples comes from the most outlandish places; I know, because a cousin of mine once beat up a policeman and was sentenced to the quarries. How do these townees get away with it? There must be dirty work some-where. And then honest soldiers are ordered to cheer their generosity!'

'They make things with their hands, I suppose, and a lot of them write in offices. That can be hard work, you know. I worked in an office myself when I was a boy.'

'But now you are a man you earn your living honourably by the sword. Otherwise you wouldn't be here. Soldiers and peasants, they are the only people who do anything useful. Yet somehow the townees enjoy what the peasants produce. I wish I could get to the bottom of it.'

'The Empire is full of cities, while barbarians live in villages. Surely you are proud to be a Roman?'

'I am proud to be a Praetorian, as I was proud to be a legionary. But I am not a Roman; my family is German. If I were not a soldier I would rather live among the Germans than grow corn to be taken by tax-gatherers to feed idle townees.'

'Careful, Flaccus. The tax-gatherers serve the Emperor, and the police prick up their ears when they hear anyone grumbling against high taxes.'

'The police don't interfere with Praetorians. Our job is to defend the Emperor; so long as we defend him no one minds if we grumble. Perhaps when we get out east we shall be ordered to sack one of those rich cities. Have you heard old soldiers talk about the sack of Lugdunum, after the Divine Severus had beaten the usurper Albinus? They say our present Emperor set on his Praetorians to sack Alexandria, just to teach those insolent townees not to be uppish.'

'I've heard about the sack of Lugdunum until I could scream with boredom. It's not a topic that appeals to me; my parents were killed in that campaign. When we get east I want to visit the great cities, and I hope the townees will be friendly to soldiers. There's a grove outside Antioch . . . I've heard all sorts of stories about it.'

'The townees will be friendly, while your money lasts. I have heard good reports of that brothel at Antioch. But it would be even greater fun to batter the whole place level with the ground, and set those stuck-up educated townees to scratching the earth for a living.'

I did not pursue the conversation. We would be marching side by side for many days and it was better to be silent than to quarrel. I knew that most soldiers shared Flaccus's low opinion of cities; but I myself wanted to see the wonders of the world, not to destroy them.

At Thessalonica we halted for a few days, hoping to find ships to take us across to Ephesus. But it was too wintry for sailing, and in the end we trudged on to the ruins of Byzantium, destroyed by the Divine Severus during his war with the usurper Niger; and so over the Bosporus to Nicomedia. But while we waited at Thessalonica we were shown another spectacle; its splendour finally convinced me of the worth of great cities, for only a great city could have staged it.

What we saw was a whole day of chariot-racing, an amusement common in Greek cities; though in the west everyone prefers gladiators, and Rome is the only western city rich enough to afford racing as well as blood. The Thessalonica circus is so big, a furlong from end to end, that there was plenty of room and we had good seats. My place was opposite the far turn, where thrilling accidents happen. Nobody else wanted it. The experts struggle for places near the winning post, where it is easier to lay bets and collect your winnings after the finish.

The principal race of the day was for four-horse chariots, eight times up and down the circus, a course of two miles in all. Twelve chariots started, four from each of the three factions of Thessalonica. A lot of money was at stake, and the charioteers went all out. I have never before seen anything so exciting. Only three chariots finished, but that was in accordance with the tactics of the race; their allies of the same colour had sacrificed themselves by sprinting at the start or by blocking rivals at the turn. Five other teams were pulled up when they lagged behind; but four were upset, at a cost of eight horses and a charioteer gravely injured. And it was all done by graceful young men, displaying their naked bodies to the best advantage; a much more gratifying sight than a lot of beefy hairy gladiators snorting and grunting to look fierce.

I knew something about horses, rather more than is known by the average infantry soldier. But I had never driven any kind of vehicle. This seemed to me the most magnificent sport in the world. Now that I would be in the east for a long stay I determined to get to the bottom of this business of chariot-racing.

In Nicomedia I managed to sneak another half-day at the races, which are held frequently in all eastern cities. But we were marching fast, on the last lap of our journey. At the beginning of autumn we had left the Rhine; now the grass had started to grow. We must hurry if we were to reach Antioch in time for the spring campaign.

We came down through the Cilician Gates in the first days of April. A day's march from Antioch we went into camp to clean our armour and draw new boots for our ceremonial arrival at imperial headquarters. When the great day came we fell in on parade in review order, with extra special attention to turnout; after the inspection we got ready to march off.

Just then a courier galloped up in a great hurry and spoke to the centurion in command. He stood us at ease while he talked with the other centurions and a few of the senior *principales*. Then we were once more called to attention, while he gave out fresh orders.

'Soldiers, the Purple is vacant. The news has just reached Antioch that yesterday our beloved Caracalla was murdered, as he rode to worship the Sun in the great temple at Carrhae. In this dangerous crisis the joint Praetorian Praefects call on all loyal soldiers to assist them. In half an hour we march; but we shall march in battle order. Load your ceremonial armour on the baggage mules, and fall in again prepared for action.'

CHAPTER THREE
The Available Candidate

Our centurions kept us marching at attention until a tribune came out from the camp to take over. He allowed us to march at ease, but in silence; no singing, and no talk above a whisper. So we arrived at imperial headquarters with no common plan. We were the kind of soldiers every officer likes to command, efficient and smart on parade, but as soon as we broke ranks powerless individuals.

We knew that the next Emperor would be chosen by the army, and that the legions would probably follow the lead of the Praetorians. The constitutional theory I learned as a child is that the Roman People entrust their sovereign power to an individual, and that his nomination by the Senate makes him Emperor. Occasionally the theory squares with the facts: if an Emperor dies in Rome, in his bed, after his death has been foreseen. But within living memory the Divine Severus had been made Emperor by the swords of the Danubian legions, and the imperial field army in Britain had chosen Caracalla to succeed his mighty father. There is only one field army (perhaps it would be better if we had two, since the Germans often attack us while we are fighting the Parthians). If the soldiers at Antioch chose a ruler, the Senate and the garrison troops in the west must acquiesce in our choice.

The new reign would begin with a handsome donative to the army which controlled the succession. Unfortunately it was a large army; the share of each man would be small. On the other hand, if we could agree among ourselves we would not have to fight anyone else.

That is what each of us was thinking as we marched into camp. As soon as we were dismissed we all began to say it.

But we had our own affairs to settle before we could make Emperors. We must find our huts, report to our centurions, and stow our baggage tidily. I was assigned to the eightieth century, in the fortieth maniple, and I was the only new arrival in my ten-man hut.

At that time the Praetorian foot made up about 10,000 men. There was in addition a troop of Praetorian horse, and even a detachment of engineers and road-makers, so that the corps could campaign as a unit; but nobody considers troopers or catapult-winders to be genuine Praetorians. The corps as it stood was not yet twenty-five years old; after the disgraceful affair of Didius Julianus the Divine Severus disbanded the rascals who had sold the Purple and formed a new guard from his favourite western legions. Of course there was hardly anyone left in the ranks from that re-founding, since the normal term of service is sixteen years; but we had old soldiers in plenty, and they were strenuous in keeping up the traditions of the most famous unit in the Roman army.

As soon as I reported with my baggage, the centurion stormed at me because my helmet was insufficiently polished, and the *optio*, his assistant, shouted that I would cut firewood for the next month unless I stood properly at attention. So I hauled out of my baggage two small jars of wine, explaining that on the Rhine it was the custom for new arrivals to offer a libation in gratitude for a safe journey. Would they kindly see that these jars were poured at the next sacrifice? After that our relations became friendly, and I was dismissed to my hut. Parade was an hour after dawn, and during this crisis all troops would be confined to camp.

When I offered my bribe so blatantly I took a chance; but after sixteen years in the army I thought I could sum up a strange centurion. By bedtime I had realised that the Praetorians as Caracalla had left them were no longer a first-class corps. Two men came into the hut drunk, though we were confined to camp in readiness for immediate action; even after I had paid my footing with my third and last jar of wine another comrade suggested that a small gift of money all round was expected from every newcomer. When I would not pay he tried to threaten me; but he was too slow on his feet to make a good bully. After I had prodded him in the stomach with the blunt end of a javelin he went away to grumble in a corner.

The six other men in the hut were lazy, experienced, artful old soldiers. Their equipment was so splendidly polished that I exclaimed in wonder; until the man who slept on my left, a German named Rufus, told me that cuirasses were no longer worn on service, and that helmets were protected by canvas covers. In other words, this shining armour was worn only for show. The hut was very neat, the men themselves very clean; each had in front of his bed-place a pair of boots upside down, showing burnished nails on the side. But these boots remained always undisturbed, while another pair was worn for drill.

All the same, these parade-ground soldiers had once been picked as good fighting-men. They were stalwart fellows, bulging with fat and muscle; it would be difficult to kill them, and impossible to frighten them.

They seemed stupid and not very likeable; but Fate had set me down to sleep between Rufus and the draught from the door which is always the lot of a newcomer, so I might as well make friends with him. I said something banal about the sudden death of the Emperor and then let him run on while I made up my bed.

He gave me the official version of the murder, which was quite evidently not the whole story. On a journey Caracalla had dismounted to relieve himself; out of respect his guards withdrew a short way. Suddenly a soldier of the bodyguard, one Martialis, ran up and stabbed him with a dagger; whereupon a fool of an archer silenced the murderer with an arrow in the

throat. Or was the archer a fool? Had he killed Martialis so that
the real designer of the plot should be forever unknown? The
story was full of loose ends. Rufus added that Martialis had a
grievance; he had been disappointed of promotion to the rank
of centurion. That proved nothing. Every soldier in the army,
except me, wants to be a centurion; it doesn't make them
murder Emperors.

'And who will rule us now?' I asked idly, to keep the
conversation alive.

'You, or me?' answered Rufus with a throaty German
chuckle. 'My claim is as good as the next man's. Caracalla left
no son. But we must be led by a soldier, and a good one. The
Parthians are marching.'

'Is there a good soldier among our commanders?'

He shrugged and spat. 'Adventus is Praetorian Praefect. He's
old, and sick, and he has never won a battle. I don't think he
wants to rule us. He hasn't offered anyone a bribe, so no one
will shout for him.'

'We'd better put it up to auction,' I said lazily.

It is always a waste of time to be facetious with a German.

'That would be a good plan,' said Rufus seriously, 'if it hadn't
been done before. The men who sold their swords to Julianus
didn't fight for him when they were needed. The next Emperor
must pay us well, but we ought to choose him for other reasons.
It might be anyone, so long as he's a good soldier.'

I did not reply that all the good soldiers were on the Rhine.
Instead I thought it wise to lay the foundation of a reputation
for loyalty. 'I shall obey orders, and leave the rest to the officers.
If the Senate makes an election that might be the best way out.
Here I suppose the senior authority is the Praetorian Praefect?'

'If those townees in Rome interfere we shall cut their throats,'
said Rufus angrily. 'The Emperor leads the soldiers and the
soldiers choose him.'

So that unpleasant enmity between soldiers and citizens
existed even out here, where the cities were so beautiful and

prosperous. I was sad to learn it. But at that moment the trumpet sounded for Lights Out.

Next morning I paraded with my century. It was a very slack parade. Because of the heat we were excused from wearing armour, and no soldier can put his heart into drill while he wears sloppy linen. We made a few tactical movements, keeping line but moving very slowly. From my point of view there was one good thing about the Praetorians; in battle I ought to be safe with these experienced middle-aged warriors on either side of me. But I did not see how we could be dangerous to any foe capable of retiring at the double.

In the middle of the morning we were assembled before the tribunal to listen to speeches. This, one of the gravest hardships in the life of the modern soldier, hits the Praetorians even more severely than the frontier legions. I saw with surprise *two* officers wearing the insignia of Praetorian Praefect, who were waiting with great wads of written notes clasped in their hands. I whispered to Rufus beside me: 'How many Praefects are there? Will they all make speeches?'

He answered in his ordinary voice, though we had been told to keep silence. 'The old boy is Adventus, who commands us. The other fellow is Macrinus. He looks after the civil side, the law-courts and all the rest of the nonsense they have loaded on to the army.'

Then an *optio* barked at him to keep his mouth shut; but he did not take his name, even when Rufus shrugged with what on the frontier would have been called dumb insolence. With no Emperor to back them our N.C.O.s had very little authority.

Adventus spoke at length, and Macrinus followed; it was the usual stuff about the glory of Eternal Rome. I did not listen closely. Only at the end was I aware of a stir among the troops, as though they were hearing something important. I pricked up my ears. Macrinus was concluding with these words:

'And therefore, gallant defenders of civilisation, the imperial power now lies in your hands. The army makes the Emperor;

but the Praetorians choose for the army. Nevertheless, it seems to us that ten thousand men, untrained in eloquence, cannot fruitfully discuss such a grave matter. The Praetorians speak for the army, but we Praefects speak for the Praetorians. I shall confer with my colleague. Tomorrow we shall have fixed on a man worthy to be Emperor. Until tomorrow, you are dismissed. You must remain within the camp, and drunkenness will be severely punished.'

After the centurions had called us to attention for the usual salute, we were dismissed where we stood, the whole 10,000 of us, instead of marching by maniples to our quarters. Of course that led to disorder. Some men climbed out over the palisade, and another group quietly and efficiently stole a butt of wine from the officers' mess. The rest of us drifted in a body to the regimental canteens. We were all out of reach before the orderly officer could catch a detail for guard duty.

As we parted I heard Rufus mutter: 'Macrinus for Emperor! That's why he stood us down without waiting to post guards. Tonight will be Saturnalia. Shall you and I take turns in guarding our kit in the hut?'

That seemed a sensible precaution. I did not suppose then, and I do not suppose now, that Macrinus dismissed us too soon merely to give us an opportunity for riot; it was just that he was a civilian lawyer, and did not remember that in a large and crowded camp some soldiers ought to be on duty all the time.

I earned the good opinion of my centurion by passing the evening quietly in my quarters. I was afraid of getting into a fight if I went to the canteen, and I did not want to explore the unknown city of Antioch on a night when there would be no law or order. I heard later that the citizens had called out their militia and barred soldiers from the gates, so I did not miss anything.

On the following morning we fell in for a ceremonial parade. Helmets and cuirasses were splendidly burnished, but some of the men inside looked frightful; unshaven, not yet sober, with black eyes and bloody noses. If a frontier legion had paraded in such a state, the men would have been sent on a long route march over the mountains. Here, in the imperial field army, our officers looked the other way. I felt ashamed, and not quite sure that the ranks of the Praetorians would be a safe place in battle.

But the scruffy parade served its purpose. As soon as we were before the tribunal Macrinus appeared, wearing full armour with a wreath of laurel instead of a helmet. Adventus came forward to begin the usual speech; instead of listening I looked hard at the man who would be our next Emperor. He was younger than I had supposed yesterday, not more than fifty at the outside. That was a point in his favour. Even an incompetent ruler is better than a series of short reigns. His cuirass, which did not fit him, must have been borrowed; but then we all knew that he was by trade a lawyer, not a soldier. His face appeared obstinate and at the same time weak, which would never do; though at the moment he was of course very happy. Adventus finished his remarks, and Macrinus came forward to acknowledge our cheers.

In the old days I had seen at close quarters the Divine Severus, a great soldier who defeated all the enemies of Rome; and the Divine Caracalla; who was undoubtedly a rake and a rogue, but also a brave and energetic leader. I made a quick decision. As a soldier I was vowed to serve Eternal Rome; in the past I had sworn to serve two worthy leaders. I would not give my allegiance to this petulant lawyer.

Adventus and the senior officers were pressing forward to take oath before Macrinus. Stepping out of rank, I saluted my centurion. 'Permission to fall out, sir,' I snapped in a most military manner. 'A touch of dysentery, sir, brought on by the change of climate.'

He peered into my face and sniffed my breath. 'You are the man who stayed in all last night, so it's not a hangover. Very well, you may go to the rear. Don't let it happen again. Next time you feel ill report sick before parade, not in the middle of an imperial ceremony.'

I marched smartly off the parade ground, to hide behind the

35

officers' mess until the oath-taking was finished. While the troops were giving three cheers for the new Emperor I slipped quietly back to my place in the ranks. We remained on parade, just in case of accidents, until the news had been announced to the legions beyond the Praetorian camp. But in matters of this kind legionaries follow the lead of Praetorians; as soon as we heard them cheering the new Emperor we were marched back to our quarters and dismissed.

There were no more duties that day, and no need for further military precautions. Our donative would not be distributed until the morning, for it took a long time to count into little packets such a great sum of money, practically the whole of the war-chest collected for the invasion of Parthia. But those of us who had money of our own were free to visit Antioch. I still had three gold pieces. This seemed a good opportunity to visit the great city, while peace was undisturbed and everyone in a good temper.

I set out alone, in the usual walking-out dress of tunic and sword. There was no companion I wished to take with me, and if I was to talk with citizens it would be useless to go with a group of soldiers. I was not planning a debauch among the brothels. I could have that sort of evening in Germany, any time I looked for it. Tonight I wished to see the wonders of civilisation, and I wished to see them in peace.

Antioch is the finest city in the east, after Rome the finest city in the world. Tall colonnades line the main streets, and on the citadel stand great temples and statues. The famous suburb of Daphne was a blaze of light and noise, and in another direction I caught a glimpse of a fine circus. But tonight I wanted to see a city, a place where educated men lived the good life which philosophers describe; the suburbs could wait for another time. The Parthian War has lasted on and off for more than 200 years, and there would be plenty of opportunities for a Praetorian to see the curious delights of Syria.

I felt amazingly free. No one would guess that I had dodged

off parade to avoid swearing allegiance to Macrinus; for none of my comrades would scruple to take an oath of loyalty in the morning and start a rebellion in the afternoon. In my blood lurks a Gallic nobleman who takes a different view. That made my secret freedom all the more precious. Since my boyhood, when the army rescued me from starvation, there had always been someone with a claim on my loyalty. After twenty years of obedience it was wonderful to be completely independent.

Sunset found me loitering in a pillared square, listening while two or three philosophers displayed their skill before an idle crowd. I was disappointed to note that they were not arguing in earnest; each was too eager to get off a witty epigram to bother about finding the truth. When they finished a boy passed a collecting-bowl, and I understood that this had been a performance, not a search for wisdom. I would have liked to enrol for a proper course of philosophy; but these were held in the morning, when I would be on parade, and anyway no teacher would enrol a brutal soldier, even though the soldier offered a good fee.

Before the menace of the collecting-bowl the crowd drifted away; and though I honestly put in a small silver coin I realised there was no more wisdom to come. It was time for supper, and I felt hungry. I strolled down the street, looking for a cookshop that sold solid meals as well as drinks.

On a corner I found quite a good place, with a charcoal grill at the entrance and a long room behind. The customers reclined on couches instead of standing close to the bar, which marked it as a real eating-house. Standing by the grill I felt a little shy; for the couches were grouped in threes and I did not want to intrude on a private party.

A big black-bearded man stood near, chatting with the cook. He saw my hesitation, and spoke with a friendly smile: 'You are the soldier who was listening in Orators' Row? I suppose you are seeing the wonders of Antioch? But you yourself are one of the wonders of the east. A soldier – and interested in rhetoric! Would you care to make a third at my table and tell us how on

37

earth you found yourself in the army? By the way, in case you are worrying about the bill, it is the custom here that each guest orders and pays for himself.'

'Thank you very much, sir,' I said in my best Greek. 'My name is Julius Duratius, and I have just arrived from Germany to join the Praetorians. I should be delighted to share your table, and to hear more about your fine city.'

'I am Claudius Demetrius, and my friend at the table is Antonius Hippias. Roman citizens, as you can see from our names; which is odd when you come to think of it. Have you ever seen Rome? I haven't. By the way, I manage an imperial estate. Hippias leads caravans to the east; or rather, nowadays he sits on a cushion in his office while his men bring the caravans to him. So now you know all about us. What part of the west do you come from? You didn't learn your Greek in Germany.'

It was delightful to recline, with a wreath on my head, discussing serious topics as the watered wine went round. I was dining as Plato had dined. This was a most respectable eating-house. There were no women in the room, not even by the grill; for in the east cooking is man's work. The slaves who waited on us were bearded men, not painted boys. My father would have been at ease in this place. If the Divine Severus had kept faith with Albinus, or chosen some other province as the scene of his civil war, I also would have supped regularly on a clean couch, served by clean-handed slaves.

When they heard of the misfortunes of my youth my companions were politely sympathetic; though they pointed out that in middle life I had done well enough for myself. But of course what they really wanted to hear was a first-hand account of the elevation of the new Emperor.

As I was telling them what I could remember of the speech of Macrinus (I had not listened, except to note that it was the usual speech; perhaps my version improved on the original) Demetrius suddenly sprang from his couch. A pimply young man was hovering by our table. What I had said was harmless enough, and the young man looked equally harmless; so that though I had noticed his eavesdropping I did not care. But the burly Demetrius seized him by his little pink nose and pulled his head down until it touched my thigh. 'There, sniff it. That's the sword of a Praetorian. If the police bother us that sword will come out of its scabbard.'

'Bloody informers,' muttered Hippias, as the young man scuttled away. 'When they see citizens talking to a soldier they come buzzing round like flies. If you shoo one away, another takes his place. But don't you think you have been imprudent, Demetrius?'

'Not particularly. My wife has a cousin in the police. Our talk was harmless enough, and I shall explain that I assaulted the agent not because I had anything to hide but because he was so damned clumsy. Standing there with his ears flapping! It was an insult to intelligent men, an insult to our discretion.'

'Well, now that we have cleared the air perhaps you can tell us, Duratius, whether the army is really loyal to Macrinus? He seems such a curious choice. A lawyer, and of very low birth. He isn't even a Senator. In Rome the Senate may take that as an insult.'

'Not a Senator? I never noticed. Soldiers are vague about civilian honours. All the same Praetorian Praefect is quite a high rank, or so we think in the army.' I answered casually, trying to make up my mind whether it was safe to be indiscreet.

'Don't badger an honest soldier,' said Demetrius. 'It's all very well for you, with a camel waiting to take you over the frontier. Macrinus is the best Emperor we have, and we all love him ... A curious choice all the same, as Hippias says.'

'He won because he had no one to beat,' I answered, taking the plunge. 'If there's nothing in his favour there's nothing against him. We were looking for an Emperor, and we look first to our commanding officers. Adventus could have had the Purple, but he would rather retire. The next in line was his legal colleague, who got it.'

'Well, we need an Emperor,' Hippias answered. 'Heaven preserve us from two rival Emperors, at least in Syria. Anyone is better than a civil war. I gather he's not too old, good for another twenty years. That will give the treasury time to form his donative.'

'If he increases the taxes there will be trouble,' said Demetrius moodily. 'I suppose the soldiers would be delighted if they were ordered to punish Antioch for rebellion?'

'I'm afraid so. I have just arrived from Germany, but they still talk of the fun they had in Alexandria. All the same, do these taxes affect you? Surely your imperial domain is not taxed?'

'I pay no tax, naturally. The property I manage already belongs to the Emperor. I don't suppose Hippias pays very much. The law allows him to keep an office in Parthia. Soldiers never pay tax, of course. Let's look round this expensive eating-house and see if we can spot a tax-payer. No, everyone here lives off the government in one way or another. No tax-payer could afford to dine here.'

'Then why do you dread an increase in the taxes?' I asked.

'Because whenever money is taken from Syria every Syrian is impoverished, and I am a Syrian. I sell to tax-payers, Hippias buys from tax-payers. This donative means that there will be no money about this year. But if we have a long reign the country will slowly recover.'

'You are quite sure there is no other candidate?' asked Hippias. 'No threat of civil war? It's odd that no one spoke up for the house of Severus. Caracalla was a disappointment, but I should have thought the family was still popular with the army.'

'Of course the whole army reveres the Divine Severus, and the soldiers had no reason to dislike Caracalla. Do you mean the family still survives? Macrinus wouldn't stand a chance against a Severus. Perhaps that's why we never heard of this man. He'll be dead as soon as the Emperor can lay hands on him; unless indeed he has already begun a civil war.'

'There's no *man* that I know of,' answered Hippias. 'But the Empress Julia Domna is here in Antioch: the widow of Severus and mother of Caracalla. Is there a chance that the troops would follow her?'

'No. Soldiers can't follow a woman. They would think it unmanly. But any male kin of hers might make trouble.'

'She has no male kin,' said Demetrius firmly. 'I thought of her as soon as I heard Caracalla was dead, and I made inquiries. She bore only the two sons. Caracalla took care of Geta, and persons unknown have taken care of Caracalla. Neither of them left legitimate sons. There may be bastards knocking about, but there are no acknowledged descendants of the Divine Severus.'

'Wait a moment,' Hippias put in, speaking with some excitement. 'At Emesa the line of the high priests still continues. I was there not long ago. The whole establishment carries on, in the name of some infant. Now, if the Empress was the daughter of the old high priest, this infant must be kin to her.'

'Yes, but the kinship is very remote. I can tell you about the child,' said Demetrius. 'The Empress has a sister. The sister married, but bore daughters only. Her two daughters married, and each had produced a son. That's good enough for the priests at Emesa, who will stretch a point to continue the line of their sacred rulers. But this infant high priest is no kin to the Divine Severus – he is the great-nephew of the Empress. Would such a claim mean anything to the army?'

'No, it's too remote, especially as the boy is unknown. If he had been old enough to hold a command in the army he might have stood a chance. But a child, and one of those oriental high priests whom most Germans see as comic figures – by the way, is he a eunuch?'

'The office is hereditary,' said Hippias drily. I blushed for my foolishness.

'So really there is very little to worry about,' Demetrius summed up. 'The donative given by the new Emperor will make us poor for a year or two, but perhaps it was worth it to get rid of Caracalla. There is no danger of civil war. We may look forward to peace and quiet.'

'Yes, peace and quiet, and that includes sleep,' said Hippias. 'It's getting late, and drunken soldiers will be on the prowl. Good night, Duratius. I didn't know there were educated citizens in the army. You ought to see that temple at Emesa. If you go to those parts look me up. I have an office there, where I spend most of my time.'

The bill was smaller than I had expected. This was the kind of place where they wanted their customers to come back. I returned alone to the camp, very proud of myself for having passed such a civilised evening.

A few days later my century formed part of the guard of honour as the Empress Julia Domna left Antioch; the widow of an Emperor and mother of another received all the honour due to her exalted rank. She was travelling to Emesa, the home of her ancestors, where she would live in royal state; for her great-nephew the high priest held the rank of client-king, ruler of his city. It was generally known that she left Antioch at the request of the Emperor, but that seemed fair enough. An Empress unrelated to the reigning monarch, living in the same city, would cause endless problems of precedence and etiquette; and there was always the chance that malcontents might use her as a figurehead. In Emesa she would be regent for the infant high priest, taking precedence of everyone; which would save conscientious chamberlains a great many worries. Although the Emperor had asked her to move, she went to Emesa of her own free will. Soldiers cannot follow a woman, but the Praetorians would never have permitted any oppression of the widow of the Divine Severus.

I stood at attention, just by the city gate; and a man who stands steady on parade sees very little of what passes before him. I caught a glimpse of the Empress, carried high in a camel-litter; she had a fierce aquiline face under a mass of white hair, and her gown of purple silk was nearly hidden by jewels. She had been worthy of her husband, more than worthy of her son. But she was a figure from the past, a historical relic, who would never again influence events. While I held my head thrown back and my eyes up I could not see the attendants who walked on foot. There were other camel-litters, but with their curtains drawn; the horsemen were mostly upper servants, of no interest to a soldier. In my old age I might bore recruits with the tale that I had seen the widow of the Divine Severus; but except for the Empress I had seen no one properly.

CHAPTER FOUR

Macrinus Augustus

Some soldiers enjoy serving in a sloppy unit; but in the long run it doesn't pay. Sooner or later you are smartened up, and the zeal of the reformers makes life unpleasant even for those who have been conscientious. The standard of discipline among Caracalla's Praetorians was really too bad to be true, and I expected a shake-up as soon as the new Emperor felt himself to be established. When it came, it was most unpleasant.

Macrinus took trouble. Adventus had retired, which gave him a free hand; our new Praefect, Ulpius Julianus, was a sound drill-master who knew the ropes. My centurion was transferred to the frontier, though he kept his rank, and the *optio* was reduced to common Praetorian. Under our new officers we exercised smartly and behaved ourselves off parade.

Then the Emperor decreed a reduction in military pay. He was careful to explain that the government would keep its contract with every serving soldier; the new rate would apply only to new recruits. No one is eligible for the Praetorians until he has done fifteen years with the legions, so of course none of us were affected. All the same, the change made us unhappy; it showed that the new government did not appreciate the army. There was the obvious danger that after a few years the administrative anomaly would be tidied away by enforcing one rate of pay for the whole army.

There was the usual drive against corruption in the quarter-master's staff. Those wretched pen-pushers can never guess right. One month they are encouraged to keep the army well found, and no questions asked; next month they are flogged for requisitioning an egg without a warrant.

It was given out in orders that cuirasses would no longer be worn on active service, at least in the climate of Syria. But they would remain as part of our full dress, so we still had the bother of keeping them burnished. Looking at it calmly, I think the change was sensible. It is possible to design a cuirass that will be proof against a spear-thrust, but then it is too heavy to be worn by infantry; the standard government issue gives very little protection. A trained soldier defends himself with his shield, and should need no further help.

On the other hand, the cuirass had been traditional legionary equipment since Rome began. We may have been better off without it, but in our own eyes we looked wrong. Legionaries are heavy infantry of the line, perhaps slow in manoeuvre but impossible to break; they take pride in the weight of their equipment, which distinguishes them from light-armed skirmishers. Besides, the Emperor was making the worst of both worlds. If we had to look after the cumbersome things we might as well wear them. The new order caused a great deal of grumbling.

The Emperor was short-tempered, attempting a difficult task for which he had not been trained. He expected his every command to be obeyed without question, and could not distinguish between negligence and open defiance. As a lawyer he had been noted for justice rather than mercy, and in particular he was hard on the slaves who looked after his office. When I did my first turn as sentry at imperial headquarters I found the atmosphere most unpleasant. In the main anteroom a clerk who had lost an important paper (on purpose, to help one of the parties in a law-suit) was tied up to be flogged to death. It was the middle of the morning, and the hall was of course crowded with petitioners; my post as sentry was within a few feet of the pillar to which the victim was bound.

I suppose the executioner had been bribed to give him a quick death; for the humblest office-clerk may have friends in high places. One of the first blows went too high, ostensibly by mistake; the heavy thong, curling round the culprit's neck; severed his jugular vein. In a few seconds the clerk was dead, but blood spurted everywhere. My armour was splashed; in the heat the mess on the floor stank abominably, while flies gathered in clouds. The Emperor decreed that the corpse should remain hanging as a warning until the law-court rose in the evening.

After I had been relieved the *optio* saw me cleaning my armour in the guardroom, and naturally inquired how a sentry dared to come off guard in such a filthy condition. I answered that it was unfair to expect good turn-out from a sentry who must stand in a shambles.

I spoke without thinking, because I was in a bad temper. The casual phrase stuck. By next morning the whole army was calling imperial headquarters The Shambles. Macrinus Augustus was never popular with his soldiers.

When he tried to enforce the letter of military law he became even less popular. At the end of April, just before the opening of the spring campaign, there was a notorious prosecution for rape; which proved that even a conscientious lawyer can make terrible mistakes in a field he does not understand.

The defenders of the Empire should never rape women whom they are pledged to protect. In military law rape is rightly a capital offence, and no good soldier should complain if a guilty comrade is executed for it. But I thank the gods that I have never judged an accusation of rape, for it is almost impossible to arrive at the truth.

I myself have never been in that kind of trouble. I am a Celt; and my blood is noble even though I have come down in the world. I hold that Duratius of the Pictones ought to be somebody, even if he isn't; it would be shameful if I had kin scattered through the world, ignorant of their high descent and unable to call on their father for help. But some of my comrades, lacking the Celtic reverence for chastity, were decidedly rough in their wooing.

The usual thing happened. A barmaid was caught with a

Praetorian, and to save her dignity gave the excuse that he had forced her. On a farm in the country the same thing happened on the same day. Even if these had been genuine rapes there was very little for the high command to worry about; in such a large army two offences a day is not a bad average. The worst element in the crime was admittedly absent; the girls were not spoiled for the marriage market, since they were already of bad reputation. But the Emperor chose to be inflexible.

In person he judged the accused, and both were convicted; though, as I have said, the evidence showed nothing worse than casual fornication. On the next day the Praetorians were paraded in a body to witness punishment.

Every Praetorian is a volunteer, who earns his bread by risking his life. Our two comrades had been unlucky; but tomorrow a Parthian arrow might find any one of us, and we knew that discipline cannot be preserved unless from time to time an offender is executed. We had all seen sudden death on the battlefield. As we took up our dressing we felt solemn, but we accepted the law we had freely sworn to obey.

Instead of an executioner with a sword we saw before us two great heaps of wood. The criminals, tied naked to stakes, were burned alive, slowly and horribly. The worst feature, from our point of view, was that the pain made these wretched men scream abjectly, going down to the lower world with cries of terror on their lips. The Judges of the Dead might mark them as cowards to all eternity. I have seen many military executions; a good soldier, when he has been caught out at last, should salute the headsman, kneel down smartly, and with hands unbound accept his fate. Then you can bury him with honour, and think kindly of him while you bid for his kit.

That was not how the Emperor Macrinus wished us to remember his justice. That evening I recalled with pleasure that I was not bound in honour to be faithful to him.

In May the imperial field army marched into the desert, to do battle with the Parthians. The dust we raised stretched on every

47

side to the horizon, and a quartermaster's clerk told me that the train was providing rations for 100,000 men, the greatest army that Rome had put into the field for many years. But by no means all of these men were warriors. Muleteers, camel-drivers and carters must have made up a full third of the total, and when we drew out in line of battle a great mass of local Arab levies guarded each flank. These Arabs of the desert come to the muster under their own chiefs, so that they are never subject to Roman discipline. Since they live by selling their swords the Emperor is compelled to hire them; for otherwise they would take service with the Parthians. But they are not to be trusted. The great desire of each leader is to preserve his own men from casualties, since his importance depends on the number of his followers; his second aim is never to find himself on the losing side.

By feeding 100,000 men the Emperor could bring into the field 40,000 genuine soldiers, Praetorians, legionaries, and auxiliaries under Roman officers; in practice that was the full strength of our army.

It was said that the Parthian host outnumbered us greatly, which frightened our muleteers; but we soldiers guessed that they also were hampered by greedy and useless non-combatants, and that genuine Parthian horse would make up only a small proportion of their numbers. In any event marching through the desert was a horrible experience; heat, dust, flies and thirst made every mile a burden. We looked forward to a big battle, which would finish the campaign; and we hardly cared which side would win, so long as we could soon get back to Syria.

Near Nisibis we made contact with the main Parthian army, led by King Artabanes. Our Arab scouts skirmished with the Arabs in Parthian pay, and by all accounts got the worst of it; though we Praetorians were too far in the rear to see what happened. Both armies drew up for a great battle. On that hot June morning I remember feeling very frightened. The heat made me dizzy and I could not keep down my breakfast; though that was no loss, since the sticky dates and hard biscuit were guaranteed to close the bowels of the toughest veteran. When Praetorians are reduced to such rations the common rankers must be really hungry. But there was no way to dodge it; by midday I would be fighting Parthians. I hoped that the infantry of the line would do better than our Arab hirelings.

Then orders were proclaimed to the whole army. A truce had been arranged. No man might advance beyond our picket line, which had been withdrawn to leave an empty space before the pickets of the enemy.

In this neutral space envoys discussed peace; though since neither the Emperor nor the Parthian King went forward to negotiate we Praetorians were spared the hazards of escort duty, which can be very dangerous during an uneasy truce. On the third day peace was announced, and the army was ordered to return to Antioch.

The peace was officially hailed as victorious. A small donative was distributed, ostensibly from the tribute of Parthia; in the following winter I saw coins which showed the Emperor Macrinus granting mercy to suppliant Parthians. But the terms of peace were never officially published, and the friendly quartermaster's clerk told me that though the Parthians did in fact hand over a few sacks of silver we Romans in return gave them heavier sacks of gold. Both countries paid compensation for past raids, but neither paid tribute. King Artabanes recognised our right to garrison Nisibis; but in return the Emperor recognised Tiridates, a pensioner of Parthia, as rightful King of Armenia. On balance Macrinus ceded more than he received. He negotiated as though Rome were the weaker party; Rome led by Macrinus was in fact weaker than Parthia.

As we marched back to Antioch the same soldiers who had been frightened of meeting the Parthian army complained that a civilian lawyer had cheated them of victory. Macrinus could do nothing right.

For the rest of a very hot summer the army remained mobilised near Antioch; and the Emperor enforced strict discipline. Men who robbed with arms in their hands were put to death, even though they had killed no one. The police tried to make burning alive the standard method of military execution, but this put the troops into such a bad humour that the innovation was dropped. All the same, life in camp was not what it had been in the gay riotous days of Caracalla. Soldiers might be punished on the complaint of mere civilians, and since there was no fighting we were employed on public works.

Praetorians in particular took that badly. We considered ourselves to be chosen heroes, whose sole duty was to win battles and safeguard the person of the Emperor. Whenever we marched we would willingly fortify our camp, for that has always been the custom. But we thought it shameful that veterans of our service should dig a road over a mountain pass, or strengthen a bridge. Discipline held, for that also is a custom of the Roman army; but any sensible man could see that it was wasteful to employ picked soldiers, drawing very high pay, at hacking through rock or hammering piles in a river-bed. Syria was full of hungry peasants who would be glad to get work; and if there was peace on the eastern frontier we should have gone to reinforce the Danube or the Rhine, where they are always short of trained men. The fact is that the Emperor wanted to stay in Antioch; and he would detach drafts for the west because he felt safer when surrounded by a numerous army.

In the autumn we heard definitely that the Parthian host had been disbanded, and the rains ended the campaigning season. The Emperor still kept us hanging about in the east, though on the Danube the Dacians were giving trouble. Instead of chastising these barbarians the Emperor freed certain Dacian hostages and made peace, to the disgust of every experienced veteran who knew that you cannot make a firm peace with Germans. The only way to cope with Germans is to kill them – or enlist them in the Roman army.

I spent most of my spare time wandering about the city of

Antioch. I soon discovered that philosophical disputations were not in fact typical of civilised life; the only men who took them seriously were a small clique of self-conscious eccentrics, or else young lawyers waiting for family influence to get them a high place in government service. Nowadays the mark of a man of culture is an informed interest in chariot-racing.

In Antioch, as elsewhere throughout the east, the racing stables are financed by clubs of supporters. The Blues were glad to make me a temporary member, since every citizen assumes that a Praetorian has money to burn. At the races I sat on the club benches and cheered my colour, but that was the least part of it. Membership of the Blues gave me the freedom of their training stables. I watched charioteers school their teams, and admired at close quarters their amazing skill. My wrists are strong, after long years of arms-drill; sometimes as a treat I was allowed to take a team of tired horses back to their loose-boxes, though of course I was never permitted to handle fresh teams eager to gallop. A few charioteers even spoke to me as an equal, which was considered a very high honour. That is odd, when you come to think of it; these charioteers all begin as bought slaves, though they have usually been freed by the time they are ready to race in public. None the less, freeborn citizens revere them.

The factions of the circus were the only truly vital institutions in Antioch. The city councillors reluctantly accepted an expensive honour which they could not refuse; the rare parades of the civic militia were perfunctory ceremonies, the sacrifices in the temples mere excuses for distributing free beef. But any citizen would work hard in his spare time, and give generously of his spare cash, to help his colour to victory at the races. When I put my subscription in the collecting box, when I held a restless team while the charioteer gathered his reins, I felt I was genuinely living as a real educated townsman.

About the middle of November my turn came round for leave. I had forty days of freedom, though I must remain in the province of Syria; and since the Emperor had recently distributed another donative, to celebrate the elevation of his ten-year-old son Diadumenus to the rank of Caesar and heir-apparent, I had plenty of money. I decided to look up Hippias the caravan-manager at his office in the sacred city of Emesa.

I journeyed in style, with my baggage on a mule. At Emesa I stopped at a good inn near the great temple. On the evening of my arrival I strolled over to pay my respects to the god; for though I serve more particularly the Three Ladies they like their followers to be polite to other divinities.

This great religious foundation is a local affair, and the rites are conducted in the local language. But there was a Greek-speaking priest lounging by the entrance, ready to entertain foreign pilgrims. The first thing he showed me was a fine marble basin, in which I was expected to deposit my offering; and he watched quite openly to see that my gift was sufficient. But priests must live, and I was under no compulsion to visit his temple. I paid up cheerfully, since a soldier gets money almost as easily as a priest.

Perhaps I was too generous. The delighted priest insisted on dragging me over the temple by myself, instead of waiting until he had collected a group of pilgrims. He told me the history of the place, with special emphasis on the antiquity of the cult.

'Emesa has been holy since the world began. This was where the Sun himself came down to see the newly-made earth, and promised to shine on what he saw. As a pledge of his promise he left us a part of his body, a part he no longer needs now that creation is finished. You will see it presently. Of course it has cooled since it fell from the sky, but there it is: a piece of sky-stone, unlike any stone found normally on earth. It fell in the garden of a virtuous man, who guarded it with all reverence. Since then, for countless generations, the descendants of this virtuous man have been hereditary high priests of the Sun-god of Emesa, the great god Elagabalus.'

'I should very much like to see your god,' I answered politely. 'Your priest must be a man of very ancient lineage. Has the office really come down from father to son since the creation of the world?'

'Not exactly,' the priest admitted with a sigh of regret. 'I don't think you would find such a lineage anywhere in the modern world. The Parthians overturned the holy dynasties of Babylon; even in Egypt the direct line of the priests of Apis was broken in the turmoil of the Greek conquest. But our high priest is undoubtedly descended from the founder of the temple, though his pedigree runs through the female line. He is a very young man, almost a child, and oddly enough he was educated to be a Roman nobleman. Now he takes an interest in his duties and promises very well. His grandmother was the daughter of a high priest, so his descent is clear.'

'Strange that a boy with such a future should be educated as a Roman,' I said with mild curiosity.

'Ah, but his Roman descent is also very distinguished. The high priest Bassianus left no son but two daughters. The elder daughter married a Roman officer who in due course achieved the Purple as the Divine Severus. The younger also married a Roman officer, now dead; her daughter is the widowed mother of our present ruler. Both the old ladies came back to the home of their childhood soon after the death of the Divine Caracalla.'

I was genuinely interested. 'Does the Empress live here now? I served under the Divine Severus, and I was one of the guard when the Empress left Antioch. When next she receives visitors I should like to pay my respects.'

'You have come too late,' the priest answered brusquely. 'The lady Julia Bassiana died a month ago. Some say she died of grief at the murder of her son, but it may have been sickness. No man knows what passes in the women's quarters. Anyway, as you will see for yourself if you stop to think, it will be unfortunate if Roman veterans come here to remind our young ruler of his imperial connections. At best it might unsettle the boy, who must work hard to learn his sacred functions. At worst it would annoy the police.'

'Very well, I shall keep away, if you think a visit would be indiscreet. I came here to see your famous temple – and to call on an acquaintance, one Hippias, who runs caravans eastward from these parts. Do you know of him?'

'I don't. Now if you want to bow before the sky-stone this is where you take off your shoes.'

The priest stopped his flow of chatter. He kept me hanging about the entry to the shrine until a group of pilgrims caught up with us, so that he could begin his usual description of the might of his god. Evidently he feared that I was a secret agent.

The god Elagabalus, who was at the same time the Sun and a small black stone, I found interesting, though not very interesting. For one thing, his identity was difficult to explain to a simple Gaul, though I believe these complications go easily into the local language. The priest was emphatic that the god had not been made by human hands; he was not an image or a symbol, but an actual fragment of the Sun's divine body. He was a bit of black stone about a foot long, shaped like a phallus. Modern philosophers hold that these stones from the sky are as natural as the stones you kick up in any field, having nothing about them of the divine. I was taught another opinion: that many objects are in a sense divine, but that such divinity is not very important. I was willing to grant the claims made for Elagabalus, but I was not impressed by them.

In Emesa the sky-stone evidently carried great weight. The pilgrims were most devout, and so was the priest who saw it every day. That morning a ram had been sacrificed, and a tethered he-goat was waiting to be killed at sunset. The god received two lives every day.

All over Syria the gods are very close to mankind; because they are not very nice gods you sometimes wish they were further off. Most of our Gallic gods live at the bottom of springs and pools, and it is hard to get in touch with them. That is the system I prefer.

I passed a pleasant evening at the inn, reclining on a couch and reading a book of travel as I sipped my wine. It is a way of life that would bore me after a month, but it is also the life I was brought up to, the life I would have led if my parents had not been killed by rebel stragglers; every now and again I liked to get away from the army and taste it.

I slept alone, in spite of hopeful suggestions from the innkeeper. In the morning I sent my muleteer to find out whether Hippias was at his Emesa office. It took most of the forenoon to get a straight answer; the office door-keeper was one of those trusted slaves who are jealous of paid menials and delight to make things difficult for them. After about three hours my man returned to say that Hippias was willing to receive me. I put on a clean tunic and went out to call.

The office stood at a corner of the caravan stable, a hollow square of stout buildings crammed with bales. Hippias had of course forgotten me, as I ought to have understood from the start; but when he saw me he made me welcome. Soon we were sitting under a shady tree, with wine and fruit before us.

While we exchanged conventional remarks about the beauties of Emesa, Hippias examined me from twinkling little eyes that lurked deep behind bushy brows. He was a very large solid man, slow-moving and too fat; yet he had an air of dashing independence. The combination puzzled me at first; a civilian is usually timid in the presence of a soldier. Then I realised that he was a civilian who earned his living on the fringe of the Empire; when he traded over the border he must himself protect his wealth. He was a civilian who did not rely on hired swords.

Abruptly he began to talk about serious things; he must have made up his mind that I could be trusted. 'You are a soldier,' he said, 'one of the Praetorians who make Emperors. I was going to say that your visit comes at an unfortunate time. My stable is nearly empty and I can't show you a good caravan. Now I shall tell you the truth. If you repeat it in Antioch perhaps they will heed a Praetorian. My stable is empty because my drivers are in Mesopotamia, and I can't persuade them to come back.'

'Can't you seek justice from the Parthian governor?' I asked.

'If my beasts had been stolen the Parthians would help me to recover them. That's not exactly what's happened. My drivers are willing to serve me; they admit that the camels are mine. But they have quite lawfully gone beyond the reach of Rome, and they refuse to come back. The Parthians will not use force to return refugees.'

'What do these men fear? Do you hire criminals? If our police are after them can't you hire others?'

'There are not many more to be hired. You cannot leave the Empire unless your papers are in order. I have a permit from the governor of Syria, permitting me to send camel-drivers into Parthia. Dozens of young men come to me, offering to take a caravan east; but I know they won't come back again. If that goes on, I shall lose my permit.'

'If they are native Syrians, why do they flee from home?'

'To escape the tax-gatherer. That's what I want you to tell them in Antioch. The Parthians rule Mesopotamia as a conquered land. They have no written law; so that even if the governor is willing to do justice you never know how a case will go. But my men, native Syrians, prefer barbarism to the Roman tax-gatherer. You must tell them that when you get back. Tell them that the taxes are too heavy.'

'I'll say so, if you like. No one will contradict me. But what can be done about it? The soldiers must be paid. As you know, that's where the money goes.'

'But surely the Emperor, a lawyer and a civilian, would *like* to reduce the taxes?'

'Our present Emperor would never dare to tamper with military expenditure. Already the soldiers distrust him, just because he is a civilian. He's the last man to do anything of the kind. I agree with you that the taxes should be reduced. But only a soldier-Emperor, certain of the army's loyalty, would be strong enough to reduce them.'

'Then I shall be open with you.' Hippias glanced down at the dagger in his belt. 'We have the wrong kind of Emperor. The Republic can prosper only under a ruler who controls the soldiers.'

'I see. Have you a candidate in mind?' I also glanced down at my scabbarded sword, lying handy on the grass beside me. If this interview took the wrong turning I might be forced to silence the only witness against me.

'Would a son of the Divine Caracalla appeal to the soldiers? If you think so, take a look at the high priest here, young Bassianus. Then when you get back to the army you can tell your comrades about him.'

'But the high priest is the grandson of the Empress's sister. That makes him first cousin to the Divine Caracalla, on the distaff side. But he does not share the blood of the Divine Severus. Only yesterday the guide at the shrine explained it all to me.'

'Nevertheless, take a look at him. And remember that his mother was at court when Caracalla was approaching manhood.'

Hippias jumped to his feet with a sudden exclamation. 'I must catch that man passing the office. I have been looking for him. Excuse me.'

There was no one by the office. But Syrians take no trouble when dealing with westerners, whom they suppose to be lacking in guile. I went back to my inn.

Just before sunset a slave brought a message to say that Hippias had been called to the frontier on urgent business; he regretted that he would be unable to meet again during my visit. I told the slave his message had been expected; but that was only because I wanted to make Hippias feel uncomfortable. He was somewhere in Emesa, and I knew that however hard I looked I would not find him.

I waited three days to see the young high priest. I was told that he visited the shrine daily, but that was for private worship; only for solemn sacrifices did he go in public procession. But the public procession would comprise also his family and his principal officers, so it was worth waiting for.

In many Syrian temples they use a strange measure of time, a cycle of seven days which does not fit properly into either the

57

month or the year; it has something to do with the seven influences of astrology. On the first day of this cycle Elagabalus was honoured with a sacrifice of unusual splendour, held at midday. I went to the temple in plenty of time, wearing my dress uniform. The crowd made way for a Praetorian and I could see everything.

The ceremony had been devised to give pleasure to a sky-stone long domiciled in Syria; I do not think it would have pleased an Olympian, or any of the lesser gods who guard the west. But then our gods are helpers of mankind against indifferent nature, while his little black stone was the Sun, who looks on everything without taking sides, or so the priest had tried to explain to me.

The purpose of the rite was the sacrifice of a bull; but in the eyes of the spectators the procession was more important than the bloodshed. The great stairway of the temple was interrupted in the middle by a sloping ramp. We stood on either side, kept back by temple guards; while the bull and his escort ascended the ramp at a slow impressive pace.

First came a band of musicians, blowing trumpets and banging on cymbals; behind them were singers. Of these none were female, though whether they were beardless boys, well-shaved youths, or eunuchs who had kept their figures I could not be sure. Eunuchs might seem inappropriate ministers for a sky-stone shaped so accurately as a phallus; but perhaps the need for the right kind of voice outweighed other considerations.

Behind the music came a long file of priests, walking two by two. They were clothed in long tunics reaching to the ankle and in tall pointed caps tied under the chin. These were certainly men, though to a westerner their dress seemed oddly feminine. There followed a small detachment of temple guards, wearing armour of an antique fashion and carrying unhandy spears and swords; they marched clumsily, and seemed ill at ease in their accoutrements. I suppose they were local peasants who put on this disguise for great occasions, to persuade the god that he still ruled in Emesa. A temple guard with any serious military value would be suppressed by the police.

Then came a little group of dancers, scattering rose-petals as they jigged. These were handsome boys; but the paint on their faces and wiggling of their bottoms showed what kind of boys they were. This sort of thing creeps in because orientals cannot think straight. First they decide that only males may serve a male god; then, because they themselves like pretty boys, they encourage some of these boys to behave as females. If Elagabalus was as manly as they supposed, he must have disliked some of his servants.

I was surprised to see two ladies walk next in the procession; they were dressed in the same long gowns and tall hats as the priests. They looked like mother and daughter, and from the acclamations of the crowd I learned their names. The elder was Maesa, sister to the late Empress; the other was Soaemias, the mother of the high priest. It seemed strange that Roman matrons, trained to the etiquette of the imperial household, should parade publicly in such outlandish clothes. I suppose they thought it better to be princesses of the ancient priestly race of Emesa rather than to be forgotten relatives of a fallen Emperor.

Now came the focal point of the procession: a great white bull, his horns gilded, garlands round his neck. Walking backward before him, since at this stage in any religious ceremony the sacrifice embodies the godhead, came a graceful youth of thirteen. As he passed I had a good view of his face, and I gasped in astonishment. The boy, though he looked childish for his age, was yet a perfect miniature of the Divine Caracalla.

This means that he was strikingly handsome. Beneath a fantastic head-dress of gauzy silk peeped a cluster of golden curls; his eyelashes fluttered like butterflies; as he moved his head I caught a glimpse of huge brimming violet eyes. The elaborate ornaments and facepaint which were part of his ritual costume made his beauty seem that of an exquisite doll. But this perfect beauty had in it nothing of the feminine; even the long embroidered gown could not conceal his manliness. The Greek sculptors of long ago would have been overjoyed to employ young Bassianus as a model.

Slowly he walked backwards. All his attention was on the guiding of the bull who was also for these few moments the Sun and the sky-stone. He did not look like a boy who had been reared in the respectable Roman court of the Divine Severus. Rumour hinted that the court of the Divine Caracalla had been less bound by convention, but even there such a figure would have seemed unusual. But if he did not look like a Roman neither did he resemble a feeble oriental. He seemed a fair servant of the gods, come down from Olympus to supervise their worship. If the Eagle of Jupiter had perched on his shoulder I would not have felt at all surprised.

There followed more priests and temple guards; but I did not linger to see them. I returned to my inn, and made arrangements to leave for Antioch in the morning.

As I rode back to the army I tried to sort out my impressions. The high priest of Emesa was a youth of fantastic beauty, with a striking resemblance to the Divine Caracalla. Hippias had indicated that among the locals there was a movement to use him as figurehead for a revolt. I did not like Macrinus, and I had been lucky enough to avoid the obligation to be faithful to him.

After long indecision I made up my mind to take no part in these dangerous intrigues. I was influenced, of course, by fear of the punishment that follows unsuccessful rebellion; but in addition it seemed to me that young Bassianus had no claim on my service. Hippias and his accomplices would put it about that the boy was Caracalla's bastard. I might owe a duty to the son of my old leader, but I did not believe this rumour of his parentage. I counted back on my fingers. The boy looked to be about thirteen. Fourteen years ago the whole imperial family, including the boy's mother and the youthful Caracalla, had been together in Rome for the Secular Games. But surely Caracalla had been very young? His father kept him pretty firmly under control. Why should he risk the Emperor's anger by seducing a lady of the imperial house, when any common girl in Rome would be his for the asking?

As far as I could recall, the Divine Caracalla was not the man to run risks for the love of a lady. In every garrison you hear gossip about the private life of the reigning Emperor, and half of these scandalous stories are meant only to amuse. But even with the usual discount for baseless rumour it seemed evident that though Caracalla often wanted a woman, he did not greatly care which woman. At the height of his power he maintained an establishment of 300 concubines; some say that in addition he kept 300 boy friends, though whether they lived in a separate building or mingled with the females I do not know. A man with such inclusive tastes would not bother to seduce a cousin who must have been carefully guarded.

There was a simple explanation for the remarkable resemblance. The Divine Caracalla must have taken after his mother. That striking beauty was hereditary in the family of the high priests of Emesa.

All the same, the resemblance was there, and so was the beauty. Both would appeal to the soldiers. It was likely that we would hear more of young Bassianus.

CHAPTER FIVE

Civil War

After the army the secret police is the most expensive institution in the Empire; and every penny spent on it is wasted. In theory this enormous body of men should warn the central government of the first whisper of disaffection; if they did their duty no Emperor would ever be overthrown. In fact these creatures expose some petty conspiracies; if a rich man takes one cup of wine too many and permits flatterers to salute him with imperial acclamations, if a cohort of second-rate garrison troops forces some seedy legate into hopeless rebellion, secret agents work hard to track down the second cousins and the creditors of the rash traitors. But if a really dangerous movement takes shape they do not expose it, they join it. Thus they safeguard their power under the new ruler, after the death of the prince they are sworn to protect.

Even competent secret agents could not have saved the Divine Caracalla. He was murdered by an angry man who was willing to buy vengeance with his own life; on those terms any good swordsman can kill his ruler. The story they tell about the murder may or may not be true; but if true it explains some features of the affair which puzzled me at the time, and I give it for what it is worth.

They say that Macrinus, then Praetorian Praefect, was afflicted with astrologer-trouble, a scourge which may unexpectedly strike down any eminent man. Astrologers make a living by predicting prosperity for their clients; but if the clients are already very successful it is hard to think of greater heights for them to climb. Macrinus was already the third man in the state; so when an obscure cousin paid an astrologer to foretell the future of his famous kinsman the fool could think of nothing to say but that Macrinus would one day be Emperor.

Such a prediction is treason. A secret agent heard of it; instead of denouncing the astrologer he thought it would pay him better to denounce the Praetorian Praefect. The denunciation travelled by official post to Rome; and from there was forwarded, unopened, to imperial headquarters at Antioch. It arrived at the bottom of a bulging mailbag. Caracalla, just setting out to hunt, threw the bag to Macrinus, telling him to read the letters and report anything of interest. The only chance for Macrinus was to act before his master heard of the charge; for no one so denounced is ever acquitted. On the same day the local police denounced the discontented soldier Martialis. Instead of ordering his arrest the Praetorian Praefect got in touch with him.

Thus Caracalla died because he could not be bothered to open his letters; the agents had done their duty. It may be a true story, or it may be an excuse put out by the police.

There can be no excuse for the negligence of the agents in the following winter. During the ten-day holiday of Saturnalia the troops talked of nothing but the claims of this marvellous youth at Emesa. He was Caracalla's acknowledged son; at his birth it had been prophesied that he, and he alone, could overcome the Parthians; his divine origin was shown forth in his supernatural beauty; he was brave and accomplished, and as hereditary high priest of Emesa he was possessed of such enormous private wealth that from his own resources he could distribute a donative richer than the oldest veteran could recall.

That was what every soldier in the camp was saying. Soon the officers heard of it. At last it reached even the headquarters staff, who were as usual out of touch with the feelings of the troops. The citizens of Antioch discussed it in every tavern. When eventually someone told the Emperor Macrinus the whole of

Syria, soldier and civilian, knew that the Divine Caracalla had returned to earth to reclaim the Purple.

Even then no official action was taken; though there was an official point of view, which was expounded by hundreds of busy and unreliable agents. You could not visit a tavern without being approached by some dirty little loafer, who would stand you a drink and explain that the country people round Emesa had been seduced by Parthian gold; the high priest was a mere child, incapable of mischief, but wicked Parthians were using him; however, the Emperor was taking prudent measures; a garrison would be stationed in Emesa, and then the excitement would vanish.

In January a full legion, the Third Gallican, went into camp at Raphanae near Emesa. The army as a whole, and the Praetorians in particular, were disappointed to hear of it. Now that there was peace with the Parthians we had hoped that imperial headquarters would move back to Europe; most of us had been reared on the Rhenish or Danubian frontiers, which are always in danger while the field army is in Asia. It seemed that the Emperor intended to linger in Syria until the whole east was at peace; and that would mean a very long stay.

At the beginning of April a comet appeared in the sky, which is supposed to foretell a change of dynasty; it was not a very bright comet, but then Macrinus was not a very great Emperor. I myself cannot believe that the Sky is deeply concerned about which man should command the Roman army, but public opinion was against me and the supporters of the established order were disheartened.

On the 12th of April the sun was eclipsed. The astrologers were taken by surprise, though as a rule they can foretell eclipses of the moon. However, such events have been reported in the past, and there is a routine for dealing with them. A ceremonial parade was ordered, to witness the expiatory sacrifices which would be offered by the Emperor in person. No one in the army felt very worried. An eclipse of the sun is indeed an adverse omen; but it is such a general omen, foretelling hard

64

times for the whole world, that it is unlikely to harm obscure private soldiers.

It took six days to collect a hecatomb of bulls, for the long Parthian War had diminished the herds of Syria. When all was in readiness we paraded before an altar in the open air, while the Emperor personally conducted the sacrifice. In the ancient Roman ritual nine victims were the maximum for the most solemn occasions; but the modern Greeks are in love with size for its own sake (though their ancestors were more moderate) and a hecatomb, a full hundred of victims, is considered necessary for any important religious event.

Six days of consultation had not devised a seemly ritual. Every priest must have added some minor deity whom it would be unwise to neglect; the introductory prayers went on and on. When the killing began that also threatened to continue to all eternity. The Emperor must personally dedicate each bull, sprinkle its head with barley and pronounce the words of sanctification; and there were a hundred bulls. Macrinus did not shirk his duty, but he was not handy at it. After the blood of a few bulls had been spilled the rest played up, frightened by the smell. Attendants wrestled to hold them, but the elderly and pacific Emperor was obviously nervous when he must approach their heads. The burly, half-naked killers who wielded the pole-axes became exhausted. There should have been relief butchers standing by, but because of some muddle two men must kill a hundred bulls. The later victims were butchered so clumsily that we seemed to be watching a fight between men and bulls rather than a solemn offering to the gods.

We were kept standing rigid at the Present until men began to faint in the ranks; but a lot of bulls were still alive when the Praefect changed his mind and brought us down to Attention. Then the Emperor, intent on keeping clear of the horns, made three efforts to sprinkle the head of one lively beast. Someone in the rear rank raised the low derisive catcall that greets a clumsy gladiator. You can make that noise without moving your lips – at least any old soldier can. Soon the whole parade, nearly

10,000 Praetorians, were mocking their sovereign while he was engaged in the service of the gods.

The officers were furious, but while they and everyone else must stand steady on parade there was nothing they could do. As the pole-axe flashed over the head of the last beast a legate snapped: 'Prepare to march off in column of route', an order which permits officers to turn about and face their men. At once there was such utter silence that we could hear the thump as the bull fell.

After such an important ceremony we looked for an allocution from the Emperor; but he hurried from the field without even giving us the order to march off. The Praefect took over. He displayed his anger by calling us up to the Present half a dozen times, and telling us how badly we did it. We were hot and tired and bored, and impatient to get off parade. Again catcalls murmured elusively through the ranks, even though our officers were now facing us.

The Praetorian Praefect knew that his men were working themselves up to open insubordination, and he was anxious to get us marched off before the trouble grew worse. But there was a further delay, as a civilian clerk scuttled over the wide parade ground with a written message. Soldiers often hoot any civilian who crosses the parade ground, even when there is no particular excuse for bad behaviour; in our present humour we hurried that office boy along on a real gale of whistling.

The Praefect read the message, and with a wooden face commanded silence in the ranks. He got it, too, for we could see that this was something serious. In a firm but expressionless voice he bellowed: 'Addition to standing orders. Pay attention. The Third Gallican Legion is to be treated as a hostile force. Any sentry sighting an enemy patrol is to give the general alarm without delay, and is authorised to make use of his weapons. Parade, prepare to march off.'

We marched off in silence, keeping the correct intervals. War had begun, and that recalls any trained soldier to his duty. But as my maniple neared the edge of the parade ground I could hear ahead of me a roar like a waterfall. My comrades, marching at ease, were discussing the latest news.

In my opinion there was nothing to be discussed. The Third Gallicans had been sent into camp to overawe the people of Emesa; if they were now hostile they must have gone over to young Bassianus. Soldiers do not often declare for a pretender in the province actually occupied by the imperial field army; such mutinies break out usually in a province that considers itself neglected. But there could be no other explanation. Within a few days I would be fighting for the first time in the ranks of the Praetorians.

In fact we did not at once go into action. Instead the Emperor moved his quarters from the city of Antioch to the middle of the camp, where I suppose he felt safer; and the Praetorian Praefect marched against Emesa with three legions.

That is quite the wrong way to fight a civil war. Macrinus represented nothing in particular, no special cause or programme for the better government of the Republic. His followers would be fighting only to maintain him as Emperor, and if he did not bother to lead them they could not be expected to fight for him with enthusiasm. I expected early news of defeat. I was surprised to hear that Julianus, the Praetorian Praefect, had formed the siege of Emesa and pressed hard on the rebel city.

Meanwhile Syria suffered the usual rigours of civil war. Soldiers requisitioned supplies and transport all over the province, though the revolt was confined to the neighbourhood of Emesa. Praetorians keep better discipline than the legions; our patrols never burned friendly villages, though we helped ourselves to anything of value we might find in them. When I happened to see Scythian auxiliaries selling peasant girls in the Antioch market I sickened of this pointless war.

Presently my turn came round again for sentry at imperial headquarters, which was not a duty anyone enjoyed. The quick temper of Macrinus made it positively dangerous; even though you heard all the latest news it could be boring to listen, standing at attention, while a deputation from some ruined village bored the Emperor with their grievances.

With my usual bad luck I drew the afternoon watch. At night even a sentry can snatch some rest, and in the morning there is an interesting bustle of couriers. Two hours in the imperial anteroom, while the court dozes during the heat of the day, foreshadows eternity.

Of course a few petitioners appeared; there is never an hour of the day or night when someone is not wanting to see the Emperor. I told them to wait, and most of them sat down in a corner.

Then a junior officer bustled in, a commissioned centurion. In the Praetorians our centurions are all promoted rankers, at the end of their career; but every legion has a few of these young men, who join the army as centurions and hope to rise to high command. I don't like them. They join the army only because their families have influence, and most of them take advantage of it by making subordinates do their work while they hang round headquarters intriguing for promotion.

This young man wore field equipment, covered with dust; his shoulder-badge was missing, so that I could not identify his legion. But as he strode quickly up the hall he was obviously on duty.

'The Emperor is resting, I suppose?' he said casually as he returned my salute. 'There's no need to disturb him. I bring good news, but it can wait for an hour or so. The guard-commander can take my bag. When he has signed for it I shall go and clean up, in case the Emperor wants to speak to me after he wakes.'

Of course a commissioned centurion would not miss an opportunity of reporting in person to the Emperor; equally he would want to look his best at this important interview. The *principalis* in charge came out from the guardroom and signed for the message-bag, which was left at my feet so that the

Emperor might see it as soon as he left his chamber. The officer strode rapidly away.

Afterwards police agents badgered me to describe him, and the *principalis* who let him go was charged with culpable neglect of duty; though events moved so rapidly that he never stood his trial. But you will see from my account that the whole transaction was quite normal. Even if we had wished to detain the messenger, a *principalis* must get hold of another commissioned officer to make the arrest of a commissioned centurion.

I stood for the best part of an hour with the bag at my feet. It was a large bag filled with some round object, too big to be a despatch. From the buzzing of the flies I guessed that this was a severed head; such things are brought to an Emperor fairly frequently. It was sad that Bassianus, that beautiful boy, would never attain manhood. I wondered idly whether his severed head would still retain its astonishing beauty.

Then the Emperor bustled out of his chamber. He was in more than his usual bad temper, as happens when elderly men rise from a midday nap. When he saw my bag he ordered his valet to cut the strings, without waiting for the *principalis* to report in due form. I was standing rigidly at the Present, so that I could not move my head; but he was directly in front of me, and I could see him.

Groping in the bag, the valet first fished out a message. 'My Lord,' he said, 'this bears the personal signet of the Praetorian Praefect. He writes as follows: From the victorious Praefect Ulpius Julianus to his august Emperor, greeting. I enclose with my greeting the head and front of all these troubles.'

'Now which will that be?' muttered the Emperor to himself. 'Little Bassianus, or that legate who went over to him? Julianus should have been more explicit. Well, what are you waiting for? Pull out the head and let me see it.'

The head that came out was so battered that at first no one could recognise it. 'It's Julianus himself!' the Emperor gasped, and fainted.

The guard turned out, valets came running; the Emperor was

carried off and the anteroom cleared. Then the secret police took over. Luckily they concentrated on the guard-commander, not on the ranker who happened to have been sentry. Their reasoning was sound as far as it went. A plotter may know in advance who will command the guard on a particular day, he cannot guess which sentry will be on duty. What the police could not grasp was that any serving soldier would know the routine for the reception of a message while the Emperor is resting, and that any centurion with calm nerves could get away without being identified.

A tribune at the head of a double guard took charge of the imperial apartments, and we were marched back to our huts with a black mark on our records. In theory we were confined to quarters until the police had finished with us; but since the whole army was getting ready for battle we were no worse off than our comrades. The canteens were closed, and everyone was standing by.

Within an hour all the Praetorians knew the story; and all regarded it as a very good joke. Julianus had not been our commander long enough to earn popularity, and anyway a Praetorian Praefect without a head seems funny in himself, at least to Praetorians. We admired the enemy's audacity. We were delighted to recall that the Emperor Macrinus, that civilian lawyer, had fainted from terror in his own anteroom, in the midst of his mighty army.

All the same, we were willing to fight for our Emperor. It is the privilege of Praetorians to bestow the Purple; we might have chosen a second-rate leader, but it was not for mere legionaries to overrule our choice. That night we sharpened our swords and the heads of our javelins.

Now that it had come to open war we heard the story of the beginning of the revolt, a story hitherto hushed up by the secret police. On the day of the eclipse Bassianus, or rather his advisers, had made the first move. An eclipse ought to be a bad omen for the Sun, but at least it makes people think of him. The boy visited the camp of the Third Gallican Legion; the legate in command, one Eutychianus, recognised him as son and heir of the Divine Caracalla and therefore rightful Emperor. The boy needed to do nothing more than show himself to the soldiers; overcome by his divine beauty, they clamoured to fight for him.

Then the army of Julianus changed sides, winning the trust of their new leader by the traditional method of offering him the head of his predecessor. That gave Eutychianus four legions, a formidable force; in addition he had a host of Syrian volunteers of little military value.

Soon we would meet in head-on collision, as the increasing rebel army marched against imperial headquarters at Antioch. It was unusual for a rebel leader to take the initiative in this way, instead of recruiting more troops in the districts he occupied, until the Emperor in possession marched against him, according to the normal pattern of civil war.

Perhaps the pattern was broken because the last serious civil war had ended so long ago. In the deserts of Africa or the mountains of Asia bands of insurgents are hunted every year; but the last campaign in which either side had a chance of victory had been the clash between Severus and Albinus which destroyed my family. That was more than twenty years ago; even among the Praetorians no one had fought in it, except a few elderly craftsmen who no longer took the field, armourers and farriers. These historical landmarks went about telling the soldiers that to meet trained Roman troops was a very different matter from chasing undisciplined barbarians; our enemies would use the same tricks of fence, learned from the same instructors, and we would be confused by trumpet-calls taken from our own drill-books.

No Praetorian felt apprehensive; we picked veterans must easily overcome common legionaries. At the beginning of June we left Antioch in high spirits, ready to destroy any presumptuous Syrians who would not obey the master we had chosen to rule the Roman world.

The Emperor led his troops in person; which was perhaps a

pity, for he was no soldier. But now that the head of Julianus was with one army and his body with the other there was no experienced professional officer to take command in his name. We knew that the legate Eutychianus led the rebels, a veteran who had risen from the ranks, a man of low birth (which did not disqualify him in our eyes), a sound regimental officer who had never held an independent command. Unless he was a tactician of genius, and there was no reason to suppose so, our army of picked men ought to beat his army of common legionaries. We thought of Eutychianus as our adversary; he had used a pretty boy to win local popularity, but if he managed to keep his troops together the child would soon disappear.

We did a full march, and camped in the open plain near a village named Immae. The heat of a Syrian June was appalling, but that would affect our enemies even more severely. We marched light, leaving our heavy baggage in Antioch; they had brought their train 130 miles from Emesa. The Emperor had chosen a featureless plain for the engagement, I suppose because an inexperienced soldier finds it easier to control troops on a field as much like a parade ground as he can find. The enemy had collected rather more of the untrustworthy local horse than we had been able to hire, so we would have been better off with our flanks protected by some obstacle. But unless we sheltered behind the walls of Antioch (and for the reigning Emperor to stand on the defensive would be a confession of defeat) there was no strong position in the neighbourhood; or if there was, our civilian Emperor lacked the skill to find it.

Our camp was fortified very sketchily. The rampart would never have done on the frontier; but the heat made us lazy and our officers thought only of keeping us in a good humour. Anyway, in such a campaign a strong camp would be wasted; if we won, the rebellion must collapse, and if by some unlikely chance we were checked, we would fall back into Asia to gather reinforcements.

We had only a light train, but supplies were plentiful. We ate a good breakfast, after a night made unpleasant by the intense heat. Then, at our leisure, we formed line of battle.

The Emperor attempted no tactical finesse. He formed his whole army in line; Praetorians in the centre, legions on either side, and beyond the legions our irregular horse. He himself with his battle standard took post behind the centre of the line, where messengers could quickly find him; but he led only a small mounted bodyguard, not a reserve which might influence the battle. By mid-morning, with the sun high and the heat worse than ever, we could see the enemy approaching under a dense cloud of dust.

My century happened to be posted in the front line, and as a new recruit I was of course in the front rank. It seemed odd that at my age I should be considered a novice; but most Praetorians have passed forty, and at thirty-five I was in fact one of the youngest men in the corps. I would have a very fine view of the action, but before sunset I would have earned every penny of my daily pay.

Eutychianus brought on his army in the normal order, with his four legions in the centre and his Syrian auxiliaries on the wings. He had a great mass of cavalry, and Arab lancers mounted on camels; we disregarded them, for Arabs are dangerous only to a flying foe.

The Praetorians were calm and businesslike; it is comforting to know that your corps is the finest fighting-machine in the world, even if there is a chance that you personally will be killed before the inevitable victory. We stood on the defensive; but we were forbidden to plant stakes, or dig a trench, since we were to counter-attack as soon as we had brought the foe to a halt.

Our worst trouble was the heat. It was a still, windless day, and dust rose in clouds even over the foot; round horses and camels it billowed like smoke from a burning city. Once battle had been joined in the centre we should be unable to see the flanks. That did not matter. We were Praetorians; we could protect ourselves even if our cavalry were driven from the field.

The enemy horse charged from 200 yards, the distance laid

73

down in the manual. Their centre advanced at a walk until they were within long javelin-range. Then they too charged, all together, in a level and well-controlled line. This battle would be fought according to the drill-book; and naturally, since the Emperor was a civilian and Eutychianus a promoted ranker.

I was still trying to see the action as a whole, wondering why men who considered themselves worthy to rule the Republic could not think up some stratagem instead of colliding like two angry bulls, when a javelin struck the ground at my feet. Now I must guard my head, not look about me.

We cast our javelins just as the lines met, so that nearly every one told; steady veterans can wait until it seems too late, knowing that the enemy will falter as they receive the volley and leave time for swords to be drawn. The attacking legion checked even before we cast; they were empty-handed, after loosing their volley at long range, and they flinched as they saw our arms come up. As soon as our swords were out we jumped forward; the two lines clashed with equal impetus.

It was very nicely done, though I say it myself. Only Praetorians could have waited so long, and then moved so swiftly.

I killed a rebel with a brisk one-two, a cut at his head to bring his shield up followed by a thrust to the belly. Then I stood my ground, so as not to get in advance of our line. My comrades on either side also halted, and the battle was at a standstill. Every man in both armies had got over his beginner's nerves. We fenced cautiously, shields well forward and hilts low.

I tried to hear what was happening on the flanks, where the noise indicated that the enemy were driving back our horse. But noise can be misleading. Anyway, it did not matter; we could cope with the legionaries on our front.

Then the rebels put in their supports; much too soon, for the engagement had lasted barely half an hour. Our second line moved up to help us, and we held our ground.

Now there was no room for fencing. Two dense lines of overlapping shields faced one another, and cautious prods brought few casualties. Long training kept us in formation; but our opponents, also well trained, still pressed us. At moments the rigid lines drew apart to reform, and during one of these I looked round me; dust rose far behind our flanks, and I could hear war-cries in the rear. Evidently our wings had been routed. The Praetorians, alone in our original position, were in danger of encirclement.

Then I was thrusting at a sweaty dust-stained face that grinned at me over a legionary shield. With a lucky blow I dislodged his helmet, and then instinctively cut at the white forehead (in a dozen skirmishes on the frontier I had rallied beside a white forehead, the mark that distinguishes a helmet-wearing Roman from a barbarian). Before the edge could land I turned it, for the man before me looked curiously familiar. He was the double of an old comrade who had once helped me to build a fire during a Caledonian snowstorm. No comrades of mine would be serving in the Third Gallican, who had been stationed in the east for a generation. But the likeness may not have been an accident; sons follow their fathers into the army. Anyway, even if he was a stranger he was a fellow-soldier, a man whom I would instinctively ask for help if ever I got lost in another snowstorm. Why on earth should I kill him now, just because he had lost his helmet in fair fight?

The man saw I had spared his life. Lifting his sword in mocking-salute he gasped: 'Thank you, Praetorian, but don't drop your guard. Bassianus Augustus!'

'Macrinus Augustus!' I answered, parrying his clumsy thrust. The young man, probably seeing his first battle, was terribly excited, and he pranced about so energetically that he was on the verge of exhaustion. For a few more passes our swords rattled together; then, because it was his life or mine, I beat down a weak parry and got my point into his throat. He looked more than ever like my old comrade as he fell.

Our third line came forward to our support just at the right moment, when the troops already engaged were fought out and the next push must decide the battle. This third line was made up of the veterans of the veteran Praetorians, grizzled stiff-moving men who for thirty years had lived by the sword; their skins were as tough as the average cuirass, and though they bent their knees with difficulty an elephant could not have knocked them off balance. Quietly and methodically, without losing their breath or hurting the bunions on their gnarled feet, they set about breaking that legion.

But they could not follow up swiftly. In a moment a widening gap showed between the hostile fronts. The Third Gallicans, a very good legion, had disengaged to reform. As they picked up their dressing and closed in over the fallen they passed their ensigns to the front, and out of the corner of my eye I caught sight of the great legionary Eagle, twelve feet of gleaming brass and silver. From the position of the Eagle I knew what would come next. As we charged the Eagle-bearer would hurl it among us; then he and all his comrades would go down fighting in a last desperate bid for victory.

Three mounted leaders galloped up to encourage the failing rebels; or rather, as I saw at a second glance, two camel-riders and a horseman. They were such curious figures that for a hundred yards on either side the victorious Praetorians paused in their advance to look at them.

A tall white dromedary bore an elderly lady wrapped in gorgeous silks; but she wore also a helmet of oriental design and carried a curved scimitar studded with jewels. Under the helmet her face showed black rather than brown, so weather-beaten was it; but the proud curved nose, the obstinate chin, the abundant white hair were familiar. Less than a year ago I had seen her at Emesa. She was the lady Maesa, sister to the Empress Julia Domna.

A smaller camel carried an open litter, and in it a most beautiful woman. Her arms were bare, and a flimsy jewelled breastplate left most of her bosom exposed; her skin gleamed white, for all her life she had been careful to keep in the shade. None the less she also wore a queer little apology for a helmet, and waved a tiny sword. I knew her also. She was the lady Soaemias, the lady Maesa's daughter.

The horse was a black stallion of the tall Nisaean breed from the far side of the desert. His rider, the child Bassianus, wore the gilded cuirass and purple cloak of an Emperor, and waved a genuine sharp sword as big as himself. He was bare-headed, his golden curls waving with the speed of his gallop. He smiled happily amid the dust and blood; handsome, confident, gay, he looked like Cupid wearing the armour of Mars.

He looked also remarkably like the Divine Caracalla; or rather, he looked like the Caracalla we veterans remembered, the dashing young soldier we had raised to the Purple in Britain, before hard living and ruthless suspicion had lined his face with cruelty.

I was suddenly ashamed of myself. We old men, with no joy left in us, dully did our duty, fighting bloodily and craftily for an Emperor we despised; and in doing our duty we would crush these vital, energetic aristocrats, this kindred in which grandmothers rode to battle, this stock of the fairest race on earth. Why should we kill them, just to earn a few more gold pieces from the civilian Macrinus? At that moment I trod on something squashy; it was the belly of the young legionary I had killed, but after he was down someone had made sure of him by ripping him from collarbone to navel. His face, unscarred by some freak of chance, smiled up at me as though he would answer my greeting; he looked more than ever like the comrade with whom I had shared a fire in the snowbound north. And absolute knowledge of where my duty lay came into my mind, as suddenly and mysteriously as though the Ladies whispered into my ear what I must do.

I took five paces to the front, then turned to shout to my astonished comrades. 'Praetorians,' I yelled, 'here is the Emperor we fight against. Isn't he a better man than the Emperor we fight for? Once you took oath to the Divine Caracalla. Look, here is Caracalla come again! My sword and my life for Bassianus Caracalla Augustus!'

Rufus was the first to follow my lead. Sentimental Germans are easily swayed by male beauty. 'Bassianus Augustus!' he shouted, and the man on his left took up the cry. Then my whole century moved forward in line, turned about, and gave a shout of 'Bassianus Augustus!'

That was the end of the battle. For a few minutes longer the two sides faced one another, while the handsome young horseman made his steed caracole between them. Then a Praetorian tribune banged his sword into its scabbard with an emphatic thump, and led his whole cohort to join the Third Gallicans. The Praetorians faced about in a body. As we stood still the dust began to settle.

The beautiful child shaded his eyes and went through a pantomime of looking earnestly about. Then he called, in a clear boyish treble: 'Soldiers, did you fight for some other Emperor? Will you lead me to him? I would like to meet my rival.'

As one man we looked towards the little hillock in the rear, where Macrinus had been stationed before the enemy charged us. The hillock stood empty, save for the imperial battleflag, deserted and planted in the ground.

'Soldiers,' the boy continued, 'you fought for nothing. Your leader ran away, leaving you to die so that he might have a longer start. But we'll catch him all the same, if you help me. Will you?'

The cheering left no doubt of our answer.

'Then you accept my orders?' he went on, with astonishing self-possession for one of his years. 'Right ... I command you to march back to your camp. Clean up the place, and get back as soon as possible to peacetime routine. By sunset you will be employed on your normal duties, the safeguarding of the Emperor's person. I shall sleep tonight at imperial field headquarters.'

He had said exactly the right thing (and he must have composed the speech himself). He took it for granted that we would be loyal to him, and at the same time reminded us of our privilege. When he told us to 'clean up the place' he gave us licence to kill unpopular officers, but when he added that he would be with us that evening he implied that the disorder must be quickly ended. He was the kind of Emperor we needed.

Centurions began to push us into formation, ready to march off; our senior officers, who were mounted, disappeared over the horizon at full gallop. Never mind, we could still plunder their baggage when we got back to camp. My century began to form on me as marker, and I felt sad that my brief moment of distinction was ended. But before I could disappear once more into the ranks the boy reined up beside me.

'You were the first to make up your mind, I saw you,' he said bending down from his horse. 'Here, take this ring. Show it to the sentry when you come to imperial headquarters this evening. Come an hour after sunset. I want to have a chat with you, about war and politics and the army and the Republic in general. Don't be shy. I expect you tonight. That's an order.'

He must have seen, from one look at me, the kind of man I am. I don't like to be prominent, because it's dangerous. All my instincts, after long years of service, tell me to avoid senior officers and their headquarters. But orders are orders, especially when given by the Emperor in person. I fell in with my century and marched back to camp; then the acting-Praefect himself told me I was excused duty for the rest of the day. He sealed a requisition on the stores, which entitled me to draw a complete new outfit for 'an individual ceremonial parade in the presence of the Emperor.'

Some of my comrades advised me to go as I was, with a dented shield and the crest of my helmet shorn away. But a complete new outfit without stoppage of pay was a pleasant windfall, too good to be wasted, and I thought that perhaps a young boy who knew nothing of warfare might be more impressed by a spotless soldier under a tall plume of stiffened horsehair than by a battered veteran whose greaves stank of sweat. Besides, the notches in my sword and the dents in my shield had been acquired while I was killing his adherents.

When I was ready, with a jug of wine inside me to give me courage and a lump of fresh pork on top of the wine to keep it from going to my head, everything I wore was in mint condition. I had even got hold of a ceremonial cuirass, the only one in the stores; for most of them had been left with the heavy baggage in Antioch.

The room into which I was shown had been the private chamber of the Emperor Macrinus (last reported galloping for Cilicia, ahead of a very small bodyguard). It was cozily furnished with couches and chairs; tall lamps burned perfumed oil; at one side a great unglazed window let in what coolness can be found in a Syrian June.

But my first impression was that the room was very hot and very crowded. There were many more people than I had expected and among them a number of women; for that matter, the men also looked out of place in an armed camp, for they wore long epicene gowns of oriental pattern. These people sat or reclined at their ease, instead of standing like courtiers in the presence of their ruler; and at the far end of the room, where one would expect the imperial throne, was a little cabinet of carved wood surrounded by tall candles and smoking incense.

Then I picked out the Emperor, the only figure still in armour. He came forward, seized me by the hand, and prevented me when I tried to kneel. 'Now then, Duratius,' he said gaily, 'stand there in the middle and let us all take a look at you. I have been reading your record. You puzzled your commanding officers, and I want to know whether you will puzzle *me*? "Recommended for promotion and consistently refused it; conduct exemplary, no ambition." That's how they summed you up. Some ancient philosophers would have been anxious to meet you.'

Once again I was struck by the superhuman beauty of this marvellous boy. He radiated happiness and wellbeing. Physically he was perfect; but a perfect miniature man, with nothing feminine about him. His broad shoulders and narrow hips set off his armour, and his legs never tangled with the sword on his thigh.

'Well, what can I do for you?' he went on cheerfully, squatting cross-legged on a little stool. 'Tonight I am Emperor, and I can give you nearly anything you ask for. Not quite anything, because some posts are already filled. I have a very good Praetorian Praefect, and a first-class secretary of state. But would you like to be Praefect of Rome, or governor of a province, or even, since you seem to be keen on soldiering, legate in command of a legion? What shall it be? You have only to ask. They tell me the governor of Egypt does no work and draws a very fine salary.'

I had come prepared to be offered promotion, though not on this imperial scale; and I had made up my mind what I wanted.

'I should like to be a centurion, employed,' I answered in the clipped tone of a soldier on parade. Then, seeing him smile encouragement, I went on to give my reasons. 'You see, my Lord, I don't want to be a great man. I don't mind giving orders but I don't like making enemies. Non-commissioned rank would suit me best. Everyone agrees that of the non-commissioned ranks an employed centurion has the best job in the army. No drilling in the rain, no getting your equipment dirty. But centurion in a legion would do, if you can't find an employed post for me.'

The boy looked puzzled. Suddenly I understood that he did not know what I meant by 'employment', though on the frontier a child of six would have heard all about it. A man lounging on a couch interposed: 'My Lord, he means that he wants a fulltime appointment that will keep him off parade, an appointment that carries with it the rank of centurion. Shall I invent one for him, if you are willing to grant his request?'

'Certainly,' said the Emperor. 'But it must be a job at court. I like this Duratius, and I want to see more of him.'

'Very well, Centurion,' said the stranger. 'I am Eutychianus, the new Praetorian Praefect. You are appointed a supernumerary guard-commander, with special charge of the instructors who will teach military drill and fencing to our mighty Emperor. Move your kit to headquarters this evening. Later on we can go more fully into the scope of your duties.'

'That's splendid,' said the boy, beaming. 'Now if you are to live with us at court you must get to know us all. This is the head of the family, my grandmother, the Augusta Maesa. Here is my mother, the lady Soaemias. She will be an Augusta presently, when I announce her promotion. The Praetorian Praefect has already introduced himself. Over there is master Gannys, who has taught me all I know. He will be my secretary of state. The rest are just family slaves or freedmen, very nice people but I need not introduce them separately.'

I was busy saluting all round, so as not to offend any of these powerful advisers. I saw a smile of encouragement on the face of the Augusta, and a grin of relief for a moment lightened the Emperor's stately beauty. He was very young, and during this series of introductions he had been working hard to remember his manners.

The lady Soaemias spoke: 'The Augusta is of course the head of our family. But I think, dear, you should also point out to this gallant soldier the divine protector who maintains our greatness.'

'Of course I must. How could I have forgotten? Duratius, will you now worship Elagabalus, who has fostered our family for countless generations and today has given me the mastery of the world? You worship him by kissing the ground before his pedestal. There is no need for you to sacrifice. He and I arranged this morning that every man killed today would be devoted to him as a sacrifice.'

I knelt down to kiss the ground as directed. I was glad that I had been ordered to perform the rite in private, for such worship of a bit of black stone might be considered comical by the army at large. As I got up again I looked closely at the new guardian of the Republic. Elagabalus was perky and perhaps benignant, an erect phallus gleaming with perfumed oil; a wreath of fresh roses gave him a rakish air. As a god he would appeal to young boys, but I felt that Rome under his guardianship might be in for some surprising experiences.

'Isn't he a beauty?' cooed the Emperor. 'He has done everything for my family; though of course Eutychianus and Gannys helped, and so did my soldiers. I want all my subjects to share the gratitude I feel to him. Do you think, Grandma, that it would please him if I were to rule in his name? Shall I call myself the Emperor High Priest of Elagabalus? Or would that sound odd in Rome?'

'Not "Emperor High Priest". That's too much of a mouthful,' the old lady answered with decision. 'Why not just the Emperor Elagabalus? Then you and I and all your friends will know that the god rules through your agency, but the common people will suppose that you are just another Emperor – though of course wiser and better in every way than your predecessors.'

'That's it. Someone put it into writing. The god and I shall reign jointly, under the single name of the Emperor Elagabalus. Which of us has inspired any particular decree will be known only to the god and myself. The Emperor Elagabalus – the Romans will see nothing peculiar in the name.'

They would find it very odd indeed, I said to myself. We have been ruled by Emperors sprung from every province, Africans and Spaniards and Illyrians. There was nothing against a Syrian Emperor. But hitherto our rulers had at least borne Roman names. Yet this assembly of intelligent Syrians saw nothing strange in the name Elagabalus, since it was famous all over Syria.

I continued to stand about, because no one told me to sit or gave me permission to withdraw. It seemed to me that the Romans would be in for a good many surprises. They might think they were ruled by a young Syrian, until they found out that he was junior partner in a firm controlled by a black stone phallus; they would never find out, unless Eutcyhianus was mad enough to publish it, that the Emperor regarded his grandmother as head of the family (in Roman law she would be a minor, under the guardianship of her grandson). He seemed also inclined to take orders from his mother. I hoped this gang of foreigners, human and divine, would combine to make a tolerable Emperor. In any case, I had freely given my allegiance; my honour as a Gallic nobleman committed me to stand or fall with them.

Just then another handsome lady burst into the room.

'Mother,' she called, 'I hope I don't interrupt anything important; but a deputation from the citizens of Antioch keeps on offering me bags of gold if only I can get them a word with the Emperor.'

'You can't get them a word with the Emperor, Aunt Mamea,' said the boy. 'I am talking to a soldier. Any soldier is more important than a deputation of flabby civilians.'

'That's what you think, little Bassy. Your grandmother will be more prudent. Mother, this is really a very grand deputation. Besides the city council they have sent the leaders of the circus factions and the commander of the militia.'

Now I could place the newcomer; yet another of these managing females who would not be popular in Rome. But at least her nephew's manner indicated that he did not regard her as another feminine head of the family.

'We must deal with them at once,' said Gannys, a flashy, soft, handsome man who wore too much jewellery. 'Perhaps Mamea need not bring them in here. If we are to receive a solemn deputation we ought to stand in rank while only the Emperor sits. (Sit down, Bassy, and look dignified.) Go and find out what they want. When we have decided whether to grant their request we can have them brought in to hear our answer.'

His eyes sought agreement from the Augusta; but cursorily, as though he knew she would endorse any instructions he might give.

'Yes, Mamea, find out, what they want. And you, Bassy, do as your tutor tells you,' answered the head of the family.

'Very well, I shall sit down,' said the boy, flouncing across the room. 'But you must remember that in future I am to be addressed as Elagabalus. Anyone who calls me Bassianus will be guilty of disrespect, and "Bassy" will be punished as the gravest form of high treason. Find out what these people want and don't bother me. But send in the leaders of the circus factions. I should like a little chat about racing.'

'The races can wait, Elagabalus Augustus,' his grandmother answered with a quelling glance. 'The sun has not yet risen on your Empire, and unless you heed the advice of your natural guardians you may be overthrown before it does.'

'Just as you say, Grandma. Business first if that is your advice. But I want to know how they train racehorses.'

Mamea went out and soon came back again.

'They want to offer a ransom, to avert the sack of Antioch,' she reported.

'We can't avert the sack,' Eutychianus put in at once. 'We might control the Syrians. But the legions, and above all the Praetorians, will consider Antioch fair prize of war. You don't want your reign to begin with a mutiny.'

'But Antioch must *not* be sacked,' said our young ruler. 'If such a terrible crime is committed both the Sun-god and I myself will withdraw our protection from the Empire, and then where will you be? I liked the place when I saw it in the days of Daddy Caracalla, and I look forward to seeing it again. Even the soldiers must know that they will get more fun out of the splendid circus than from a heap of smoking ruins. Eutychianus, you understand soldiers. Think up one of your famous arrangements, so that the city is unharmed.'

'I doubt I can arrange it,' said the Praetorian Praefect thoughtfully. 'Perhaps if the ransom were big enough ... But here is a Praetorian. What do you think, my man?'

'Praetorians can be persuaded, sir. We are veterans, who have sacked many cities at one time or another. The spoil comes to very little when it is divided among a whole army. Besides, we also know Antioch and like it. Offer a good ransom, and see.'

'If the Praetorians agree it will be easy. The legions will follow their lead. In that case we could manage a peaceful entry.'

'How much?' asked the Emperor suddenly, looking at me with a shrewdness that sat curiously on his boyish face.

'Well, my Lord ... five hundred drachmae a man? That's more than we would get from a sack.'

'Splendid. Get it out of the deputation, Eutychianus. Antioch can find it, if they try hard enough. I don't want bloodshed in my Empire. A good time for all will be the policy of my government. Duratius, take this blank tablet. Here is my seal at the bottom. Use it to get what you need from the paymaster, and be here in the morning when I ask for you. Until further notice you are posted to imperial headquarters. Sleep well, and enjoy yourself.'

As I walked back to my hut I thought that under our new ruler most of his subjects would enjoy themselves. What would really puzzle the Romans would be to find the seat of authority; the Emperor had so many unofficial colleagues.

CHAPTER SIX

Winter in Nicomedia

The Emperor was genuinely anxious to learn the squad-drill and sword exercises which are part of the elementary education of every Roman youth. As a child in the imperial household he had made a beginning, but the two years at Emesa had interrupted his studies. There the priests of the sky-stone had taught him their ritual; they had also taught him to read easily in Greek, Latin and Aramaic. He knew many queer legends about the beginning of the world and the odd family life of oriental divinities. But he had forgotten the words of command which every little Roman picks up from listening by a parade ground; and as high priest he carried a curved scimitar, so that in his fencing he relied on the edge and neglected the point in a most un-Roman fashion.

Therefore my post at court, though it had been invented for me, was not exactly a sinecure. Someone at Praetorian head-quarters chose sober, well-spoken, gentle drillmasters and fencing instructors; but the chosen teachers reported to me before they began their task, and I was present during the lessons to make sure that no harm came to the Emperor, either to his body or to his self-esteem. I was something between a special bodyguard and the pedagogue who looks after the behaviour of a young nobleman.

I began to see life from a new point of view. Since the age of fourteen I had lived in intimate contact with comrades rougher and less educated than myself. I had been the clever one, knowing the answer to all difficult questions; and this is very harmful to the character. Now I found myself the slow simple soldier among a crowd of quick-witted beautiful young people, whose talk was full of allusions and references I could not follow. Their flippancy both delighted and shocked me, and the effort to keep up with them sharpened my brain.

The most striking characteristic of the imperial family was a breath-taking beauty. The Augusta, though a grandmother, was none the less a most beautiful lady. Nearly everyday she went riding, and she had allowed her face to get as brown as any man's; but the exercise kept her waist slim and her movements vigorous. She was not tall, but she held herself very straight. She could sink into a pile of cushions without hesitation, and spring erect as easily as a young athlete. Sitting in her chair of state she looked like a statue of Demeter, very wise and motherly but at the same time stern and awesome.

Her daughter Soaemias was beautiful in quite a different fashion. She was a peach, beginning to turn a shade over-ripe. Her skin, never touched by the sun, glowed pink and white, and her body was curve after soft inviting curve. On a cushion she looked eminently desirable, though standing she was a shade too plump. Her mass of golden hair and her huge violet eyes would have made her an outstanding figure in any other setting; at court she was overshadowed by the majesty of her mother and by the golden adolescence of her son.

I cannot begin to describe the young Elagabalus. It is enough to say that I could gaze at him all day long, as one takes pleasure in gazing on a magnificent animal. He had in fact suffered one slight but irreparable disfigurement; like all the other ministers of the sky-stone he had been circumcised. Greeks in particular think this is a very ugly mutilation, and it is of course un-Roman. But it showed only when the Emperor stripped for exercise in the gymnasium, and I found I could overlook it quite easily. On public occasions any great man will wear at least some wisp of cloth round his loins; though Elagabalus, who took pride in his beauty, was inclined to wear very little.

His aunt, the lady Mamea, was another beautiful woman, in a

style intermediate between her mother and her sister. She was soft and pink like the lady Soaemias, but her thin face held some of the Augusta's dignity. She did not pass all her time lolling on cushions, but neither was she fond of exercise; instead she took thought for the better government of the Republic. She was always suggesting reforms, reforms that were never put into effect because long ago her family had decided that her advice was not worth following. She was the only member of the court who was not thoroughly happy. She had no useful work to do, and no authority; for the Emperor, who listened with deference to his mother and grandmother, was often impatient with his talkative aunt.

She spent much of her time with her only child. Little Alexianus was nine years old, only four years younger than his cousin the Emperor. But he was more childish in every way, a baby for his years; though a good obedient baby, with a flair for decorous behaviour in public. He could be trusted to receive deputations or preside over sacrifices. In fact he was a very useful child to have about the place, capable of performing imperial functions but incapable of influencing policy. Since he was also of the family of the high priests of Emesa he also was beautiful; but his regular features showed none of the winning charm of Elagabalus.

The ladies Soaemias and Mamea were widows. Their husbands had been mildly distinguished soldiers; but in that family, ruled by the grandmother, sons-in-law can never have played an important part. Nobody spoke of them. Their task had been to beget sons who would carry on the sacred line of the high priesthood; now the task had been accomplished they were as completely forgotten as the drone who has fathered a queen bee. I believe they had died in the ordinary course of nature; if their wives had murdered them someone would have told me all about it. In that court gossip had free rein, and the most discreditable stories were told of the great.

Most of these discreditable stories involved Gannys, who was officially the Emperor's tutor. In truth he had taken over all the male duties in that female household. There was no attempt to conceal the fact that he slept with the Augusta, and it was whispered that in addition he consoled her widowed daughters. He had commanded the little band of Syrian volunteers who first proclaimed the new Emperor, and he had engineered the boy's appearance on the ramparts at Raphanae which won over the Third Gallican Legion; so that at one time he had seemed important. But nowadays he was a kind of bailiff or managing clerk, who decided practical matters too trivial for the attention of his superiors; though the Emperor or any of the three ruling ladies would countermand his orders whenever they chose.

Gannys was no fool. All the same, he could not hold down a responsible post, because he did not understand Romans. He came from some barbarous mountain in Asia, and spoke Greek with a thick accent; Latin he could barely understand. As a professional stallion he took great care of his health, always sweating in the bath to keep his waist trim and gobbling little doses of medicine between meals. He was well educated. He was tall and dark, and moved very gracefully; even I could see that a Syrian would find him dashing and attractive. But his vanity, and his foreign upbringing, led him to wear such extraordinary clothes that he had to be kept in the background for fear that the soldiers would laugh at him. It was hard to remember that this creature, languishing under a high turban crowned with peacock's feathers, his eyes painted and false ringlets tumbling over his neck, had risked his life to start a hazardous rebellion.

Eutychianus, the last member of the council, was another Asiatic who spoke Latin as a foreign language. All the same, he was an ordinary Roman, of the kind that has become ordinary during my lifetime. He had enlisted as a common soldier, won a commission for bravery in the field, and risen by merit to command the Third Gallicans. Once he had declared for Bassianus-Elagabalus he naturally overshadowed the civilian Gannys. As far as I know he never crept into the bed of any of the ruling ladies; he was not a member of the imperial household, but rather their trusted military adviser. Now he was

Praetorian Praefect, which under an Emperor of such inexperience made him in practice commander-in-chief. It was obvious that sooner or later he must clash with Gannys; there was no room for two males in that feminine court. But for the time being the administration was still so insecure that all its adherents must work together in harmony.

Though my position was humble I knew all that passed. Never can there have been a court which made less attempt to keep secret its counsels. In a sense the Emperor ruled, for the army would support him in battle; if he had asked for the head of the Praetorian Praefect he would have got it. But a thirteen-year-old boy cannot rule an Empire. Nothing was done against the will of Elagabalus, but a great many decisions must be made in matters to which he was indifferent.

The driving force was the Augusta, though she was scrupulous to get the Emperor's warrant for everything she did. She was too wise to ask her grandson to spend long hours in council; instead she sought him out wherever he might be and whatever he might be doing. Often when he was learning his arms-drill the Augusta would come in with a sheaf of papers for his seal. Usually he asked what was in them, though he never disagreed with what she had written; sometimes he would seal them without inquiry. As discreetly as possible I told him how the Divine Caracalla had been murdered, as a warning that an Emperor should look through his correspondence. He was sharp enough to see what I meant, and frank enough to explain his lack of suspicion.

'The Augusta enjoys ruling,' he said with a grin, 'and she cannot rule save as my grandmother. I suppose you fear she might marry Gannys, give him the Purple, and rule as his consort. That wouldn't work, you know. If Gannys replaced me he would have no need of an Augusta. Anyway the soldiers would murder him. They don't like his embroidered skirts, though I think he looks sweet in them. Besides, though the Augusta likes Gannys, I think she likes me even more.'

'I wasn't thinking of Gannys, my lord,' I answered. 'Eutychianus holds the post held by Macrinus under the Divine Caracalla. The soldiers might follow a promoted ranker.'

The fencing instructor was listening with his ears flapping. He was new to the manners of this carefree court.

'The Augusta does not like Eutychianus,' said the Emperor with decision. 'He's a good soldier, and I shall keep him on to run my army. But he will never fit in with the rest of us; he's too serious. No one who worships the sky-stone would want Eutychianus for Emperor. I trust him because he lacks appeal. Besides, I really do work very hard at being Emperor. While the family remains united no one can overthrow me. . . . Now then, what's your name, instructor, let's see if I can cut the crest from your helmet.'

To be a member of that court was to hold high rank, for within the imperial household all were equal. The Emperor was always seeking advice, though he did not always follow it; but he would seek it from anyone who happened to be passing. Petitioners found him easily, but they were sometimes surprised to hear him discuss their problems with the boy who carried his sunshade, with a casual slave at the door, perhaps with the Augusta or the Praetorian Praefect. We addressed him as 'my lord' and got out of his way going through doors; otherwise there was no etiquette at all. It was difficult to wait on him, because at any moment he might catch hold of a dish or a jug of wine and himself pass it round the company. I learned to be considerate even to grubby slave-girls; for if the Emperor heard you being haughty to a housemaid (he knew them all by name, and how their love-affairs were prospering) he might order you to hold her bucket for her next time she scrubbed the floor.

Of course the reason for this friendliness was that Elagabalus thought of himself as a god among mortals. A slave girl was infinitely beneath him, but so was a Praetorian Praefect. A god cannot be bothered with petty differences of rank among his worshippers. Since the Emperor was benevolently inclined towards the whole human race he treated us with an all-embracing kindliness.

During those first days of the new reign events favoured us. Every soldier of the imperial field army was willing to die for this beautiful young god, who seemed Caracalla come again without the cruelty that had marred Caracalla's last years. At the same time he managed to keep his popularity with the provincials. Our entry into Antioch had passed off in perfect peace, though everyone had expected trouble. The citizens produced the very large ransom demanded, and the soldiers were satisfied with their payment of 500 drachmae a man. All the world knew that the young Emperor had himself devised the compromise. It was many years since an Emperor had protected a city from the rapacity of loyal soldiers.

Even such a successful revolution brought a few executions, though they were kept to a minimum. Macrinus was arrested in Asia; the local police started to send him back to Antioch, until the Emperor sent word that he should be killed immediately to put him out of his misery. This was done, painlessly and without torture, somewhere along the road. The usurper left neither supporters nor mourners.

The merciful Emperor was distressed when he heard of the fate of young Diadumenus. His father had sent the child eastward to seek refuge in Parthia, whose king is usually glad to welcome a Roman pretender. But this time the Parthian commander on the frontier chose to stand on the letter of the regulations. He would not permit the fugitive to enter without a valid passport; while they argued on the river-bank someone cut off the boy's head and sent it to Antioch in hope of a reward. The child was not to blame for his usurpation; all the same, he had been a usurper. When his father gave him the title of Caesar he compelled his son to share in the dangerous trade of Empire.

It was rather more surprising to learn that while we had been fighting in Syria no less than five pretenders had claimed the Purple in other provinces of the Roman world. It seemed such a futile enterprise. Macrinus might defeat Elagabalus; but which-ever side won must provide the next Emperor, since the field army was concentrated in Syria. A claimant who set himself at the head of a provincial garrison deserved death as the punishment for sheer stupidity.

Macrinus, Diadumenus, the five pretenders, all had forfeited their lives in a gamble for high stakes. In addition five prominent soldiers were killed, including the governor of Syria and the acting Praetorian Praefect, successor to the unlucky Julianus; these last were so closely identified with Macrinus that they must share his fate, though Elagabalus regretted it.

There was no persecution of the kindred and backers of these defeated rivals. The police were warned that further denuncia-tions would be disregarded.

Just when all the citizens of Antioch were embracing one another in the streets, and offering hecatombs in gratitude for the return of the Golden Age, a courier arrived from Rome. When he was brought before the Emperor the poor man was in a pitiful state of terror; but he had been arrested as he landed from his ship and could not escape. The letter he carried proved to be the reply of the Senate to an earlier message from Macrinus, a message giving news of the outbreak of civil war. The Senators sent their best wishes to the legitimate Emperor, so sorely beset by ungrateful Syrians, and to prove their loyalty decreed the extermination of the whole house of Antoninus Severus wherever it might be found.

The Emperor Elagabalus returned a dignified reply. He suggested that the Senate had been misinformed concerning the true state of affairs; but he promised amnesty and forgiveness for anything done to further the cause of Macrinus, during the time when Macrinus commanded the Roman army. The answer was composed by a joint session of all the Emperor's advisers, and we chuckled a good deal as we went over the wording. The Senators must be grateful for the imperial clemency, but at the same time they were roughly reminded that the army, not the Senate, bestowed the Purple. For one reason or another, no one in the imperial household liked or admired Senators.

Meanwhile the Parthians were glad to confirm the peace first concluded with the fallen Macrinus. They were having trouble with their conquered subjects, and our agents informed us that they were in no condition to renew the war. The Emperor was able to put Syria on a peace footing, to end military requisitioning and dismiss the local levies. The legions of the field army set out by slow stages to march back to Europe, which pleased the men in the ranks. The faithful Third Gallicans and the cohorts that had murdered Julianus were promoted to form a new corps, the Alban Legions. These would normally be stationed in Italy, though not actually in Rome. They would accompany the Emperor whenever he took the field. In fact they would be a kind of outer guard, below the Praetorians but above the common legions of the line.

All this was accomplished without extra taxation, though often the demobilisation of an army and the donatives that mark a new reign are as burdensome to the taxpayer as a great campaign. Of course the cities of the east offered the usual complimentary presents, which in legal theory are voluntary and so do not count as extra taxation; and the private fortunes of the usurpers and pretenders brought in something useful to the treasury. The Parthians very wisely sent a handsome present, which might be labelled tribute from a defeated foe; they saved themselves money in the long run by making it easy for the Emperor to despatch his field army to Europe. But the great savings of expense was that the maintenance of the imperial household cost the taxpayer nothing. The Emperor and all his family lived on the revenues of the temple at Emesa.

Eutychianus commanded the army on its long march by way of the Cilician Gates. The imperial household, including myself, journeyed by sea. This had been decided after the usual frank and public discussion in council; a discussion in which I, or for that matter any passing footman, might be asked to join. There was a problem in etiquette to be solved. The Emperor had announced that the sky-stone, the other Elagabalus, would lead the expedition; since it was the god who ruled through his high priest as agent. The Augusta said that such honour paid to a foreign god would irritate the Romans, and might even cause discontent in the army. When they asked for my opinion I answered that the soldiers would take anything from the heir of the Divine Severus, though perhaps they might not like his god; but that indeed the Romans, and especially the Senators, would be irritated.

'There you are, Elagabalus,' said the Augusta, triumphantly. 'Duratius knows what he's talking about, and he says that if we pay too much honour to our god we shall anger the Romans. You may not allow him to lead your army from one end of the Empire to the other.'

'The god will come with me to Rome. There he will assume dominion over the whole earth. If you won't let me do that, Grandma, he will go back to Emesa and I shall go with him.'

'Of course our god will come to Rome,' answered the Augusta with a rapt look on her face. 'We owe him everything, and unless we show ourselves grateful he may withdraw his favour. But we must move tactfully. Go to Rome yourself, and make sure of your power before you proclaim his dominion over the whole earth.'

'I wish you wouldn't all talk about *our* god,' said the Emperor pettishly. 'He is *my* god, for I am his high priest. I have been circumcised in his honour, which was painful at the time and still mars my beauty. I learned all those long prayers and difficult dances to please him. What have you done for him, any of you others?'

He looked triumphantly at his mother and his aunt, who as usual sat beside the Augusta. 'We are kin to the high priest,' said Mamea sharply. 'You are high priest because you are your mother's son. If you gave us our proper place in the government we could do more to help both you and *our* god.'

It was a sore point with the lady Mamea that she was not Augusta, though the Emperor was always promising to promote her. A more tactful woman would have realised that he would never grant her the title, though he could not bring himself to make a definite refusal.

'I don't want to be equal in precedence with my own mother,' said the lady Soaemias with a simper. 'It is enough for me to be the mother of the Emperor. Without me you would never have come into the world, my dear, and then the Romans would be in a very bad way.'

The lady Mamea snorted. The lady Soaemias spoke so placidly that it was always hard to know whether she was being deliberately spiteful or merely tactless.

'You yourself have a fine son, Mamea,' said the Augusta, 'though little Alexianus is not so beautiful as his cousin the Emperor.'

'He's good, and that's more important than being beautiful,' Mamea answered with a sniff. 'I am only the Emperor's aunt, but I also am descended from the high priests of Elagabalus. I ought to have some title to distinguish me from the common herd.'

'An unfortunate metaphor, auntie darling. How can we distinguish you from the herd? Would you like to be known as the chief cow?' The Emperor hooted with laughter at his own wit.

'This is getting us nowhere,' Gannys put in from the corner where he lounged. 'Elagabalus, you must apologise to your aunt. You don't want to be known as the boorish Emperor, do you? But we were discussing how to get the sky-stone honourably to Rome, without offending the army. It's quite simple. There is no need for the Emperor to march with his men. Why don't we all go by sea?'

Everyone cheered up at the suggestion. It would be much more comfortable for the ladies than bumping over rutted roads in carriages, and we would have all our baggage handy by us. There was the added advantage that the Emperor might install his sky-stone on the poop, and give him command of the flagship, without anyone noticing it except a few sailors. Sailors are despised by the army, and not very highly valued by the Senate, so that no one need mind what they thought.

Our ships voyaged slowly along the Asiatic coast, putting in at every rich port to receive an address of welcome and the customary present. I travelled on a troopship with the body-guard, so I saw little of my young lord and his extraordinary family. By the time we reached Smyrna the season was grown late; the Emperor changed his mind, and decided to join his army. Then in Nicomedia he changed his mind again, because the autumn was rainy and cold. In October he would celebrate his fourteenth birthday, which would call for lengthy festivities. It was decreed that the court would remain in Nicomedia until spring, lodging in the great palace of the ancient Kings of Bithynia.

On the eve of that fourteenth birthday the Augusta sent for me. I was taken down long corridors to a small room at the very end of the palace, a hot little boudoir crammed with cushions. A slave-girl stood by the door, ready to run errands, and Gannys lounged as usual in a corner; but the Augusta, perched sideways on a tall stool as though she were riding a camel, spoke to me without bothering about eavesdroppers.

'Tomorrow the Emperor will be fourteen, Duratius,' she said abruptly. 'In Syria that makes him a man. Yet in some ways he is still absurdly childish. It's time he grew up. I want your help in that, for I know he listens to you. He *plays* at everything. Can you persuade him to be serious? I don't want him to govern the Empire. Gannys and I can do that, and he's still too young for it. But he ought to have some adult interests. For example, is he attracted to girls?'

'I really don't know, Augusta. He talks to me about war, and about chariot-racing. I can make him work at his drill, if I don't push him too hard. But I am not his tutor in serious subjects, and if I bore him he won't listen to me at all.'

'That's a dig at me, I suppose,' drawled Gannys. 'I never imagined an imperial household would be so catty. Even a hired drillmaster makes sarcastic remarks about the only educated man in this barbarous establishment.'

'When I want your opinion I'll ask for it,' the Augusta snapped. 'If you spent more time educating my grandson, instead of lolling on cushions in ladies' boudoirs, the Emperor would be more of a man.'

'Oh, very well. I'm only a professional scholar, with years of study in Alexandria behind me. When it comes to serious discussion I must leave the field to ladies and centurions.'

Gannys scrambled to his feet and went out in a huff.

'That man is getting too big for his boots,' said the Augusta coolly. 'Take notice, Duratius. You need not try to make the Emperor subservient to his tutor. There would be no harm in encouraging a little independence in that quarter. But to get back to the main problem. Can't we get the Emperor to take interest in something more adult than chariot-racing? Do you think it would help him to grow up if he were married to some nice girl? Have you noticed him chasing even a bad girl, which might lead him to appreciate a nice one?'

A bit of gossip clicked into place in my mind. Only this morning a valet had told me, as a funny story, that recently the Augusta had sent for Gannys in the middle of the night; he could not be found because he was in the bed of the lady Soaemias. The morals of these ladies were no concern of mine, yet it might be important to remember that Gannys was on the way out.

But I must answer the Augusta's question. She was shrewd enough to deserve the truth even though it might not please her.

'I have never noticed the Emperor chase a girl, madam. It would not be very noticeable, would it? I mean, an Emperor does not have to run very fast to catch any girl, does he?'

'You know what I mean. Don't fence with me, Duratius. Is the Emperor a man? It's hard for a grandmother to see whether her grandson has grown up.'

'I know what you mean, madam, and still I can't answer. I

99

have seen him gaze after a pretty slave-girl, but only as he gazes at a fine statue. As you know, he has a horror of ugliness, and won't have ugly people near him if it can be avoided. But if you really want my candid opinion it's boys he likes, not girls.'

'There's no harm in that, except that one day he must father a family. There's only little Alexianus to carry on the ancient line of the high priests of Emesa. Soon the Emperor must make a suitable marriage, though it need not interfere with his private amusements. I'll be frank with you, Duratius. When I think of our entry into Rome I feel nervous. We are foreigners, and utterly alone. The army is on our side, of course; but soldiers are fickle. I don't understand Romans, and some of their great families wield a lot of influence. As soon as we get to Rome I want the Emperor to marry the daughter of some great house. Then we can fill the magistracies with our own kinsmen. It's absurd that at present I don't know a single Consular.'

'I suppose those old families matter, madam. As a soldier I wouldn't know. The Emperor must marry, of course, and it would be fitting if he marries the daughter of a great house. I shall do my best to put the idea into his mind.'

'I want you to do more than that. I want you to teach the Emperor that marriage can be a pleasure. Tomorrow he is fourteen and the day will be filled with celebrations. The day after tomorrow I want you to take him to a smart brothel, and see he has a good time. That's an order, from the Augusta. Now be off, and don't chatter about what I have told you.'

The Emperor had himself devised the ritual for his fourteenth birthday, for which precedent was lacking; as a result it turned out to be a festival rather in honour of the sky-stone than of a mortal ruler (that Elagabalus might mean either of them or both was a perpetual stumbling-block to busy courtiers). In the morning the sky-stone was carried into the great Temple of Jupiter. With the rest of the court I was in the procession that followed his litter, and we westerners were shocked to see that the image of Jove, Father of Gods and Men, had been overturned to provide a plinth for the little black phallus. Then the Emperor in person waved incense before his patron, and the whole congregation was pushed into line for a dance. It was not much of a dance; we just hopped and shuffled where we stood for a very few minutes. The Syrians took it all as a matter of course, but again the westerners found it embarrassing. There were a few Praetorian sentries on duty. I had a word with them afterwards to remind them that I had great influence with the Emperor, and that any soldier who told funny stories about a dancing centurion might expect to find his military career beset with misfortune.

Then the Emperor offered a hecatomb, not of bulls but of flamingoes: big birds from Egypt of a striking pink colour. I had never before seen them offered in sacrifice; I believe the Emperor himself thought of the novelty. It was a good idea, all the same. The Parthian War had fallen heavily on the east, and there was a shortage of horned cattle; nobody would want a hundred bulls to be killed at once, even though the Emperor paid for them honestly. The flamingoes, dead or alive, were of no use to anyone; though I believe the Alexandrians charged a high price for them.

After the sacrifice there were long prayers and even longer hymns; during which the worshippers must remain standing in their places. But it was no worse than a ceremonial parade, and those of us with a military training endured it fairly well. At long last even the Emperor thought his sky-stone had been sufficiently honoured. The procession formed up again to march back to the palace and settle down to feasting.

Throughout the day the Emperor remained the high priest. I never saw him relax and enjoy himself, even when the most skilled orators in Asia made graceful speeches in his honour. He drank very little, and before he ate anything went through the ritual of offering it to his god. I have nothing against that sky-stone, but I could never take it seriously; to me it will never be more than a smutty joke. The Emperor quite genuinely worshipped it. You might say that he loved it, though love is an odd word to use for the relationship between a worshipper and his god.

The rest of the court had a very gay time, for the food and drink were excellent and plentiful. Our ruler was all that could be desired, beautiful and intelligent and high-spirited and merciful. If he was not yet very wise that hardly mattered. The Emperor leads the army, but we were at peace with all our neighbours. In civil affairs only one policy was possible: to raise enough money to buy the army's loyalty, and in the process ruin as few civilians as possible. At fourteen Elagabalus could do that as well as the next man.

Best of all, we felt secure. Elagabalus did not turn against his friends, and if he tried to his grandmother would stop him. Throughout the world his rule was accepted; all the pretenders were dead, nowhere did a province rise in arms. During that autumn civilisation was at peace.

On the next morning I reported as usual to take the Emperor to his sword exercise. He was still in a very affable mood, and I had no difficulty in introducing the subject of a night out. He answered at once that it would be great fun, but that he did not want sour looks from his grandmother. 'The Augusta will not object, my lord,' said I; at which he gave me a shrewd look and at once consented. Every Syrian is quick to take a hint.

The evening had been planned with care. The Augusta had given me a heavy bag of gold, and I had seen to it that we would be expected. There were a few discreet patrols in the low quarter of the town, but I had decided to risk taking no escort.

Alone, the two of us slipped out of a postern. We walked through dark streets to our destination, and no one recognised us. But in a palace these things always leak out, and at the Nine Muses we found Mother Gyges waiting to greet us. She had crowded the doorway with torch-bearers, and turned away all her other customers. I was a little sorry that the Emperor would not see ordinary night life, but at least we could count on a special entertainment.

Mother Gyges had everything under control. She was a mountaineer from the Caucasus, and a most uninhibited woman. The story goes that she was a courtesan of outstanding beauty, until she got mixed up in a brawl that cost her one eye. A remorseful syndicate of past lovers put up the money to buy her a good brothel. She prospered because she knew what men like, never robbed her customers, and would throw out even a policeman, if he became quarrelsome in his cups. In her hands the Emperor would be safe, as well as, I hoped, amused.

As we sat over supper in the main room a dozen girls did the usual dances, which I need not describe in detail. As a matter of fact I was myself a little embarrassed. I was not used to this kind of company. With a companion of my own age I might have been jolly; but the Emperor stared at everything in wonder, and asked awkward questions.

To liven the pace, Mother Gyges announced a fight between a buxom negress and a tall German girl with a very white skin. She called me into a corner to explain the attraction.

'It's hard to rouse such a child,' she said, 'but this fetches everyone. It's the speciality of the house. We keep the German in a cellar, so that her skin is always white. Bruises show on it after a few minutes. Of course the fight's fixed, and she loses. When it's over they come out to drink with the guests. You can see it as an omen for the new reign. If the Emperor is stern he will pick the strapping black, if he's kindly he will choose the battered white. But if he's anything of a man he will take one of them.'

Mother Gyges realised that I was on duty; she did not press me to choose a girl for myself. I enjoy a night out with a party of congenial comrades, but my dignity will not allow me to hire a girl in cold blood.

The wrestling was a very good show; if I had not known it was rehearsed I would have taken it for a desperate struggle. When at last the German was hurled against the wall, to lie as though stunned, everyone in the room clapped with enthusiasm. Presently the two naked, sweating women knelt before the

Emperor, holding out their hands for the expected tip. He gave them a few gold pieces as solemnly as if he were distributing a military donative, and then engaged the German in conversation. After a whispered exchange she led him to a curtained alcove. Grinning, Mother Gyges muttered: 'I've never known it fail.'

Then I had to listen to her complaints about the police, and the even heavier bribes demanded by the officers of the Praetorians while the court was in Nicomedia. I was able to content her without bothering the Emperor. The bag of gold I carried for expenses had been sealed with the imperial signet. A little work with a hot knife transferred the wax to a sheet of parchment; on it we drew up instructions to every police authority in the Empire, informing them that Mother Gyges was a personal friend of the Emperor.

For half an hour I drank very happily with the girls, while the old bawd told stories of her past. Then the Emperor and his German came back to join us; but in answer to my look of inquiry the girl shook her head.

The Emperor, who was a little drunk, talked incessantly. 'I must free Gunda,' he babbled. 'Fancy, she was enslaved as a baby by my father, the Divine Caracalla, so it's only fair that his son should set her free. What's her price, Mother Gyges? Hand it over, Duratius. There, my dear, you are free. Where will you go now?'

'If you free her, my lord, you must also give her enough money to start her own brothel. It's the only trade she knows, and of course she can't marry.' Before the Emperor freed every girl who caught his fancy I thought it prudent to point out the difficulties.

'Oh no,' cried the girl. 'I like working here. Mother Gyges would never turn me away. But it will be nice to work for proper wages, and keep all my tips.'

'Then everyone's happy,' I said hastily. 'The girl is free, and the Nine Muses will not have to seek more staff. It's getting late, my lord. Shall we start back for the palace?'

It was quite easy to get the Emperor away, which I had feared would be the most difficult part of my task. But it was impossible to stop him talking all the way home.

'I was sorry for poor Gunda, even though she looks so ugly: red bruises on a skin like the belly of a fish, and that horrible female softness that reminds me of my wetnurse. The silly girl seemed to think I might want to caress her. Can you imagine anything more disgusting? There's a smell about women that turns my stomach. But I gave her a good tip, and her freedom, and I listened patiently to all she had to say. They keep her in the dark, you know, to preserve her pallor; and when she fights that negress she always loses. Isn't there a law against cruelty to slaves? If not, there ought to be and I shall make one.'

'There are any number of laws against cruelty to slaves, dating back to the time of the Divine Augustus. Since a slave cannot give evidence in court it's a little difficult to enforce them. But that German trollop was not ill-used. Now she is free she wants to go on doing for wages what she did as a slave. By the way, my lord, was there no one there who took your fancy? When you went off with Gunda I never guessed it was to listen to the story of her life.'

'That was a nice little boy who took our cloaks at the door, but all the women were frightful. I know why we made this expedition. The Augusta arranged it, to find out whether I am a man. Well, you can tell my grandmother that I am a man, but that I don't like women. Never bother me with this kind of thing again. But I am not angry with you. You carried out orders, and you didn't badger me to stay in a place that disgusts me. Besides, I have learned how some of my subjects live. It isn't slavery that does the damage. That's just as well, because if it was we couldn't cure it. Civilisation rests on slavery, as any philosopher will tell you. No, it isn't slavery, it's the hard life of the harlot, whether slave or free. One day I shall do something for the poor creatures. The really horrible things they must do to please silly men!'

'Without those horrible things no man would be born, my lord. And it's a fact that most people enjoy them.'

'Yes, but I am not most people. I am the high priest of Elagabalus; and when Elagabalus does not need me I am Emperor of the Roman People. I shall never touch a woman for my own pleasure. Tell the Augusta, so that she drops the subject for ever. All the same, now that I am a grown-up man, fourteen years old, I recognise the responsibility laid on me. When the time comes I shall marry, solely to beget heirs. That is a duty which I owe to the sacred line of the priest-kings, which has continued in Emesa since time began.'

I would have to tell the Augusta that the evening had ended in failure; but I could reassure her that the Emperor was willing to face marriage. Since he disliked all women he would not object if the bride chosen for him were personally unattractive.

CHAPTER SEVEN

Gannys Drops Out

By midwinter there was a feeling of strain at the palace. The Augusta was making her grandson learn too many things at once. The household of the Divine Caracalla must have been a ramshackle establishment, for the Emperor, who had been reared in it for the first ten years of his life, knew nothing of Roman etiquette or even of Roman daily life. When he was in a good mood he had exquisite manners; but they were Syrian manners, as used in the temple of Emesa. Instead of returning a military salute he would give his hand to be kissed by the sentry; if he was pleased with me he would embrace me on both cheeks. He was ignorant of the sacred constitution bequeathed to us by our ancestors; he mixed up praetors and Consuls, and was surprised to hear they were appointed annually. Though he could read and write with fluency, he had never read the Latin classics. He could not always recall correctly the sphere of influence of an Olympian god; he was capable of asking Minerva to calm the sea, or Neptune to help with his lessons.

Since he would enter Rome in the spring, when the Augusta wished him to behave like a young Roman, his lessons were long. Eutychianus taught him high politics, with special emphasis on the distribution of the army and the relative strength of the different provincial forces; he also tried to teach him finance. The Emperor was intelligent, and his good memory retained what he had learned; soon he could repeat the battle order of the western legions, and the precedence of the provincial governors. Concerning finance he learned little, for there is little to be learned. Citizens *look* rich; the army always needs more money, and usually gets it; yet there is never enough to go round, and both citizens and soldiers perpetually complain of poverty. I think that is all that the wisest man can say about the finance of the Empire.

Eutychianus found the Emperor an apt pupil, because he was teaching him real things, things which would help him to hold the Purple. Gannys had a harder task, for what he taught was ultimately nonsense. At bottom, it is impossible to believe that a Consul is greater than a praetor, since neither of them wields the slightest power. The Senate is called the Emperor's colleague in government; but the Emperor can have any Senator killed without trial. Jupiter on the Capitol may be the supreme ruler and protector of the Roman People; but no one truly expects any help from him . . . Nevertheless, the Augusta had commanded Gannys to teach the Emperor everything a Roman noble ought to know, and the long hours in the classroom bored the poor boy dreadfully.

His lessons in drill and swordplay gradually ceased as the cold weather made it unpleasant to hang about out of doors. He had learned how to call a parade to attention, how to pick out a fault or two while inspecting a guard of honour, and how to order the men to march off when the function was over. I could not teach him how to lead the Roman army to victory, and there seemed to be no point in teaching him the tactical handling of a cohort in the presence of the enemy. If the worst came to the worst he knew how to wave his sword and charge in front, because he had done exactly that at Immae. The late Macrinus held the Purple for a year without knowing even so much.

Though the Emperor no longer practised his drill I saw more of him than ever. He had chosen me as his companion in the arduous task of learning all about chariot-racing. In that we started more or less level, and I did my best to keep up with his quick brain. We were both good horsemen; neither of us knew how much a horse should eat or how you keep him fit; neither of us had the slightest idea of how to control a chariot.

The trouble is that, though everyone watches the races, the actual job of driving a racing chariot is one of those stigmatised by our ancestors as ignoble. A man who drives a racing chariot is debarred from public office, unworthy of commissioned rank in the army, and in general considered disgraceful. Therefore the only people who learn to drive chariots are slaves; though by the time they are successful some admirer has usually bought their freedom.

Since the Emperor was set on learning how to drive a chariot the Augusta arranged that he should learn in private. In the morning he did his amusing lessons with Eutychianus, or his dull lessons with Gannys; in the afternoon he went out to a high-walled private park, where his servants had laid out a full racecourse of a furlong each way, with proper turning posts. There the freedmen employed by the circus factions of Nicomedia taught him how to guide four horses, attached to a flimsy car that will fall to pieces if you overturn it.

The Emperor graciously allowed me to watch, because the experts said I was too old and heavy to make a good driver. So I did not risk my life daily as he did. It is physically impossible to control a four-horse chariot, though a clever driver can persuade the horses to comply with his wishes. If you are riding and your horse bolts you can tug at the bit until you break his jaw or turn him over. When a chariot is going at speed the horses will pull you as readily by the reins as by the traces; they stop only because the driver dominates their stupid minds.

Some of the little slave-boys of Nicomedia could make a team of four fresh horses obey them instantly. I don't know how they did it, and they themselves could not explain; the horses knew what was wanted from them and were eager to please their drivers. I thought at first that it might be because slaves are not afraid of breaking their necks; but then the Emperor picked up the knack, and he had more to lose by sudden death than anyone else in the world. I suppose it is a combination of courage and dexterity and being able to think as a horse thinks. Whatever it is, the Emperor possessed it.

He was enthralled by his new amusement. When sunset drove us from the racecourse he would potter about the stables by lantern-light, fussing over the horses he had driven. Chariot-driving may be an ignoble calling; but it is difficult and dangerous, and the Emperor had mastered it.

I admired his courage and skill, and he liked me the more for my admiration. That crowded household was full of people who loved him, who loved him with the fierce, stifling devotion of a Syrian lady for her helpless infant; but none of the assorted relatives who helped him to govern the Empire admired him as a man. In their eyes he was still little Bassianus, who was doing very well in a job really too difficult for him.

He liked me for another reason; I never asked him for anything. I did not seek power or promotion; surrounded as I was by all that money can buy, I had no need to ask even for money. My centurion's pay went straight into my savings, invested in the British branch of a banking syndicate; I kept quiet about it, and no one would look in Britain for the fortune I was rumoured to be accumulating. I spent nothing on clothes; whenever I wanted to look smart I could draw another gorgeous cuirass from the quartermaster. I spent nothing on food or drink; I had only to clap my hands for a slave to bring me roast pheasant or Chian wine. When suitors pressed bribes on me which I could not refuse without offence, I at once passed on the money to a sensible slave, for preference one who was saving to buy his freedom. Even the palace servants did not hate me, as they hate most low-born favourites of the great.

The ladies trusted me as an informal bodyguard, and disregarded me as a man. They were very busy, and they had no time to eliminate friends of the Emperor who were not their rivals as rulers.

There was a great deal of ruling to be done from Nicomedia, and most of it was done by the ladies. Official correspondence went first to the Augusta, but a petitioner with a grievance might get hold of any member of the family. There were few important decisions of policy; the aim of the new government was peace abroad and retrenchment at home. The Germans were still afraid of us and the Parthians in trouble with their own subjects; we could have peace unless we wished to attack. The army was content with its lavish pay. Only the Senate in Rome was a little offended with the Emperor, or so our spies informed us; and for a very absurd reason.

When the Senate received the Emperor's generous pardon for their letter in support of Macrinus they of course voted statues in gratitude for his clemency. But nobody in Rome knew what he looked like. At their request the Emperor sent them a portrait; and by some silly slip he sent off, without consulting any of his elders, the picture of himself that he liked best. Eutychianus or Gannys, or even I myself if I had heard of it in time, would have prevented the mistake. The picture showed him in his robes as high priest of his sky-stone, with his face painted and his hair curled and his neck hidden by splendid but unmanly jewellery. Someone who saw it started a rumour that the Emperor was a eunuch, and every stuffy Senator agreed that he could not be a true son of Romulus.

It was after this episode that the Augusta insisted on opening all letters. The lady Soaemias was willing to leave everything to her mother, so long as she might find salaries for the handsome young men who consoled her widowhood. Only the lady Mamea stood on her right to be consulted. She had been the first to see that the Emperor was unlikely to beget a son, which would make her Alexianus his natural heir. But it would be silly to set up Alexianus as a rival in the same field; a gay, beautiful boy will not win the love of soldiers who already serve a gay, beautiful young Emperor. The lady Mamea began to cultivate, at long range, the respectable opinion of Rome. As tutors for her son she sought worthy, frowsy, Latin-speaking sages who knew the Twelve Tables by heart.

The Augusta made every decision of importance; in this she had no rival, for no one else at court wanted to take on the laborious task of governing the civilised world. But all the others, even Gannys, thought they were entitled to get special treatment for their friends. Sometimes there was trouble, when different men received the same appointment from different patrons; then the Augusta, as head of the family, would straighten things out. But she took care never to overrule the Emperor. In name the Emperor must be supreme, for the Roman People will never consent to be governed by a woman.

The Emperor very seldom wanted a job for a friend; the reward he preferred to give was money. He got that in handfuls from the military chest, which was controlled by the Praetorian Praefect. There was always enough in this chest for the Emperor's personal needs, and for the soldiers' pay. No government money was spent on anything else.

The Emperor had made a number of new friends, though so far they were not greedy. Practically everyone who worked in the racing stables, slave or free, got a gold piece from him whenever he went down to look at the horses. Of course they praised the Emperor's driving, and allowed him to take out their most valuable teams. But there was no flattery in this; for the Emperor was rapidly becoming the best chariot-driver in Nicomedia.

He took up particularly with one driver, a freedman named Gordius. This fellow was at the peak of his career, I suppose in his late twenties; for by thirty most drivers are too old for the racecourse. At any rate, he was completely an adult, which made him seem much older than the boyish Emperor. By birth he was some kind of eastern barbarian, though he spoke Greek like any Bithynian. He was chief driver for the Greens, and had been given his freedom some years before. But the most important thing about him was that he was strikingly handsome.

The Emperor quite genuinely fell in love with him. What was even more strange, Gordius quite genuinely loved the Emperor. There was nothing unequal about their relationship, nothing of the abasement that you normally find in an affair between ruler and subject. At first this puzzled me, as I watched them strolling hand-in-hand beside the racecourse. Then I understood. Gordius was the leading charioteer in Nicomedia; he already had the admiration and devotion of everyone interested in racing. At the stables he was the Emperor's equal. He had embarked on a friendship with a beautiful boy, a rich and splendid boy certainly, but one who could offer him nothing he lacked.

As usual, the Emperor did as he pleased without worrying about public opinion. Before the New Year he had fetched Gordius to the palace and installed him in the imperial bedchamber; so that no one at court could pretend ignorance of their relationship. There was one consolation; Gordius was not added to the family council which was trying to rule the civilised world. He would not resign the duties which made him the most popular figure in Nicomedia; for most of the day he was busy at the stables.

The Augusta was worried by this addition to the family circle. One morning as I passed through the garden I found her strolling with Eutychianus and Gannys, and she called to me to join them. There had been a time, not long ago, when I would have felt abashed in the presence of the Praetorian Praefect; but Eutychianus, once he saw that I was not trying to displace him, took pains to put me at my ease. Of course no true soldier can be abashed by a female, even if the female happens to be Augusta and the grandmother of the Emperor. When Maesa asked my opinion I answered without embarrassment.

'We have been discussing the Emperor's new concubine,' she began, with a frankness that came oddly from such a venerable figure. 'What do you think of him, Duratius? More important, what do you suppose they will think of him in Rome?'

'Why should they think anything, one way or another?' said Eutychianus quickly. 'There's nothing strange in an Emperor having a boy-friend. In Egypt they still worship Antinous. Does anyone regard the cult as a slight on the memory of the Divine Hadrianus? No one will object to Gordius, so long as he is not too greedy.'

'But this is quite different,' said Gannys angrily, and I understood that I had been called in to arbitrate on a quarrel among the great. 'Hadrianus was a famous ruler in middle age, and Antinous a dancing-boy with no ambition. Gordius is ten years older than his lover. Everyone will see him as the dominant partner. Will the Romans submit quietly to the rule of an Asiatic charioteer?'

'Well, will they, Duratius?' said the Augusta quietly. 'That's what we are arguing about, because we are none of us true Romans. Your family have been citizens for centuries, and you come from the Romanised west. Tell us how you think the citizens will regard this affair.'

'What will happen to Gordius if you decide against him?' I asked, trying not to commit myself in this quarrel.

'Some fatal accident – at least, it will look like an accident,' Eutychianus answered grimly.

'Then the Emperor will find another to take his place,' I said, glad to find a way of escape, 'and the successor may not be so easy to manage. Gordius the famous charioteer does not need money, and if he were eager for power he would have shown it already. Augusta, you ought to know your own grandson. He is indifferent to women, but he is not a eunuch. There will always be a boy-friend in the palace. The Romans will put up with it, as they have put up with worse behaviour from past Emperors. Let the Emperor have his way in this little matter, and then he will not bother you by interfering in the government of the Republic.'

'Nobody minds boy-friends,' Gannys muttered angrily. 'A man-friend ten years older than his lover is a different matter. I still think we ought to get rid of him. But if you insist I shall drop the idea. Instead I shall give my pupil a good talking-to.'

At that moment the Emperor himself came into the garden. Such encounters happened constantly in that crowded palace where no one enforced the rules of etiquette. He was arm-in-arm with Gordius; which did not make the meeting any more cheerful.

'Hallo,' he called with a grin. 'Do I interrupt a council of state? No, it can't be that. You have Duratius with you, and he's too sensible to waste time on politics. The man I am looking for is Eutychianus. I have a job for the Praetorians, and after all my lessons I know that I must give orders to the troops through the usual channels. If the Praetorians must undertake a mission, then their Praefect must organise it. That's right, isn't it?'

'Tut, tut, my lord, have you begun a war without informing your council? But whoever you want us to fight the Praetorians will destroy them,' Eutychianus answered, also grinning.

'Oh, I don't want to fight anybody. This is a different kind of job. I've been talking to Gordius, and he mentioned that he has never tasted fresh mullet. It seems that no one else in Nicomedia has ever eaten them either. Just think of it! One of the nicest fish, and my unfortunate subjects in these parts don't even know what they look like! So I decided to give everyone down at the stable a real feast of mullet.'

'Why not? But where do my Praetorians come in?' asked Eutychianus.

'They will fetch the mullet. I consulted the fishmongers, and they explained that there are no mullet to be caught within a hundred miles of Nicomedia, and it's too expensive to bring them to market from the coast before they go bad. But if the Praetorians bring them we can give away the fish. The transport will cost nothing. Praetorians get paid every day, whether they do anything useful or not.'

Gannys frowned. 'It's out of the question, my lord. It's the kind of silly freak that makes an Emperor unpopular, and the soldiers will be hurt in their dignity at having to carry fish for civilians.'

'On the contrary, the troops will think it great fun, if we explain the plan to them properly. We'll offer a prize for the first wagon to reach Nicomedia, and let the cohorts compete for it,' said Eutychianus jovially. 'You must come with us, my lord, and we'll show you how Praetorians can move when they hurry. For that matter, we might carry water-casks on the waggons, and see if we can get your fish here alive.'

'Splendid. I'll come with you, on the warhorse I rode at Immae. Gordius can drive his chariot at the back, to pick up anyone who falls out. The town council of Nicomedia will pay for the fish. The army transports it free of charge. We have enough wine in the palace to give free drinks with the feast. A very fine party, which they won't forget in a hurry, and it will cost the treasury nothing at all.'

'It's a silly idea, and the palace will be drunk dry. Augusta, will you forbid this prank?' snapped Gannys.

'The Emperor has commanded. How can I forbid?' said the Augusta quickly. She frowned at the tactless tutor. We all knew that the Emperor might never be openly overruled; the Augusta governed only because he found governing a bore. If he saw himself as subordinate to his grandmother he would soon displace her.

The mullet-feast was a great success. The Praetorians were proud to show their speed; by spacing out their transport they moved several casks of fish more than eighty miles in twelve hours. The Emperor galloped up and down the road, waving his sword and distributing gold pieces. The local peasants stood by to cheer, impressed by the might of the Roman army. Gordius picked up an elderly veteran whose foot had been crushed by a waggon-wheel, and brought him into the camp hospital at full gallop; the old boy had never ridden in a chariot before, and played up by pretending, before a large audience, to have fallen madly in love with the handsome driver. The poor of Nicomedia filled their bellies with free food, and if mullet was not what they would have chosen they were all the same grateful for the imperial largess. By midnight half the town was drunk, but in a good-tempered way, without quarrels. Everyone in the palace came to cheer, with the exception of Gannys.

I suppose Gannys had turned sour because of some disappointment in his love-life; the Augusta and her daughters now had a great many stalwart courtiers, and a man who had ruled undisputed among the elderly priests of Emesa could not cope with competition. Whatever the reason, he was very difficult to live with. He was also losing his touch with the Emperor. Since he spent the day moping in the palace he did not see his pupil behaving like a grown man among the racehorses. He thought he could still bully the child in his care; and he was mistaken.

I was there when the trouble came to a head. I had knocked on the schoolroom door to remind the Emperor that he had an engagement at the stables, to watch an important gallop. He called to me to come in. I entered to find him alone with his tutor, who was in a towering rage.

'No, my lord, you can't get away from your lessons so easily,' Gannys shouted as he saw the boy pick up his cloak. 'Everyone knows about the great Hannibal, and your last answer put him in the First Punic War. I don't care if they can't begin racing until you have gone round with your little bucket to pick up the dung. That's all they let you do at the stables, I understand. You must stay here until you can repeat without mistake all the great battles in which Hannibal commanded.'

On other occasions the Emperor had been kept in the schoolroom until he knew his task. He was sensible enough to obey, for he wanted to know the outlines of Roman history. He might have obeyed this time, if it had not been for the sneer at his horsemanship.

'I drive a four-horse chariot as well as anyone in Nicomedia,' he answered fiercely. 'Duratius, you have seen me doing it. Tell this fool he is wrong. Of course I examine the horse-droppings, as a good driver should. A horse can't tell you when his stomach is upset, and it's a way of checking his health. As for you, Gannys, you don't know the difference between a cow-pat and a camel-turd, for all that your mother was a she-camel.'

I don't know why that particular insult always rouses a Syrian. It is untrue on the face of it; and they listen unmoved to the most frightful descriptions of their fathers. But I have never heard it spoken without a fight following. Gannys turned white. With eyes blazing he strode over to the Emperor.

He looked so menacing that I stepped forward to get between them, to save the poor fool from the deadly crime of laying hands on his master. I was not quick enough. Towering over the boy, he raised his hand to strike. Then he checked, for the Emperor had drawn a dagger from his tunic.

As Gannys withdrew the Emperor took a step to follow, holding his dagger poised like a sword. They were both mad with anger and quite reckless of consequences. 'You little bastard,' shouted Gannys as he backed against the farther wall. 'I'm glad I'm not your father. I don't know who was your father, among the hundreds who enjoyed your mother before me. Now drop that dagger, or you will be sorry for it.'

Since the Emperor still came on, Gannys drew his own dagger from his wide Syrian waistband. I had been staring in stupid surprise, but now I saw where my duty lay. My centurion's sword was on my thigh, as usual. I drew it as I jumped across the room.

For the only time in my life I brought off a stroke that even veterans boast of; though in battle, against an adversary who wears a helmet, it is almost impossible of performance. A horizontal sweep of my sword cut through Gannys' neckbone and sank deep into his throat. I did not exactly cut off his head with one stroke but I was not far off it. He collapsed in a fountain of blood, and before I could interfere the Emperor was worrying at the tattered neck with his little dress dagger. When the head came free he waved it to get the blood out, like a public executioner. Then he held it by the hair, staring at me.

'Together we have killed a traitor,' he said solemnly. 'Is this the first man you have killed? Of course not, what a silly question. On the frontier you killed masses of barbarians. All the same, he is the first man I have killed, and I shall remember today all my life. It's not difficult to kill a man, is it? But it's not nearly so much fun as I had expected.'

'He drew steel on you, my lord. I am your bodyguard. We could have done nothing else. We didn't kill him for fun; killing is always a miserable business. Let's never do it again unless we are driven to it. It's a great pity you were driven to it just now. Why did you say his mother was a camel? You know that a Syrian can't take that lying down.'

'Why couldn't Gannys take it lying down? Such a man ought to swallow any insult. He was only the palace stallion. Oh, do you think the Augusta will be cross with me?'

'She won't be cross because Gannys is dead, my lord. Lately she has been thinking of getting rid of him. She may be upset because you cut off his head with your own hands. An Emperor should order his soldiers to do these things.'

'There wasn't time, was there? Though you acted very quickly, I might not have managed it without your help. But now we must go and tell the Augusta, before she hears of it from some servant.'

I noted that the Emperor had slain Gannys. Well, if that was to be the official version I need not defend my own part in the affair.

In search of his grandmother the Emperor wandered through the palace, the severed head dangling from his hand. I walked half a pace behind him, still holding my bloody sword; it was a good sword, and I did not want to risk dulling the edge by putting it back in the scabbard dirty. We must have made a very frightening procession.

We found the Augusta at her dressing-table. Her maids shrieked with well-bred horror, to prove that they were not common slaves but refined attendants. The Augusta herself was more curious than dismayed.

'Whose head is that, my lord? Gannys, isn't it? Don't you think you have been rather too violent? If you have outgrown the tutor who taught you as a child you might easily have dismissed him. To kill him seems to show a lack of reverence for learning. And really I must ask you not to bring carrion into my private apartments. Stick the thing on a spike if you want, but don't carry it about as though you were fond of it.'

'He attacked me with a dagger, so I killed him with my own dagger. That's all,' said the Emperor sulkily. His grandmother had only to raise her eyebrows and he saw himself as a naughty little boy.

'Then you did right to kill him, and it was brave of you to kill such a big man. Now let Duratius take away that horrid head and dispose of it in the manner usual for such trophies. Then I'll send these maids packing and you can tell me all about it in private.'

I went out with the shuddering maids, who could not make up their minds whether to avoid me with horror or to make up to me so as to learn the inside story of this terrible event. Then I found Eutychianus, and together we arranged that the head and body of the unfortunate Gannys should be decently burned, and the ashes sent to his kin in Syria. The sooner the whole thing was forgotten the better for everyone, and especially for the Emperor; it would never do if he should develop a liking for killing his subjects with his own hands.

Later I escorted the Emperor to the stables. He seemed subdued; he would not drive a team but instead pottered about among the loose-boxes. He did not mention Gannys, either to me or to the lads who chatted with him. He came back early, and announced that he would spend the evening with Gordius in his private apartments, and did not wish to be disturbed.

I put on my dress uniform and sat down to wait in my bedroom. I knew the Augusta would send for me, to find out what really had happened. At a knock on my door I sprang up and tucked my helmet under my arm, ready for the summons to the presence. Instead of a chamberlain the Augusta walked in, alone.

She wore a black gown and kerchief, like any respectable Syrian housewife; no jewellery, and no facepaint, so that her sunburned skin seemed darker than ever. Without speaking she squatted cross-legged in a corner, her back against the wall. She was completely at her ease, but there was nothing about her of the great imperial ruler.

'Why did you kill him this morning?' she asked abruptly. 'I mean, why this morning in particular? Was it really necessary to kill him in the presence of the Emperor? Couldn't you have waited until you got him alone?'

I told her the whole story. She listened without interruption. When I had finished she sighed.

'So that's what really happened. My grandson spoke so excitedly that I could not make out what Gannys had done to offend. Poor man, he hadn't a chance, had he? But it was your duty to kill him once he had drawn his dagger. Does the Emperor really think he killed him single-handed?'

'That I can't tell you, Augusta. It is no part of my duty to contradict anything said by the Emperor. Had the Emperor killed him, he would have acted correctly. I saw the daggers.'

'I suppose my grandson was jealous of him. He wants all the love of all his family. Some Romans may be shocked at the idea of mother and daughter sharing a man. That's what we did, you know, and it's silly to try to conceal it. But we were faithful to our husbands while they lived; and widows of the imperial family are allowed a certain relaxation.'

If Soaemias had been faithful to her husband then the Emperor was not the son of the Divine Caracalla. The Augusta ought to know the facts, and it seemed that she was being frank with me. I noted this, in case it should come in useful one day; but I did not say anything that might check the flow of confidences.

'The Emperor has killed a courtier with his own hands, or that's what he thinks,' she went on. 'Did he enjoy it? Will he want to do it again and again? We can't tell. Duratius, I want you to help me to handle my grandson. At present his subjects like him, and he knows it. He enjoys being popular, and he will do his best to please them. But if he loses his temper and does something abominably cruel, so that the people hate him, he will go on from one evil deed to another, just to spite the tiresome grown-ups. There are so many respectable men and institutions that he despises already.' She sighed.

'My lady, couldn't you tell him that it is wrong for an Emperor to kill evil-doers with his own hands? Forbid him to carry a weapon. He doesn't need one.'

'You are like all the others, Duratius. I thought you had been with us long enough to understand this court. You see me giving orders right and left, without consulting the Emperor. So you suppose I govern the Republic. I don't. I can't control the Emperor. No one can control the Emperor. What would happen if he saw me as an obstacle, coming between him and his pleasures or his work? The soldiers will obey him in anything, because they believe him to be Caracalla come again. Did you learn about Nero when you were at school?'

'Not a great deal, my lady. But I recall that he murdered his mother. I had no idea things were so bad.'

'They are not – now. That's because I never thwart him. He lets me rule in his name because for the present he is not interested in ruling. I spoke to him once about the disgrace of living openly with a lover ten years older than himself. But I saw he was growing angry, and I gave way immediately. Now I am gracious when I meet Gordius, and ask him polite questions about the prospects of the Green faction.'

'Can't you make my lord see, tactfully, that he is not yet quite a man?' I asked hopefully. It was hard to believe that the Augusta feared the grandson who treated her with such deference.

'Of course I can't. Anyway, he does not think of himself as a man. He is the chosen minister of the divine sky-stone, and he feels that with its help he can do anything. That's not strange, when you remember what he has already accomplished. Eutychianus and a legion came over to him, just because he showed himself to the soldiers and asked for their allegiance. Then he led his army in a pitched battle, and in fair fight won the Purple. All before his fourteenth birthday! How can you expect him to heed the advice of his elders?'

'He has sound principles,' I said, trying to be cheerful. 'He is brave and compassionate. He likes happy faces round him. So far he has not spent a great deal of money.'

'That may change when we get to Rome. Perhaps that beastly amphitheatre will teach him cruelty. We have nothing like it in Syria.'

'What he needs, my lady, is a new interest. He's fond of horses, but he's too intelligent to regard chariot-racing as the chief end of man. Shall I try to persuade him to make war on the Germans?'

'That won't do. I could not be with him, and while he was on campaign he might forget me. In Rome I shall find him a bride. If she pleases him he may forget these revolting young men.'

'Quite so, my lady. But marriage is no more worthy to be the occupation of a powerful ruler than chariot-racing. Can't we find some other hobby for him?'

The Augusta frowned, and I saw I had been tactless. But what I said was true; marriage may be the chief interest of a woman, but a real man must live his life in public.

'What about the sky-stone?' I continued. 'He thinks more of being high priest than of being Emperor. Can we encourage his interest in religion?'

'The Romans do not take kindly to eastern gods. All the same, it's an idea. When we get to Rome I shall keep him busy with his bride, and with organising a fitting cult for the sky-stone who gave him the Purple. Then he won't have time for his wild ideas about bringing back the Golden Age to this sordid world.'

The Augusta got to her feet before I could help her to rise. She went away without another word, to resume the stealthy padding up and down the palace corridors which showed that she was worried. I believe she called privately on Eutychianus and Gordius, and on both her daughters, before at last she went to bed.

It proved to be only too easy to encourage the Emperor in his religious duties. On the very next day he announced that solemn worship would be offered to the Sun-god on every seventh day, as had been the custom of Emesa. For the present this would be private worship only, offered by those who were already his dedicated servants; in other words, he added after he had read this from a scroll, everyone in the palace must attend but he would not bother the ordinary citizens of Nicomedia.

Three days later we assembled in the throne room, where once the Greek kings of Bithynia had reigned in state. I was among the crowd of slaves, freedmen, and guards who stood near the door of the hall. The god was brought in with great pomp, on a litter decorated with ivory, as though he were a magistrate of the Roman People. Eight senior officers of the Praetorians bore the litter. Behind it came first the Emperor, then the ladies of his family and little Alexianus, then a group of local priests. Three hundred of the regular priests of Emesa were on their way to Nicomedia, and when they arrived they would accompany us to Rome; in the meantime local servants of the Olympian gods could make themselves useful, for they knew at least the technique of sacrificing and burning incense.

I never mind attending a sacrifice. It may go on rather too long, but you are sure of a feast when at last it ends. Unfortunately sacrifice played a minor part in the worship of this Sun-god. Instead he liked to be praised to his face, in a fulsome strain that a god of better breeding might have found embarrassing. At least I consider the hymns sung at these ceremonies fulsome, but that may be the fault of the translation. The originals were in the Aramaic tongue.

The Emperor and his family sang these hymns, for no one else present was familiar with the language. While they sang the local priests placed the phallus upright on the marble chair that had once been the throne of the kings of Bithynia. The Emperor offered burning incense, and then withdrew by a side-door while the ladies continued their hymn.

We knew that the Emperor had gone to change his clothes. In his eyes one of the greatest attractions of the high priesthood was that it permitted him to wear the most elaborate vestments. There is a limit to what even an Emperor can wear as the dress of everyday without being considered mad; but what the high priest should wear had been decreed by the god long ago.

After a few minutes he came back again. We westerners

gasped in amazement, even though we were familiar with the ritual of Syrian temples. On his head was a mitre at least two feet high, made of moulded Egyptian paper and gilded. Round his neck were so many jewelled collars that he must hold his chin in the air. A long purple cloak, also fastened round his neck, floated behind him; from the way he managed it there must have been little weights in the hem. His breast was covered by a vest of purple silk, which ended at the heavy gold belt round his loins. On his feet were purple buskins, studded with gems. Between belt and boots he wore nothing at all.

Nobody notices a completely naked man. It is a mark of civilisation to take exercise with no clothes on, and we laugh at the Persians who consider it indecent. But to be covered above the navel and nude below will look indecent in any part of the world; even the most carefree athlete wraps something round his waist before he goes into a temple. The Emperor looked like a half-plucked fowl. Two things made his nudity even more striking: his legs had been depilated; and he had stuck on himself, in the appropriate place, an enormous phallus of gilded leather.

In this remarkable get-up the commander of the Roman army performed an intricate and athletic dance, to the music of flutes and cymbals.

There was no denying that he looked impressive as he went through his act of worship. His lips and eyebrows had been gilded, his cheeks and chin stained purple, so that he hardly seemed a human being. The long cloak fluttered like beating wings. I was ready to believe that the heavenly messengers of the Sun-god, if such beings exist, must look like Elagabalus the High Priest.

Then Gordius sprang out from the side-door to partner his lover in the dance. At once the rite lost all dignity. Gordius was a beefy, heavy-muscled man, burned brown and gleaming with oil in contrast to the white powdered flesh of the Emperor. He wore nothing but three wreaths of lilies, on his brow, neck, and loins. The two of them had rehearsed the dance in private, but

Gordius was a horseman who seldom used his legs. He pranced very clumsily.

At last the Emperor came to a stop, panting and exhausted. He turned to face the packed crowd by the door. 'Who's next?' he called. 'We must keep this up till midday. The Sun-god likes it. He has just told me so.'

The three imperial ladies moved to the front. The Augusta began a slow stately dance, curtseying and bowing and beckoning with her arms very gracefully. Her daughters danced with her, and little Alexianus hopped a few steps; but the Augusta, who had been reared in the temple at Emesa, was the only one who really understood the business. The Emperor watched them, his hand caressing the sky-stone as though it were the shoulder of Gordius. 'That's splendid,' he shouted. 'Grandma, you're wonderful. But at your age you can't be expected to go on very long. Who's next? Let the next dancers come to the front.'

With my hand on my swordhilt I walked firmly to the door. A row of tall footmen stood before it, and at first seemed inclined to keep it shut. I prodded one of them in the stomach with my thumb, whispering: 'Praetorian on duty. Get out of my way.' They opened one side of the double door just wide enough for me to slip through.

In the afternoon I went down to the stables with the Emperor and Gordius. The Emperor was all smiles as we set out, but as soon as we were alone he turned on me.

'Duratius, you refused to honour the Sun-god. You knew that everybody was supposed to dance. Eutychianus, your commander, danced very gracefully, considering his lack of practice. Why did you leave the parade without asking for permission to dismiss?'

I halted to face him, standing stiff at attention save that my hand rested once more on the hilt of my sword. 'My lord,' I said firmly, 'I did not know that this morning's function was a military parade. There seemed to be a great many civilians present. I apologise for leaving without asking to be dismissed.

All the same, my lord, there is a fundamental law of the Empire that you must learn, since at present you are ignorant of it. Soldiers never dance in public. There it is. Even an Emperor must get used to it.'

'I see,' he said with a frown. 'The Praetorian Praefect danced to please me, and he is soldier enough for anybody. You know that I am your commanding officer, and that disobedience to orders is a capital offence?'

'I know that, my lord. I can only hope that you will forgive me when you have heard my explanation. The Praetorian Praefect is indeed a soldier, but such a great one that he has many civilian functions. I should have said that no soldier of the rank of centurion or under dances in public. If we had been in the habit of dancing for the Emperor Macrinus we might not have changed sides on the battlefield of Immae.'

'Very well. Soldiers do not dance. I shall remember that, and never again order them to do it. But everyone else shall dance, and in particular those stupid proud Senators who were shocked to see my picture decked in the jewels my god has bestowed on me. They shall recognise the might of the sky-stone, the veritable phallus of the Sun. I shan't let them take refuge in the excuse that he was unknown to father Romulus. Now we all know him. Do you, Duratius, acknowledge his might even though you will not dance for him?'

'Of course I acknowledge his might, my lord. I will do anything within reason to please him.'

'That's something, at any rate,' said the Emperor, smiling. 'This morning he told me that he would like to see you drive a four-horse chariot. In private, of course, so that you are not in any way degraded. We shall arrange it as soon as we get to the stables.'

Gordius grinned also, and clapped me on the back. I had rounded a dangerous corner. When the Emperor was crossed he seldom sought the heads of his opponents, for at bottom he was merciful; but he did like to make them look ridiculous. By falling out of a chariot I could win forgiveness for my defiance.

Two hours later we came back to the palace very good friends. Of course my team had bolted with me, and at the furlong post the whole affair had capsized. But I cut the reins and was thrown clear. Except for bruises all down my right side, from shoulder to ankle, I was none the worse. The team did not suffer, for the Emperor and Gordius were waiting by the post; they dashed in to calm the frightened horses before they could kick one another.

The lady Soaemias was waiting for her son. She could never reconcile herself to the perils of chariot-racing, and was always unhappy until she had seen him return safe and sound. But she was also afraid of him, and avoided an interview unless he commanded her to speak with him. Now she waved a greeting from the portico and then disappeared down a corridor. Later in the evening I met her, wandering vaguely with a handsome young officer who carried a bowl of fruit and snow.

'Do you want to see me?' she asked with a distracted air. 'We are just going to picnic in the library, and I haven't time to hear a petition. Oh no, of course, you are Duratius. You can approach the Emperor whenever you wish. But tell me, is it true that you disobeyed an imperial command? Will you be punished?'

'That's not quite what happened, my lady,' I answered respectfully. 'I did not disobey an imperial command. All I did was to persuade the Emperor to change his mind. In future serving soldiers will be excused dancing, at all ceremonies designed to honour the sky-stone.'

'That was clever of you,' she said with a giggle. 'It's difficult to persuade my son to change his mind. I can't do it. But don't you like our hymns and dances? In Syria everyone thinks them great fun. Oh well, I mustn't keep you, since you have no petition.'

The Augusta saw more clearly what had passed. When she ran into me that same evening she came quickly to the point.

'Duratius, you have saved us from disaster. Eutychianus has confessed to me that the legions would revolt if ordered to dance in honour of the sky-stone. I don't know why they should feel so strongly, but it is so. Eutychianus feared to disobey the Emperor, but he admits that what you did was right. But you have done more than correct a mistake, you have taught the Emperor that there are limits to his power. It should have been done long ago, but none of us was brave enough to do it. Is there any reward I can give you?'

'Well, my lady, I wouldn't refuse a hundred gold pieces, if you can spare them. Money always comes in handy. Otherwise I am very well as I am. Certainly I don't want promotion.'

The slave who called me next morning brought the gold pieces. In future the Augusta was very gracious whenever we met.

CHAPTER EIGHT

A God Approaches Rome

𝒞

In the spring Eutychianus began to prepare for the long overland march to Rome. We would be a large company. Besides the Praetorians, who always guard the Emperor, the Alban Legions, the soldiers who had first acknowledged our sovereign, would march with us to their privileged quarters in Italy. It was a considerable business to assemble adequate supplies along the Via Egnatia, and to provide horses and draught oxen.

The serious planning was done at military headquarters, but the Emperor made his personal contribution. One morning I was chatting with the sentries in the guardroom; for with very little else to do I tried to make myself useful by keeping in touch with the feelings of the common soldiers. Suddenly there was a knock on the door and one of the Augusta's maids put her head in.

Her welcome made her blush all over; she had to wait until the greetings had died down before she could deliver her message. One does not usually send a pretty slave-girl to carry orders to soldiers, but I was not surprised to hear she bore a command from the Emperor. When he was struck by a bright idea he would send his orders by the first person he met; one got used to that sort of thing in the palace of Nicomedia.

'Imperial command. Meeting of the privy council in half an hour,' she stammered, blushing more than before.

'Well, what about it? What are we supposed to do?' said the

guard commander sharply. Soldiers resent having their orders delivered by slaves, though it happens constantly.

'I suppose they want you to mount an extra guard on the council chamber. Is that it, my dear?' I said, trying to be helpful.

'No. The message was for you, Duratius. The Emperor commands you to attend,' she answered.

At the consternation on my face the soldiers burst out laughing. The centurion of the guard quickly gave them something to do, for fear they should get out of hand. 'Strip, privy councillor,' he barked at me as though we were on parade. 'Greaves, boots, cuirass, helmet, baldric – take them off, the lot of them. Now, two men to each piece of armour and really get down to it. You have a quarter of an hour, no more. The privy councillor Duratius must have the smartest turn-out ever seen on a Praetorian. He's the first centurion of the corps to attend the privy council, and he will do us credit.'

That gave me a few minutes to collect my thoughts. It was absurd that a centurion should be a member of the imperial privy council, a venerable institution founded by the Divine Augustus. But there would be nothing strange in the Emperor discussing affairs of state with his family and friends, as he frequently did over the supper table. The Emperor was merely being flippant in a serious matter, and not for the first time. This kind of behaviour would not make him popular when at last he reached Rome. I would drop a hint that he must take seriously the sacred constitution bequeathed to us by our ancestors; the Senate in Rome takes it very seriously indeed.

When I reached the door of the imperial council chamber, the regulation five minutes before the advertised time of parade, I looked very splendid. But of course I entered the room last, and took the lowest place at the long table.

There was nothing strange about the group assembled, except that the Emperor should choose to call us his privy council. He took the head of the table, with the Augusta on his right and his mother on his left. Beyond the lady Soaemias sat the lady Mamea her sister, and next to her the freedman

Gordius; beyond the Augusta sat the Praetorian Praefect, and then the chief priest of the local shrine of Cybele, who was of course a eunuch. I sat below the eunuch. In the centre of the table, on a little stand of precious ivory, the polished sky-stone presided over the meeting.

The Emperor produced an enormous sheet of paper, covered on both sides with close-set writing, much blotted. He peered at it, turning it round until he found the beginning, which was apparently in the middle of the sheet. Then he pushed it away from him, and spoke in his official voice.

'It has been brought to my attention,' he began pompously, 'that the court lacks a code of etiquette. Before my solemn progress through my dominions and my state entry into Rome that shall be remedied. There are no useful precedents. We cannot follow the ritual of the usurper Macrinus, and the customs enforced by Caracalla, my divine father, were in many respects imperfect. So here are my instructions on this important subject.' He began to read. 'The Emperor, the commander-in-chief of the armed forces, will receive from the soldiers the normal salute due to a general officer. The Emperor, president of the Senate, will be greeted by civilians with the decent respect due to a Senator . . . There, what do you think of that?' he added in his normal tone.

'It will be popular. But can you go right back to the etiquette of the Divine Augustus, after more than two hundred years?' asked Eutychianus doubtfully. He was the only councillor who recognised the sweeping nature of the change suggested by the Emperor; except myself, and I was determined to express no opinion, if I could help it.

'Perhaps we can't, though there will be cheers from the Senate at this stage of the proclamation,' said the Emperor with a giggle. 'But wait. I haven't nearly finished.' Once more he read. 'The Emperor, as Emperor, is no more than leader of the Senate. But the Emperor now reigning gloriously is also high priest of the sacred sky-stone Elagabalus, the veritable phallus of the Sun, by which long ago he created the whole world. As high priest and partner of the all-conquering Sun the Emperor should be approached by all citizens with the deference due to a divinity. When he wears the insignia of his priesthood, and this will be always save when he is in military dress, citizens will greet him by kissing his shoes. This order does not apply to the army.'

The Emperor put down his paper and looked round the table.

'There's a lot more of it, but I'm not satisfied with the details. That's why I called this council. Now that you've got the general idea we must work out a full code of court etiquette, to cover all contingencies.'

The silence was broken at last by the lady Soaemias, too stupid to recognise the perils of the Emperor's proposal.

'That's a very nice composition, my dear,' she said gently. 'Did you write it all by yourself? Have you remembered to put in that I am to be granted the rank of Augusta?'

'Gordius and I made it up entirely by ourselves,' said the Emperor proudly. 'But it was written by the clerk who checks the forage-bills at the stables. I'm afraid it's rather blotted. He doesn't usually write such long pieces.'

'You must have it rewritten, my lord,' said the Augusta. 'We can't send that dirty piece of paper to the Senate. I suggest that you give it to me, and I will get the best clerks in the chancery to make out a summary. You don't want to fill in all the details before you reach Rome. You can work them out as occasion arises. You may find that some ceremonies bring inconvenience to yourself, and it will be easier to make changes before everything has been promulgated.'

'I don't mind personal inconvenience if it brings honour to the Sun-god,' answered the Emperor. 'But you are right as usual, grandma. I shall leave the whole affair in your hands.'

'And my rank of Augusta?' his mother reminded him. 'Why don't you promulgate that now, at this meeting?'

'I have been thinking about it,' said the Emperor with a smirk. 'In fact I had a long consultation with my most trusted councillor, Gordius. We don't think it wise that such a high rank should be multiplied. There should be only one Augusta. So I propose to grant you the splendid title of Clarissima. That will be nearly as grand as Augusta. But not quite so grand, because the daughter of a high priest should take precedence of the mother of a high priest. That is my imperial decision.'

He gazed at us sternly, while the oafish Gordius grinned.

'Is there any other business, my lord?' asked Eutychianus. 'I have a great deal to arrange about the journey, besides this important proclamation. Unless you have further instructions I should like to get back to my desk.' His face was fixed and expressionless, as though he were on parade.

'No other business, except for one minor point. We shall take with us the local priests of Cybele, and pick up more from the shrines we pass on the way. Their place in the column will be immediately before the litter which carries the sky-stone. Thus the Sun-god will have suitable courtiers on his journey . . . Oh, and by the way, Duratius hasn't opened his mouth. I make you a privy councillor, a tremendous honour for a centurion, and you don't advise me. Tell us your views, Duratius.'

'I am not fit to advise on civilian matters, my lord. The code of etiquette as it applies to the army seems to me excellent. Since the days of the Divine Augustus soldiers have honoured the Emperor as their commander, while paying little regard to his religious functions.'

Eutychianus turned on me a long cold stare; the others paid no attention. The Emperor had commanded me to speak and I had spoken. But no one was interested in my opinions.

Before we left Nicomedia the Emperor gave a great party to his friends the charioteers. Though he wished only charioteers and grooms to be present the Augusta begged him to bring a guard. So as a compromise I was given a couch at the first table, with the Emperor himself and Gordius. I reclined awkwardly in full armour, with my sword handy. Not one of these raffish sportsmen would murder the Emperor of his own free-will, but such men can be cheaply bribed. Though I could not guard the Emperor from assassination I could ensure that his assassin died instantly; in such company that was precaution enough.

The Emperor's friendship for me had been cooling; Gordius was a better authority on racehorses, and I had withstood him in the matter of dancing before his god. But tonight he was in such high spirits that he had to talk freely. Besides, Gordius was mildly in disgrace, and the punishment devised for him would lose its point unless the Emperor could explain it. He chatted with me on the old footing.

Gordius, taking advantage of his new grandeur, had been raiding the palace kitchens for supplies of the rare Arabian sugar. As a result he had begun to grow fat; and the Emperor, who took pride in his lover's excellent figure, had ordered him to reduce. This feast would inaugurate his new diet.

The excellent *hors-d'oeuvres* were eaten in silence, for we were all hungry. Then the roast was carved and laid before us on individual plates, instead of being handed round for us to help ourselves as we chose. I was mildly surprised, until the Emperor's giggles made me realise that this was more than a casual change in the ordering of the meal.

'How are you doing, Gordius?' he asked.

I was eating roast beef (pork was never served in the Emperor's presence), but it was nothing special, nothing calling for comment. I looked at Gordius; he was trying to chew on a piece of wood, carved and painted to resemble meat. With a rueful grin he looked back at his master. 'At least it's excellent for the figure, my dear. Let me see what I have in my cup.'

But the Emperor had a kindly heart, for all that he enjoyed teasing his friends. The wine was genuine.

The Emperor began talking to me about his god. 'Eutychianus fears trouble. He won't say so, but I can see it. He thinks the Romans will turn against me rather than worship a god from Syria. But my grandmother sees nothing odd in the idea, and she ought to know Rome better than Eutychianus. You were brave enough to refuse to dance, so I know you won't lie just to keep me in a good temper. Do you think I can bring my Sun-god to Rome?'

'If you can't, my lord, what will you do?'

'I shall go back to Emesa, and make it the centre of the Empire. I shall let the Germans take over the west if the west proves unworthy of me.'

'Very well, my lord, if you feel so strongly about it. I just wanted to know, for you will rule more easily without your god. But you can take him to Rome, if you go about it carefully. I suppose he recognises the Olympians, even though he is their superior? See that they are not entirely neglected. Why not find places for them at his heavenly court? By all means compel the Senate to pay him deference, but do not insult the feelings of the soldiers. And be merciful about it, my lord. Remember, these Senators will do anything to save their lives; but if they think they will be killed whatever they do they might pluck up the courage to strike first.'

'That's a very sound answer,' said this fourteen-year-old boy, as judiciously as if he were an elderly legate. 'At Antioch I was merciful, more merciful than anyone had a right to expect. All my life I shall be merciful. I have promised my god that I shall never take life merely for amusement, or because I feel frightened. Under my rule there will be no executions save by due process of law. There have been none so far, and I have held the Purple for half a year. But I shall make those stuffy Romans see that a Syrian of ancient lineage is as worthy of respect as a Senator who can trace his pedigree from King Numa; and if I find them stubborn I shall make them grovel before me.' He frowned across the room, looking much older than his years.

I have remembered every word of that declaration, for it justified my loyalty. I knew the Emperor would keep a vow made to his god, and he did. No Emperor has been more merciful, or a better friend to the soldiers and the poor.

But there was another side to his nature, which he could never suppress for long. When he discussed policy he talked like an intelligent adult, but about the private life of his subjects he had the insatiable curiosity of a small boy.

At the end of the feast the usual dancing-girls performed. They were not good dancers, nor pretty, and stable boys seldom take much interest in women. But a party must end with dancing-girls, and the Emperor had provided them lest his friends should feel slighted.

'I don't see how anyone can enjoy making love to those girls,' he burst out, 'and they don't enjoy it either. I know, I have talked to them. They lead a miserable life. I can't stop slaves being miserable, that's the way the world's made. But some of these girls are free. When I get to Rome I shall do what I can to improve the condition of harlots. ... Perhaps the priests of Cybele are wiser than the rest of us. They look happy enough, and they are spared a great deal of bother. I might try joining in their dance, to see if the Mother can comfort me also. But dancing is not a subject to discuss with *you*, Duratius, is it?'

'I'm not a dancing man, my lord, that's true. But you can go into all these matters after you have taken possession of Rome. In the west you will find many interesting things to occupy your time, perhaps things more interesting than the wrongs of harlots. There's the best racing in the world, for one thing, not to mention the amphitheatre.'

He turned away from me to whisper to Gordius. I had bored him, but I had bored him on purpose. If the conversation had continued he would have begun to ask indiscreet questions about my own private life, whereas nothing he said to Gordius could make that young man feel shy.

We set off towards the end of April, and once in Europe travelled very slowly along the Via Egnatia. The Emperor had read somewhere that the Divine Nero travelled with 500 carriages, so he had ordered that his baggage must fill at least 600. But even that enormous train was not too much for the needs of such a numerous court. The Augusta brought a considerable household; the Clarissima demanded nearly as many servants; the lady Mamea and little Alexianus had the entourage of Caesars, though they lacked the title; the priests of Cybele gathered more colleagues at every halt; the sky-stone, attended by 300 Syrian priests, travelled in even greater state than the Emperor himself; Gordius, who liked company, brought a number of other stable boys.

The carriages travelled midway in the column, with the Praetorians in the van and the Alban Legions in the rear. The army and its encumbrances filled many miles of road. But during the long march every man was encouraged to persevere by seeing the Emperor several times a day.

Daily we covered the usual legionary stage of twenty miles, which was easy for me since I rode a comfortable hack. But the Emperor must have driven more nearly eighty miles than twenty. As soon as we started he set off in a fast two-horse gig, which he drove at a hand-gallop up and down the column. Sometimes he wore armour with all his badges of rank, sometimes the fantastic tunic and head-dress of his high priesthood, sometimes the billowing cloak of a racing driver with nothing at all underneath it. He loved speed, and to steer round the obstacles of the baggage train was an added thrill; he would leave the road when he came to a block, urging his team through standing crops or down a steep hillside. He was a magnificent driver, and the troops loved it; you could hear the wave of cheering travelling down the column long before he came into sight. The grooms who managed his stud were hard put to it to have a fresh team ready whenever he thundered up to change horses.

The only thing that would make him pull up and look dignified was a deputation waiting to deliver a loyal address. Every city for miles round sent councillors to greet the Emperor as soon as it was known that this pleased him; even the peasants sent their headmen, with speeches written in a queer jargon, saying how glad they were that the Emperor should pass through their fields and see with his own eyes how much of their crop they had to deliver to the tax-gatherer.

For all these loyal addresses, whether composed by skilled rhetoricians in great cities or by ignorant village school-masters, ended with a plea for protection from the tax-gatherer. It is the one subject that unites every inhabitant of the Empire, citizen or peasant – save for the minority of soldiers who depend on the taxes for their pay. I think the Emperor was surprised to discover that taxation was such a universal grievance.

The first two or three deputations were granted all they asked, forgiveness of arrears of tribute and a lightening of the future burden. Then Eutychianus woke up to what was happening; if the Emperor went on in this way Thrace and Achaea would soon contribute nothing to the revenue. At a stormy meeting of the family council it was arranged that in future some responsible adviser should drive with the Emperor in his gig.

The Augusta, in view of her age, refused to travel at full gallop; at a hint from the Praetorian Praefect, Gordius explained that any good charioteer hates to be driven as a passenger. The rest of that strangely composed council had to take a turn at galloping up and down the line every day. I think the only one who enjoyed it was little Alexianus, recently promoted to the council in recognition of his cousinhood. But the Emperor took care to drive cautiously when accompanied by his mother or his aunt.

That meant that he could let himself go only when Eutychianus or I were his companions. Soldiers are used to concealing their fright, and anyway chariots are no more dangerous than hostile swords, which we had faced often enough. The real danger was that the Emperor might kill himself. Then the army, or perhaps the Senate, would choose a successor; and the favourite Eutychianus, with the favourite Duratius, would be executed as left over from the old reign. It was unfortunate that my patron chose to live dangerously; on the other hand, he was very young, and if no accident befell him he ought to last my time. It was safer than being the chosen favourite of a senile ruler.

As he drove the Emperor never stopped talking. He was bursting with happiness, which added to his almost super-human charm. His beauty increased every day, as his superb body filled out into manhood; he had a delightful voice, and a natural felicity of expression. He wanted everyone to be as happy as he was, and he was young enough to believe that as a ruler he could bring this about.

We had been talking with a group of peasants. I had done my duty as a councillor by finding out which of the taxes oppressed them most, and the Emperor had done his duty by promising to consult with his advisers before he gave a definite answer to their plea. The spokesman of the peasants was most disap-pointed; until Gordius offered him a lift in another gig, to spare him the long walk to our next halting place. In the end we drove away leaving the peasants cheerful and grinning.

'I begin to understand,' said the Emperor, speaking quietly as a well-behaved boy should speak to an adult. 'The government has been trying to do too much. The army must be paid, of course, and that comes first. It's a very heavy burden, but the peasants would be dead if they did not pay it. But these people must also pay for schools, and universities, and games and shows, in some city that claims to be the capital of their territory; and that does them no good at all. They ought to be let off all payments, except *annona* to the army, at least until they are more prosperous.'

'That's all very well, my lord,' I answered, 'but you know what the council will say to you. The Empire is civilised because we have free education, and endowments for philosophers, and great shows and public buildings. We can abolish these things if you think them too expensive; but then we shall live like German barbarians. Besides,' I added to clinch the argument, 'do you think money wasted if it is spent on chariot-racing?'

'Well, no, of course not. We must improve the breed of horses, for the sake of our cavalry. Every racing man will tell you that if you query the expense. But I don't see why country farmers should pay for aqueducts and baths in faraway cities.'

'Because without baths there would be no city, my lord. There must be cities, everyone is agreed on that. You yourself took some pains to preserve the fine city of Antioch, when it would have been easier to let your army sack it.'

'That wasn't because it was a city. Anyway, Emesa is a finer city; perhaps one day I shall make it the capital of Syria. It would be fun to give Antioch the status of an open village. I could do it, too, with a stroke of the pen. The Divine Severus made Byzantium an open village, and it's still one. The Emperor can do anything.'

'Yes, but that makes it all the more important that his deeds shall benefit his subjects. The Divine Severus punished Byzantium because it had rebelled against him; but the historians do not praise him for it. Whereas your mercy to Antioch, which had been the headquarters of Macrinus the usurper, will be remembered as evidence of your kindness until the end of time.'

'I want to be remembered as the high priest who introduced the Sun-god to Rome. That is my real life-work. As well I want all my subjects to be happy and prosperous. They will be, when they have asked in due form for the favour of the Sun-god. My sky-stone is actually and truly the phallus of the Sun, and the Sun can make the whole world prosperous if it likes.'

'That is quite another matter, my lord, on which you know far more than I. My duty as your councillor is only to advise you against granting every petition you receive. And by the way, my lord, I am not really of sufficient rank to be a councillor, and I find the work very difficult. Would you consider dismissing me from your council, so that I may revert to the duty I know how to perform, that of centurion?'

I looked anxiously in his face as I said this; he might take it as evidence of disloyalty. But I had chosen my moment well, when he was so pleased with life that he could not suspect anyone of evil-doing.

'I need you while we are on the march,' he answered gravely. 'But as soon as we get to Rome, where the Augusta says wise advisers will be waiting for me, you may revert to your old rank.

That is my imperial decision, and you may remind me of it if I forget.'

I heaved a sigh of relief. What had been great fun in the ramshackle atmosphere of Nicomedia was looking more and more dangerous as we approached Rome. He would find wise advisers in plenty there, right enough; and if they chose to intrigue for my downfall, a simple soldier would not stand a chance against them. But the pay and allowances of an employed centurion would not tempt even the most greedy courtier. If I sank back to a humble station I might yet die of old age.

Then the Emperor whipped up his horses, and for the next half hour he was too busy driving, and I was too busy holding on, for either of us to spare breath for conversation.

By the time we reached Dyrrhachium the march had settled into a routine. At every halt the Emperor conferred with Eutychianus and the Augusta about the answer he should give to petitions. Very rarely these petitions asked pardon for convicted criminals; these could be granted without any bother. The Emperor liked mercy, and there was no danger that his mercy would encourage crime; a pardon won by direct personal appeal to the Emperor was such a rare accident that no intending brigand would count on it. All the other petitions were appeals against the tax-gatherers, and here the Emperor and his advisers asked first how the money was to be spent. If it was needed for the army of course it had to be paid; if it was to support some amenity in a city half was remitted, and the city left to struggle on with a diminished revenue; if as sometimes happened, it was to build something new, something a particular city had managed without ever since it was founded, then the whole tax was remitted. As the Praefect said, this age of iron, when the whole human race was unnaturally impoverished, was no time for building new gymnasia.

So on the whole the petitioners got something, though not all they had asked for. The Emperor was amazingly popular. For the first time in recorded history the passage of a great army and a numerous court was bringing benefit to the countryside instead of renewed poverty.

From Dyrrhachium we made an easy passage to Brundisium, and then travelled comfortably on the fine roads of Italy. July had come, and the harvest had been reaped, when we settled down for the last night of our journey. It had been a good harvest, and the peasants were glad to sell their grain to this great body of soldiers who paid cash for all they took. We were greeted with rejoicing that was genuine, and we all went happy to bed. Tomorrow a deputation from the Senate, with the curule magistrates, would escort us into Eternal Rome.

For this last stage the Emperor had decided to travel with his sky-stone, so that the magistrates might greet both of their new rulers at the same time. The Clarissima and the Augusta were borne behind him in their ornate litters. Immediately behind the Clarissima came the litter of the lady Mamea, which also carried little Alexianus; because these held no official rank they were all the more watchful of their rights as members of the imperial household. For the rest of us no official precedence had been laid down; in theory the baggage train might crowd the road in no particular order. But I had pushed my horse to the front, just behind the last official litter, and beside me Gordius drove a spanking pair of horses; all his racing friends followed him, to watch the official welcome of the Roman People.

Coming towards us I saw a small escort of foot, a little knot of horse, and a long file of litters. They had difficulty in moving; for they had to pass the marching Praetorians, who did not willingly make room for civilians. As they came nearer I saw that even their guard were almost civilians; an urban cohort, men who dress up as soldiers and then pass their time in keeping back crowds and putting out fires among crowded houses, to the contempt of real fighting legionaries. They approached to the sound of some very rude catcalls from the marching Praetorians.

But they drew up in a straight line and gave a creditable version of the imperial salute; as they should, since they spend so much of their time on parade and never see a battlefield. Through a gap in their ranks came the horsemen, young nobles representing the whole order of Roman Knights. They wore old-fashioned tunics, with the badge of their order, and carried instead of spears long poles tipped with laurel; they had been chosen for their horsemanship as well as their birth, and looked very fine in the antique mode.

Then the Consuls and the urban praetor emerged from their litters, to pay their respects to the Emperor. They wore official togas and their lictors marched before them, in accordance with the ritual that had been devised when the kings were driven from Rome more than 700 years ago. They walked with dignity, responsible men who followed the ways of their ancestors, themselves descended from Consuls and praetors. They lifted their arms in greeting, and the senior Consul began to read from a scroll.

Suddenly I noticed the expression on the face of the urban praetor, and for a moment I saw this ceremony through his eyes. Before him was a great four-wheeled cart, fantastically decorated; in the middle of the cart, under a silken awning, a little black phallus poked impudently at the sky. In front of the phallus, holding the reins of the four white stallions who drew the cart, was the master of the Roman world. The Emperor was in fact a handsome youth in his fifteenth year; but in his priestly robes he looked more like an image than a human being. His tall mitre was garnished with floating silk streamers; his huge ear-rings covered his cheeks; his eyes shone through concentric lines of blue and gold paint, and his lips also were gilded; his hands blazed with jewelled rings, and his arms were hidden by long close-fitting sleeves; his clinging tunic was belted with a wide silk sash, in which were daggers, a ceremonial whip, and the ritual divining-sceptre of his high priesthood.

Round the cart capered the half-naked eunuchs who serve Cybele, in Roman eyes creatures less than human.

Behind the high priest came the litters of his grandmother and his mother, Syrians bedizened with facepaint such as only whores use in Rome; each bore the insignia of high official rank, which in Rome is forbidden to women. They were women and rulers, a combination disgusting to all conventional Romans. Behind these again came the chosen companions of the Emperor, stable boys who were slaves or who had been slaves; skilled artists in a calling which to every Roman is ignoble.

I thought back to the battlefield of Immae. There the Emperor by his courage had shown himself a true son of the Divine Caracalla; by his beauty, a true son of Roman Mars. His grandmother might ride to war on a camel, but to soldiers long stationed in Syria that had not appeared odd. He had been as Roman as Macrinus, and a more inspiring leader.

Then at Antioch, and even more during the long winter in Nicomedia, one thing had led to another. The Emperor had grown more devoted to the service of his god, he had given rein to his liking for horses and his more ardent liking for handsome grooms. He wore the dress he felt at home in, and we became accustomed to it. He behaved as he wished, because he was the master of the world; and we fell in with his whims. No one had taken him to task for his eccentricity, or even noticed that his conduct was strange.

But it would seem very strange to these magistrates who studied to follow the ways of the ancestors. I could see the shock in their eyes. I shivered for his safety, and for my own.

CHAPTER NINE
Weddings

𝒞

I was not alone in seeing that the Emperor would make a bad impression if he entered the City wearing the ritual dress of his high priesthood. The Augusta also had noted the dismay of the Senators. After we had heard the address of welcome the whole procession was halted; when we continued the Emperor, in full armour, rode in a triumphal car. The car was drawn by the customary four white horses; but they proceeded at a stately walk, led by attendants on foot. Gordius stood beside the seated Emperor; but he held an umbrella over his master's head and might be taken by the public for a confidential slave.

The official procession comprised only the Praetorians, the Alban Legions, the Emperor and the Senators. I might have marched with the Praetorians, since my name was still on their roll; but I shrank from such a long walk in the heat of a summer afternoon. Instead I accompanied the baggage carts, which made their own way to the palace. I was in good company. The Augusta and the other imperial ladies also crept into the City with the Emperor's baggage. So did the senior partner in the government, the sky-stone with his attendant priests.

No Emperor had set foot in Rome since the Divine Caracalla set out on his Parthian campaign, nearly five years ago. That was one reason why my lord's state entry was greeted with wild enthusiasm. It meant also that we found the palace in great disorder. For more than a century the Emperor's palace in Rome has been a makeshift affair, ever since the Divine Vespasianus curried favour with the gentry by destroying

Nero's Golden House. The buildings on the Palatine crowd together in a shapeless lump, with plenty of little studies for business but not enough great halls for ceremony. When we arrived there was not even a proper ceremonial entrance, such as you find in every palace built by a petty eastern ruler. While the buildings stood empty they had in theory been looked after by a large staff of freedmen and slaves; but the freedmen had neglected their duties, and most of the slaves had run away. The place had been sketchily cleaned by the servants of the urban praetor, in readiness for its new occupant; but it was sparsely furnished, and in the kitchen, especially, much essential equipment was missing.

There was great confusion when 600 baggage carts, and the litters of the imperial ladies, all arrived together at the back door. But our servants had looked after us in strange places for every night of our 1,600 mile journey, and they treated the great palace as though it were just another halt on the road. They got fires going in the kitchen, and put up travelling beds in the cleanest rooms. Three hours after our arrival the majordomo had the trumpets blown for supper. It was nearly midnight, an odd time to begin a meal; but I set off, guided by the smell of cooked food, to find my way to the dining hall.

It was a gloomy, musty hall, a long way from the kitchen; but it was big enough to hold the numerous company. The furniture was old and battered, and not all of it very clean; but once it had been worthy of the lord of the civilised world. When I arrived boys were already handing round wine, and after a steward had shown me to a couch I felt more cheerful.

There were nine couches to a table in that crowded hall, which meant that the company must be mixed. At my table I found a tribune and three centurions from the Praetorians, and four youths from the racing stables of Nicomedia. Now that I did no regular duty I felt awkward in the presence of serving soldiers; outside the imperial household the stable boys would have been reckoned ignoble, unworthy to recline beside honourable citizens. But even these uncongenial companions showed that someone had tried to look after me; I might have been put with a clutch of stewards and clerks, Syrian pen-pushers who always got on my nerves.

We were all in very high spirits. The Praetorians could talk of nothing but the rousing reception of the crowd; the stable boys were on fire to taste the dissipations of Rome. We all felt that a function which might have turned out badly had passed off better than we had expected.

'I've never heard such cheering,' said the tribune. 'In the Camp everyone remarked on it. Tonight they will have a wonderful party; bad luck that it's my turn for palace guard. But I'll be back in quarters before all the wine is finished. The men who are for guard tomorrow are the real unlucky ones. In the morning they will have to parade sober, just when we are getting ready to enjoy ourselves.'

'Then the Emperor had a good welcome?' I asked, eager for reassurance even though I knew the answer.

'Magnificent. They shouted that he was Severus come again. They are calling him Antoninus, and that's the highest praise they can give. He looked an Antoninus, too, in his golden armour. I didn't know the boy had it in him.'

'You didn't see him at Immae. He can rise to an occasion. He's good when something is happening, something exciting enough to make him forget his funny little sky-stone.' This was one of the centurions, speaking rather too freely in the presence of a commissioned officer. It came as a shock to me, after my months as a courtier, to hear these soldiers discuss the points of their ruler so casually. I had forgotten that soldiers, and Praetorians in particular, feel that they own the Empire. They had bestowed the Purple on young Elagabalus, and if he did not please them they could take it away again.

Then the majordomo banged for silence, and we all got to our feet as the Emperor hurried in. He had taken off his armour and wore a simple Roman tunic, though the laurel wreath was still on his head. He was arm-in-arm with Gordius, but otherwise he had no attendants.

He was very happy, and as usual wanted everyone else to be happy too. A couch was ready for him at the far end of the hall, but he stopped on the way there to have a word with several friends. He shouted a greeting to the stable boys beside me, and then stopped as though reminded of something and beckoned me over to him.

'There you are, Duratius. I didn't see you in the procession. Don't you think my extra special private bodyguard ought to have been on hand when those dangerous Senators pressed round me? Never mind, perhaps you feared I might ask you to dance. Let me see, you are dismissed from the council. I don't forget my promises. All the same, the Augusta wants to see you in the morning, early, before they loose the petitioners into her anteroom. I don't know why she wants you, but she asked me to deliver the message.'

He moved on, still chatting easily. He was the Emperor, the partner of the Sun-god; he saw himself as so infinitely superior to all his subjects that he might deliver messages to centurions, or let stable boys slap him on the back, without impairing his majesty.

By the time he was gracefully arranged on his couch, beaming over the wine-cup at his faithful courtiers, the buzz of conversation was concerned only with the splendid Games which would mark his arrival in the palace of his ancestors. Even the Praetorians had forgotten their criticisms; the Emperor had only to move through a crowd and the charm and beauty of his person silenced the doubts raised by his unconventional conduct.

Sleeping in the cluttered palace was no worse than a night on campaign, and I was properly dressed in a burnished cuirass when I waited on the Augusta at sunrise. The Emperor had chosen a bedchamber at the far end of the building, with his stable boys bedded down in the anteroom and the corridor; so the Augusta had been allotted the principal state apartment, not far from the main entrance. Her maids were expecting me, and I was admitted as soon as I arrived.

The Augusta lay in an enormous carved bed, among a huddle of purple silk coverlets. Her white hair had been freshly arranged above her brown face; the toils of the journey had fined down the luxury of Nicomedia, and she looked more than ever like a benevolent goddess. She was still very tired, but not at all sleepy. As usual, she had planned in advance what she wanted to say, and she began to speak without hesitation.

'Duratius, the Emperor has very properly removed you from the council. It was an honour you did not seek, and unfitting to your rank. You know very well that you might command an army, but if you think the work beyond you I won't press you to accept promotion. That doesn't mean you can go back to being an ordinary centurion. You are marked as an imperial favourite; the soldiers would regard you as a police agent planted in the Camp. So if you want to stay in Rome, we must find you some reasonable occupation. Or if you like you can take your savings and go off to live quietly in the provinces. Are you still willing to work for the Emperor?'

'Of course I am willing, Augusta. On the battlefield of Immae I took an oath of my own free-will. Besides, I can't retire into provincial obscurity. The police would assume I had fallen from favour, and think to please the Emperor by charging me with treason. I wish to serve you in any way I can, and moreover I am so far committed that I cannot draw back.'

'I'm glad you have the sense to recognise it. We can always find work for a man who sees the world as it is. But if you are determined to remain a centurion you must do work fitting for a centurion. You can't have it both ways. No more being one of us in private, and then standing to attention before Eutychianus because you are only a humble warrant officer.'

'That will suit me, madam. Do me the justice to agree that I never sought greatness. I serve the Emperor as his private bodyguard because I have been detailed for that duty.'

'That's true. You will still be the Emperor's private body-guard. But in Rome you will live like a bodyguard, not like a minister of state. My plan is that you should lodge in the palace, but among the soldiers. You will not take post as a sentry, but the guardroom will be your living-room. You will parade as a supernumerary at the daily guard-mounting. There will be occasions when the Emperor will wish to leave the palace incognito, and then you will go with him and be responsible for his safety. But your real work,' and here she smiled at me as at a confederate, 'will be to keep in touch with the feeling of the Praetorians. I suppose the daily guard will accept you more or less as a comrade, and you can warn us if you think the army is discontented with the government. We do all we can to please the soldiers,' she added with a sigh, 'but so did every Emperor who came before us. And look at how many of them were murdered by their guards!'

'The soldiers make the Emperor, madam, so they think they have the right to unmake him. I don't see how they reconcile it with their oath, but that's how even honourable men see it. All the same, our present Emperor is extremely popular, and I don't think you need fear any movement to overthrow him. I shall talk with the officers of the daily guard, and keep my ear to the ground. If I went to live in the Camp they would dislike me as a palace spy, but here in the guardroom a palace spy is to be expected. They won't hold it against me. Neither will they say in front of me exactly what they are thinking. But I know soldiers, and I ought to be able to spot the beginning of discontent.'

'Then that's settled. You can have today off, to move into your new quarters. Tomorrow you parade at guard-mounting. You keep your centurion's rate of pay, unless you want more. I expect the Emperor will give you presents from time to time, and you will live free at the palace. Does that suit you?'

I saluted, and waited for permission to withdraw. But the Augusta had not finished with me.

'There was something else,' she said with a worried frown,

'but I can't remember everything. This palace has to govern the civilised world, and all the work falls on me. It's not woman's work, but the Emperor is too young to manage by himself. Oh yes, I remember. You ought to be told a lot of things about the policy of the new government, so that you can explain it to the soldiers. But I can't go into it now, and anyway it's not clear in my head. Someone else must do it. Who is there? The Praetorian Praefect will be busy. The Clarissima can never explain anything to anyone. How a daughter of mine came by such a muddled mind I can't understand. I know. Wait on the lady Mamea this afternoon, when she is supposed to be resting. Most of our plans were her ideas to start with, and she ought to be able to explain them. Now you may go.'

That free day to settle into the palace was a more valuable privilege than perhaps the Augusta understood. My servant laid out my baggage and bedding in a cosy little chamber near the guardroom. I foraged for suitable furniture among the deserted attics, and made friends with cooks and butlers until my private store-cupboard was well stocked. I tipped a pretty housemaid to keep my room clean, for my servant would be fully occupied in looking after my armour. I knew my way about that numerous household; I could tell who gave promises that meant nothing and who could really make life easier. By the afternoon I had things organised so that I might live softly in the palace, without too much work, and, most important of all, without attracting attention.

In the afternoon I waited in the anteroom of the lady Mamea, who had been given a distant self-contained wing where she might keep little Alexianus safe from the racket of the Emperor's supper parties. I had a long wait for her; but when she arrived she saw me first, before the other petitioners.

She sat behind a littered desk looking busy and worried and at the same time capable, like the commander of a strong garrison in a turbulent province. She smiled, and spoke politely; but she was very much the great lady instructing a common centurion. One might say that she was the only member of that court who was conscious of her dignity, and that she was too conscious of it. Though she was trying to be fair, she did not like me and considered my position deplorably irregular.

'I understand you will be talking to the soldiers, Duratius,' she began with a sniff of distaste. 'All this pandering to the opinions of mere legionaries seems to be sadly un-Roman. It was the cudgel of the centurion that conquered the Empire, in the days when discontented soldiers were flogged. But I suppose we can't go back to the good old days, in a world that grows steadily more wicked.'

'When every citizen could fight, madam, the soldiers were kept in order. Nowadays no one dares to withstand them.'

'There's no need to rub it in, even though you are a soldier yourself. But if you are to influence their opinion, which I consider a disgraceful concession, you must know what we want said to them. Pay attention. I don't want to repeat this.'

She picked up a paper, wrinkling her nose to read it.

'In the first place, the Emperor is the heir to the legitimate Antonine house, which has ruled Rome for a hundred years. He is the son of the Divine Caracalla, who was the son of the Divine Severus, who had been adopted into the Antonine house by the Divine Commodus. No one is to say that we are founding a new dynasty.' She glared at me severely, to see whether I would scruple to repeat this pack of barefaced lies. I nodded affirmatively.

'This Emperor of the ancient line will reign after the ancient fashion. There will be no innovations,' she continued with an even fiercer glare. 'The Senate will be granted its due share in the administration. The Emperor will adhere to the sacred constitution bequeathed to us by our ancestors. Our policy will be peace on the frontiers, a generous and punctual stipend to the soldiers, and, if possible, a lightening of the burden of taxation. It is no secret that the Emperor nourishes a personal devotion to the Sun-god Elagabalus, but he will fulfil his public duty to Capitoline Jove and to the other ancient guardians of the Republic. The citizens will share in the general prosperity of the state. The restoration of the rightful dynasty will shortly be celebrated with unusually splendid Games, and a generous congiary to every citizen. The Emperor will immediately take in hand the completion of the public works begun by the Divine Caracalla, which were neglected during the tyranny of the usurper Macrinus. Finally, though perhaps the soldiers will not appreciate this, the Emperor has sworn that no subject shall be put to death, save after conviction in a lawful trial.'

'You promise the return of the Golden Age, my lady,' I said solemnly. 'May I add, while I am encouraging the troops, that the Augusta will spin wool for the imperial toga?'

Mamea stared hard into my eyes and decided, wrongly, that I had not spoken ironically.

'Avoid the subject of wool-spinning; though the Augusta Livia set the example long ago, and it would be well if we could follow it. The Emperor is reluctant to wear the customary toga. You may not know that the high priests of Emesa follow the Egyptian fashion, and consider it a defilement to wear clothing of animal origin. The Emperor wears only linen or silk. But we are getting a toga made for him, of especially thick linen, which we hope will look like the usual article . . . Now I know you will be discreet, and I have given you your instructions. You will lay emphasis on the Emperor's admiration for the ancient customs that made Rome great. You will not talk about his liking for charioteers. Gordius will live in the palace, but he holds no official post.'

She turned back to her desk, and I realised that the interview was at an end.

On the way to the guardroom I ran into the Clarissima, as usual walking vaguely about with a basket of something to eat and a handsome young man to carry it for her. 'Ah, Duratius, isn't it?' she said as she saw me. 'When you see the Emperor ask him to be sure to come to my sitting-room this evening. I want him to meet some young ladies. We must hold the wedding soon, before everyone leaves Rome to avoid the heat.'

I saluted obediently. It would be no good telling her that I had not been commanded to wait on the Emperor, because she never listened to anything said to her.

After I had greeted the guard commander we talked about the weather and the crops. I had heard so many instructions of such a startling novelty, that I thought it better to wait a bit before telling the world that we had a sound traditional Emperor of the old school.

The Games held to celebrate the return of the Emperor to his faithful city were the most splendid within living memory. Eutychianus had planned them in outline; and by a useful tradition the curule aediles bore most of the cost. But it was obvious to those who knew him that the Emperor had taken a hand in the details.

I stood among the guards at the back of the imperial box, where I could see everything. The huge Flavian amphitheatre was packed with a happy and contented throng of citizens, all the more content because the proceedings opened with a congiary of startling generosity. The Emperor proclaimed that every Roman citizen present would receive a gift of 150 drachmae; and the same amount would be given to every woman, a thing that had never been done before. In those days the great amphitheatre did not hold so many spectators as it does now; damage done by an earthquake in the reign of the Divine Commodus had been left unrepaired. The new government had already taken in hand its restoration, as the most urgent public work of this peaceful reign. Even in its damaged state it held a great many people; I wondered how long the ancestral treasure of the high priests of Emesa would stand the strain.

I noted something else. The Emperor had been serious when he proposed to do something to better the hard life of Roman harlots. Respectable wives do not frequent the amphitheatre; this strange female congiary would benefit chiefly the loose women who ply their trade in every crowded place.

The Emperor's behaviour was always unexpected. After this congiary to his civilian subjects he announced a donative to the soldiers; but at the rate of a hundred drachmae a man. Some of the guards looked sour; until I whispered that a hundred drachmae was a very nice present when you had done nothing to earn it, and that soldiers would keep all they got while the civilian congiary, or most of it, would go straight to the tax-gatherer.

The events which followed in the arena gave further evidence of the Emperor's planning. Gladiators fought to the death, in pairs dotted all over the sands; because without gladiators the crowd would have rioted. But there were not very many of them and they fought all at once, so that the murdering should be quickly over. The mob demands death, but mere bloodshed without beauty did not amuse the Emperor.

The distribution of the congiary, and then the hasty slaughter of the gladiators, occupied the morning. During the dinner hour most of the gentry went home for their meal, according to the custom of Rome; but no one left the imperial box, because the Emperor had brought a picnic lunch with him. Nowadays fools quote this as evidence that Elagabalus was bloodthirsty, so bloodthirsty that he could not leave the amphitheatre even to eat. They should remember that no one is killed during the dinner hour, which is traditionally devoted to comic relief.

The comic relief devised by the Emperor was in one respect curious. It is the custom that tumblers and acrobats, of both sexes, should entertain the public with obscene dances. That was not enough for our new master. He had commanded that every obscene gesture should be carried to its logical conclusion. Even the ignoble tumblers blushed at some of the things they had to do in broad daylight, before thousands of spectators. But the crowd, squealing with delighted embarrassment, loved every minute of it.

In the afternoon wild beasts were hunted. Gladiators should be seen at close quarters, or you will miss the blood and the gaping wounds that are the attraction of the entertainment. The hunting of wild beasts can be beautiful as a spectacle, seen from the back of the imperial box; especially if the programme has been devised by a connoisseur of beauty like our young Emperor.

In the first scene mounted Arabs hunted gazelles. The crowd thought this dull because there was no danger for the hunters. But we saw some magnificent riding as the men darted and twisted after the twisting gazelles, dodging the stone walls of the arena until they rode beside their quarry to hurl their javelins.

Next men on foot hunted wild bulls. The naked hunters carried short spears and lengths of coloured cloth to throw over the bulls' eyes. Quite a number of them had been disembowelled before the bulls were killed, which put the spectators into a better temper.

Then came what was for connoisseurs the most important event of the day, the hunting of an enormous African elephant. Every Roman is familiar with elephants, for they figure in many state processions. But in fact there are very few of them in the City, because they are hard to catch and ship oversea; the same dozen or so of the beasts, mostly tame Indians, parade again and again. It was a long time since an elephant had been turned loose in the arena to be killed. His hunters were a band of black men armed with two-edged swords. In the end they got him, cutting the tendons of his hind legs from the rear; but not until he had killed a good number of the hunters. Even after he was down he took a lot of killing; his hide was almost proof against a swordstroke. Soldiers watched this with deep interest. If you campaign in Africa or the west you never know when you may have to face elephants in war; though the Parthians do not employ them and I have never seen a genuine war-elephant.

But it was not the kind of thing to interest the populace, who like to see a lot of fights going on at once in every corner of the arena. The hunting of a single animal, even if that animal was an elephant, seemed to them evidence of shameful stinginess. It was an historic occasion, to be recorded in the annals of the City; but to send the crowd home in a good temper something more lavish was needed at the finish.

The last turn of all was spectacular enough to please anybody.

Oxen drew into the arena more than fifty wheeled cages, and in each cage sat a hungry tiger. Tigers, which must be bought from beyond the Empire, are more expensive than lions which are sent to the City as part of the tribute of Africa. The loosing of the tigers was the first attraction; it gave the spectators an opportunity to bet among themselves on a more or less even chance, which always amuses them. Condemned criminals, unarmed and naked, were lined up at the far end of the arena; when a trumpet blew they raced towards the cages. Each man had to open a single cage, then run to get out of the arena by a wicket gate before he was caught by a tiger. Of course those who opened the first cages had the best chance, which made them race well. Some got away and others were caught.

Then men armed with long pikes fought the tigers. Their method was to provoke a tiger into charging, and spear him in the belly as he sprang. The hunters began with great confidence, for they had been trained to the work; but of course each man could watch only one tiger at a time, and many were killed by unexpected attacks. In fact you might say that the tigers won; when fifty-one of them had been killed there were no more hunters left on their feet. The half-dozen surviving beasts were driven back to their cages by attendants who waved blazing torches.

The amphitheatre was properly dotted with the bodies of men and animals; the sand was properly splashed with blood. For a full half-hour the citizens shouted their gratitude before they went home in an orderly manner, without rioting.

Throughout the long day the Emperor had behaved perfectly. He sat still in his place, enjoying everything but not showing too much excitement. Gordius stood beside him, and occasionally they chatted; but the young man carried a tray with drinks and the Emperor's handkerchief, so that only courtiers in the know recognised him as more than a valet. The imperial toga, arranged in graceful folds, looked as though it were made of the conventional wool. The Consuls and the other curule magistrates shared the imperial box, and the Emperor greeted them correctly. The ladies of the imperial household, even the Augusta, sat in a separate box, behind the Vestal virgins. We might all have been real Romans, born and bred on the Palatine; instead of a collection of queer foreigners from the most outlandish province of the Empire.

The Games continued for many days, until the supply of wild beasts was exhausted. But no more elephants were killed, because the Emperor had thought of another use for them. The supply of trained gladiators lasted better; the Emperor was not interested in fights between man and man, and showed as few of them as he could without irritating the populace.

After the Games in the Flavian amphitheatre we continued to celebrate the new reign by a special race-meeting in the circus. But on the morning of the first race there was a special parade at the Praetorian Camp, for the Emperor to announce his approaching marriage. The Divine Severus set the precedent of announcing these family events first to his guards, as though they also were members of the imperial family; the Senate does not like it, but the custom is too firmly established to be altered.

Since this was a family occasion the imperial household were present in force. The Augusta, wearing a purple cloak and a wreath of laurel, took the principal part. She held her grandson by the elbow as though he were still a child, and herself called the troops up to attention before announcing that Antoninus Elagabalus would shortly marry the only daughter of Julius Paulus. The Emperor blushed, looking .uncomfortable but obedient; but he summoned up the resolution to embrace his future father-in-law as though he liked it. Paula herself was not present, in accordance with the theory that a tender virgin would be frightened by the sight of soldiers in the mass.

The match was in every way suitable. Julius Paulus was an eminent lawyer of impeccable breeding. There were no black sheep in his respectable family, and yet it was not very ancient or famous; there was no danger that his kin would found a powerful faction. So long as the Emperor remained obedient to his grandmother there was a chance that he would win the friendship and support of the Senate, which no Emperor has enjoyed since the death of the Divine Marcus Aurelius.

Unfortunately the chariot races on the same afternoon introduced a disturbing influence. I saw the beginning of it; for I happened to be in close attendance on the Emperor, for the first time since we had arrived in Rome.

In the circus there has never been the formal etiquette of the amphitheatre. Watching the death of gladiators is an ancient Roman custom, tenuously connected with the worship of the gods. Watching horses race is a new diversion, introduced from foreign parts; and even the Greeks who brought it to Rome never regarded it as more than a diversion.

Therefore at the circus the Emperor might recline in comfort, instead of sitting in a chair of state. He wore a comfortable tunic instead of his ceremonial toga. He might have his friends round him, instead of placing the curule magistrates in accurate order of precedence.

Gordius squatted at his feet. The imperial ladies sat behind him. I stood at his side, the only bodyguard in the imperial box; though there were sentries within call.

The first race was not important, a sprint for three-year-olds with apprentice drivers. While the chariots were lining up for the start the Emperor chatted with me, just as in the old days at Nicomedia. He was chaffing me about my correct military turn-out.

'Must you carry a centurion's cudgel, as well as a sword? Of course you must. It's in standing orders, dress and equipment for a centurion on guard duty within the City. But suppose a wicked Senator jumped out, brandishing a dagger? Would you hit him with your cudgel, as though he were a clumsy recruit? Or would you drop your stick to draw your sword, at the risk of appearing improperly dressed in the circus?'

'Duratius would get it right at all costs,' said Gordius lazily. 'He would submit a written report to the Praetorian Praefect, asking for permission to draw his sword within the peace of the

City. Until the answer came the Emperor would rely for protection on the fists of his gallant stable boys.'

'If it was a Senator I would not need even the cudgel,' said I. 'A soldier has only to scowl from under his helmet and any Senator will run away. More likely the assassin would be another soldier, and then the cudgel would come in useful. After all, it's laid down in the manual: "the legionary should fear the cudgel of the centurion more than he fears the swords of the enemy." '

'Meanwhile I would run away, uttering the little falsetto screams that make the heart of Gordius go pit-a-pat. I wonder would he run after me, or stay behind to fight the murderer?' the Emperor continued.

'Run after you, of course, my dear, and leave fighting to those who are paid for it. Hallo, they're off. Only novices, but it may give us a pointer for next year. Let's watch.' Gordius became professional.

There was a bit of trouble as the chariots swept round the first turn. The leading Green, boxed in, wrenched his team away from the central spine to avoid a collision. His horses fought a bit, for they had been trained to keep close to the wall; by brilliant driving the young charioteer pulled them clear of the ruck. But he spurted too soon, trying to make up lost ground on the straight; his unbalanced team were not properly on their legs when he gave them the whip. One of the inner horses stumbled, and his weight on the yoke was too much for his mates. After a long complicated scramble the chariot and the four horses together rolled over in a spectacular spill right in front of the imperial box.

Accidents usually come at the turns, not in front of the imperial box half-way down the straight. The Emperor and Gordius craned to see, shouting to the sentries to run down and unyoke the horses before they could kick one another. The young driver had been thrown clear. He lay on his back, naked save for his breech-clout, for his cloak was tangled in the chariot; his cap also had fallen off, and golden curls framed a pink-and-white face. Even I thought him attractive; the Emperor was thunderstruck.

'Who's that, Gordius? I know him, he's one of the boys from Nicomedia. But he's come on, hasn't he? Odd how ten days will suddenly turn a good-looking child into a youth of amazing beauty. I ought to know, it happened to me. But tell me his name. We must have him at the palace.'

'It's young Hierocles, a Carian. He's one of my apprentices. Still a slave, you know, and not half such a good driver as he thinks he is. He need not have fallen if he hadn't been too impatient. Do you really want him at the palace?' I could sympathise with Gordius, who dared not lie to his master but was naturally reluctant to praise a rival.

The Emperor took in the situation with one of his queer flashes of adult insight. 'He shall be nursed at the palace, and when he's better we shall keep him there. But don't you worry, Gordius. He doesn't compete with you. You are my man, Hierocles shall be my boy. Does that sound very strange, Duratius? Anyway, you know what I mean. All too soon I shall be a husband. I am not looking forward to my wedding, but together the three of us will fix up something to make it more endurable.'

I smiled, and left Gordius to answer this pretty sentiment. The Emperor's private life was his own affair, and it seems to me ridiculous to hold that it is more wicked to love boys than girls. But my own tastes lie in a different direction, and I could never understand the intensity of his feeling. For that matter, the Emperor himself could not understand them. At one minute he would talk as though Gordius and all his other boy-friends were no more than casual concubines; at the next he would sigh and groan as though he were one of the famous masculine lovers of Greek legend.

Hierocles was carried to the palace in a closed litter. The Emperor remained in his box until the finish of the day's racing, so there was no occasion for scandal. That evening he supped with his two charioteers; but privately, so privately that half the court knew nothing of it. He was really doing his best to live like a conventional Roman.

Three days later I had the delicate task of passing on certain instructions to a section of Praetorians and the centurion who was to command them. They were to proceed, in all haste, to some backwoods city of Pontus; there they were to seek out the elderly slave-woman who was the mother of Hierocles. Her full and only name was, unfortunately, Ma; her owner had called her after a famous Cappadocian goddess, as some unimaginative men call their doorkeepers Cerberus and their boatmen Charon. It was a good enough name for a slave-woman, but it was hard to keep a straight face when explaining the business to soldiers. The centurion, who carried a blank draft on the provincial treasury, was to buy her at a price fixed by arbitration; then he was to see her emancipated in the court of a competent magistrate. Finally the section, transformed into a guard of honour, were to escort the old girl to Rome, treating her with the respect due to a close friend of the Emperor.

Of course the whole project was absurd. Handled in the wrong way it might have grown into an insult to honourable Praetorians, enough to set off a dangerous mutiny. I treated it as a joke, and persuaded the detail to see it in the same light. Once they felt themselves to be confederates of the Emperor, helping him in an assault on the dignity of stuffy Senators, they were quite happy to begin their journey. I saw to it that they were provided with a travel-warrant drawn in generous terms, authorising them to impress transport and requisition billets wherever they should find it convenient; they would return substantially richer than when they set off. They left willingly, and the Emperor's high-spirited sense of humour became the talk of the Camp.

But you cannot do that kind of thing too often. Soldiers like a ruler who from time to time makes respectable civilians look ridiculous; they will not submit to a flippant young joker who cannot take serious things seriously. The goings-on at the time

163

of the Emperor's wedding were kept as far as possible secret from the troops.

Those goings-on were really disgraceful, and yet I cannot find it in my heart to blame the Emperor. He had never concealed his aversion from females, and we all knew that he went through with this marriage only to please his grand-mother. He was performing an unpleasant duty, and he was entitled to a bit of his own kind of fun to make up for it. But I am sorry he brought me into it, for I was genuinely shocked by his behaviour. It made it harder for me to continue as his advocate with the Praetorians.

My troubles stemmed from the Augusta's lack of understanding while we were in Nicomedia. Because I had taken the Emperor to a brothel, a thing I would never have done if I had not been acting under orders, he saw me as a rake who would condone any kind of irregular conduct. When he commanded me, a mere centurion, to be a witness of his marriage he was merely displaying his contempt for the Roman code of precedence; but then he kept me by him to be a witness of the secret ceremonies later in the same evening, a mistake in tact of a kind he seldom committed.

His wedding to Julia Cornelia Paula was a sad, half-hearted affair, though nothing was lacking of ceremony or ritual. The bride, aged twelve, was frightened half out of her wits, and the bridegroom was openly indifferent. But all the most famous lawyers in Rome were present, preening themselves on the honour done to their profession. Paulus swelled with self-importance. The Augusta was delighted, and so was the Clarissima. The lady Mamea looked down her nose, but a Syrian lady cannot but rejoice at the marriage of her nephew; for to any Syrian an increase in the number of her kindred must be a good thing. All the patrician flamines joined in the ceremony, and the pontiffs were present in their official robes. The Emperor, the Pontifex Maximus, alone did not adhere to the set ritual. He chose to wear his vestments as high priest of his sky-stone instead of his Roman gown; and he flatly refused to share the sacred barley-cake with his bride, because, as he frankly explained, that would make divorce more difficult if later he changed his mind. They were married instead by the form customary among plebeians, which binds a couple only until the husband chooses to send back his bride.

Eminent Senators carried the torches. Nobly-born maidens accompanied the bride. The Augusta was matron of honour. Twelve white bulls were sacrificed to the twelve high gods of Olympus, and the chief Vestal offered something secret at a little tripod set apart, where no man could see what she was doing. The happy couple ought to have enjoyed all the luck that devout service of the gods can bring down.

But when the bride was escorted to the nuptial chamber, the Emperor made no move to follow her. Instead, after a very short interval for the usual drinking, he brought the feast to an end by announcing that he must go away and pray before his sky-stone. As he left the banqueting hall he motioned to me and a few others of his intimates to follow.

We trooped down corridors and across dark courtyards until we reached a distant outlying part of the palace. It was in fact a relic of Nero's Golden House, a tall vaulted room which had been a garden pavilion when all that quarter of Rome was the Emperor's private park. The Divine Vespasianus allowed the citizens to build over this park, for with Rome so crowded it seemed a hardship to keep an entire region for the Emperor's private enjoyment. But some of the outlying pavilions remain, if you know where to look for them; they are still joined to the main block by narrow private passages.

In this room we found the stable boys reclining before their wine, after a supper as good as the wedding feast. The Emperor made sure we had plenty to drink, then left us to change his clothes. When he came back I tasted my wine carefully, to make sure I had not been drugged into seeing visions.

He wore the flame-coloured tunic and stole of a maiden bride. His golden hair, in elaborate curls, hung down his back under the veil of transparent silk. His bare arms, depilated and powdered, were loaded with feminine bracelets. His toes, reddened with henna peeped from flimsy feminine sandals. A palace freedwoman, wearing the ornaments of a matron of honour, led him by the little finger on his left hand, while he feigned the reluctance of a bashful maiden on her wedding day. Behind him a rout of cleaning women, dressed as bridesmaids, chanted the wedding hymn.

From an opposite door emerged Gordius, wearing the wreath and decorated tunic of a bridegroom. His attendants were children, naked save for the Cupid's wings fixed to their shoulders. Behind them a group of the priests of Cybele joined their soprano voices in the hymn of the bridesmaids.

The stable boys laughed and cheered and shouted obscene greetings. They treated the whole affair as a boisterous joke, while Gordius continually giggled with embarrassment. But it seemed to me that the Emperor was more than half in earnest; he had so thrown himself into the part he was playing that for the time being he was genuinely a willing but bashful maiden. The business was soon over. The happy couple exchanged their vows before the chief priest of Cybele as officiant; and then immediately retired to a curtained bed in an alcove.

Bridesmaids and cupids bustled about, filling every cup with unmixed wine. I drank eagerly to steady my shaken nerves. Even the toughest stable boys were uncertain how they ought to behave. What seemed on the face of it an obscene joke might be regarded seriously by the Emperor; even his closest friends could never be sure of what he thought in any matter connected with religion. If he caught us mocking at something he believed sacred we might all find ourselves in the wrong part of the amphitheatre when the next Games came round.

The Emperor settled our doubts by sticking his head through the bed curtains. 'Drink hearty, boys,' he said with a wink. 'I'm a married woman now, and nothing can shock me. So I can tell you without blushing that the next scene follows immediately. This is my wedding night, by special command of the Augusta. By dawn I shall be most thoroughly married.'

The cupids continued to press wine on us. It must have been the middle of the night, but the windowless hall was a blaze of lamps. I felt that I had been reclining in this hot, mad, closed world for longer than I could remember; and that I would stay here, without seeing the sky, until I was an old man. Since I could expect no rational conversation from the stable boys I set myself to drink copiously enough to drown my uneasiness.

After what seemed a long interval the Emperor entered once more. He must have escaped from the curtained bed by a hidden passage, for he had again changed his dress before he emerged from the side door. Now he was wearing the dancing costume of the sky-stone's high priest, the queer get-up I had seen in Nicomedia. Once again he was naked below the waist, and his loins were decorated with that great leather phallus.

But a bridegroom's wreath encircled his mitre, and the young men attending him waved the thyrsus, the Bacchic emblem that is another version of the phallus.

From the opposite door a procession came to meet him, the bridesmaids and matron of honour who had attended him in the first ceremony. Now they escorted another figure, one which at first I failed to recognise. Someone frail and white and slender was encased in the flame-coloured bridal wrappings. It was all very odd. Was the Emperor about to take a second wife, while the mate chosen for him by his grandmother lay in his unused marriage-bed?

Then I recognised the boy Hierocles, looking as shy and frightened as the most virginal bride. If he doesn't like it why should he do it? was my first thought; until I saw there was another side to the question. I am not among those who hold that slaves are something less than men, though I can see what they mean. A man who accepts slavery when he might die free on the battlefield, by his cowardice diminishes the dignity of the human race. But an infant born into slavery should be judged by more lenient standards. Young Hierocles, slave-born, had never been in a position to disobey his master's orders. He need not be blamed for his part in tonight's extraordinary activities.

I don't like male prostitutes. Nobody does. At the same time nobody objects if a man falls in love with another man, because that has been made respectable by the example of antiquity. Gordius could be excused, for he was genuinely in love with the Emperor; he would have loved him as deeply if they had been slaves together in some Bithynian stable. Perhaps the Emperor could be excused; he was genuinely in love with Gordius, and his feeling for Hierocles had more of affection and admiration for beauty than of mere brute lust. Now I was making excuses for Hierocles, because he was frightened and young and very far from home. A post at court broadens the mind.

It was easier to forgive Hierocles because he looked so very attractive, with the blue of his eyes peeping from under long black lashes and the brown of his healthy skin setting off the bright gold of his hair. His clothing and make-up were so completely feminine that it was easy to forget that he had no right to be a blushing bride. I am a Gaul, with the Celtic distaste for unnatural love; but even I envied the Emperor the possession of so much beauty.

Once again marriage vows were exchanged before the sardonic gaze of the eunuch priest; this time with the Emperor as bridegroom. Once more the happy pair retired to the curtained bed. Once more the naked cupids came round with wine for the company. But they passed the heavy sweet wine that by custom ends a feast, and I realised that at last this odd entertainment was finished. Presently a steward announced that we had leave to depart, and servants began to extinguish the lamps. Many of the stable boys were past rousing; but those of us who could still use our legs were escorted by torchbearers to the main block of the palace. As far as I could see, the Emperor was still in his masculine marriage-bed.

Next morning I suffered from headache and spots before the eyes; but so did many other courtiers. No one remarked on my seedy appearance. At guard-mounting I stood steady, and then hoped that the worst was over and that I might sit about until an early bedtime. To my dismay, I found a note waiting for me in the guardroom after parade. I was to report immediately at the office of the Praetorian Praefect.

A stiff drink gave me confidence, if it did not improve my complexion. Deciding that if my turn-out was good enough for guard-mounting it must be good enough for the Praetorian Praefect, I hurried straight off to his office in the main block of the palace. I was expected. As I arrived a petitioner was ejected with his business half-finished, and the sentry threw open the door for me to enter.

It was a surprise to find sitting behind the littered desk not only Eutychianus but the three ladies of the imperial household. The Augusta might turn up in any government office at any time; she was trying to rule the Empire, and that meant taking a hand in everything. But Soaemias seldom bothered about anything except food and handsome young soldiers, and Mamea was too busy making friends with respectable Senators to cultivate the powerful but unfashionable Praefect. I thought it prudent to address my salute to the Augusta, though Eutychianus was the only commissioned officer present.

Eutychianus, who looked worried, fussed with his papers as though he did not know how to begin. The Augusta came immediately to the point. 'You were with my grandson last night. Tell us exactly what he did.'

I told her, in blunt soldierly language. Nothing could shock or embarrass the Augusta, and told simply the events of that night seemed mere childish naughtiness; only those who had felt the atmosphere of that isolated hall could realise that the Emperor had been in deadly earnest.

When I had finished Eutychianus snorted. 'There's not a word of truth in your ridiculous tale. Yesterday the Emperor was married. He spent last night with his bride. If you hear rumours that he did anything else you are to deny them. You are to take special pains to make sure that the Praetorians hear the correct version of events. That's an order.'

'*Sir*,' I answered, with a rigid Praetorian salute. Common

legionaries say, 'Yes sir,' when acknowledging an order, but it was a fad among the Praetorians to cut the acknowledgement as short as possible.

'What good will that do?' asked the Augusta in a tired voice. 'We have been into this already. The only way to keep the debauch a secret would be to kill all the witnesses. But the Emperor would kill *us* if we killed Gordius and Hierocles. He won't let us so much as frighten his stable boys. Probably he would protect Duratius, for that matter. The story is bound to leak out. It will be denied officially. Every Senator and civil servant who wants to keep in with the government will pretend to be convinced by the denial. But this evening all Rome will know how my grandson spent his wedding night.'

'Of course all Rome will know the truth,' snapped the Praefect, 'but if we deny it officially no one will be brave enough to contradict us.'

'I can't think what's come over my dear boy,' wailed the lady Soaemias. 'What you tell me he did isn't natural, and surely he can't have enjoyed it? That sweet girl Paula, too! So humiliating for her, a virgin after her wedding night! I shall speak to the Emperor. . . . Oh, do you think that scented young Hierocles could have cast a spell on him?'

'Now don't you start making bright suggestions, or I shall break down and scream,' said the Augusta through set teeth. 'The Emperor does not care for Paula. But then he has never loved a woman. I don't know what went wrong with him, but we must admit that he will always prefer boys. Perhaps we can persuade him to treat Paula as a wife, but he will do it only to please his family. We have been thrashing it out all morning, and we need not begin all over again in front of Duratius. This is a practical business meeting, to decide what to do next. The Emperor is the heir of the Divine Caracalla, the heir of the Antonine house who brought peace to the citizens and high pay to the soldiers. Duratius, give us your honest answer. Will the Praetorians remain loyal to the Emperor, bearing in mind his ancestry; or will they overthrow him, and us, because of his disgusting behaviour?'

'Even if the soldiers still follow him the Senate will be disgusted,' said the lady Mamea with a sniff. 'How can we rule Rome if all the gentry despise us?'

'Oh, be quiet,' snarled the Augusta. 'I could govern the civilised world if only my daughters would leave me in peace ... Now, will the soldiers continue to support us?'

I thought hard before I answered. I owed the Augusta an honest opinion, but her question was uncommonly difficult.

'The Emperor's behaviour has not strengthened his position,' I said slowly, 'but what he did was done in private. Some of those who admire him may choose to believe the official denials. Anyway, no Emperor was ever overthrown for disgusting behaviour. What the soldiers don't like is frivolity in serious matters, and especially frivolity in military matters. Most soldiers don't regard marriage as a serious matter.'

'In other words we shall be all right this time, provided the Emperor behaves in future,' said the Praefect, looking at me sharply. 'That's more or less what I said before you gave us your advice. It's really a matter for the family, not the soldiers. I command the troops, but I cannot control the Emperor's private life. He may listen to his grandmother and his mother. Make him see that it's in his own interest to behave like a conventional Roman.'

'You have left out his aunt,' said the lady Mamea. 'But then there is little I can do. His mother is the person to convince him of the pleasure of natural straightforward intercourse between man and woman.'

This downright reference to the notorious adulteries of the Clarissima silenced us all. The Augusta was the first to recover 'That will do, Duratius,' she said coldly, 'you may go. You know the official story that will go out from the palace. The Emperor is in love with his wife, a charming girl. He is fond of driving four-horse chariots, which proves that he is a youth of courage. Gordius and Hierocles are his friends, though of lowly rank, because they remind him of happy days in Nicomedia. They are freedmen, and therefore they are never seen at public functions. They do not take bribes.'

CHAPTER TEN

The Sky-Stone Takes Over

℃

The soldiers heard all about the Emperor's weddings, and believed what they heard in spite of the official denials. Rumour even managed to improve on the truth. The little naked cupids had been hurriedly collected by the unsuitable intimates the Emperor employed in such matters; these men paid top prices without bargaining, and probably took a commission from the slave-dealers. The story got about that the Emperor desperately needed children, and would buy them at any cost. Why should he need them? Obviously, as sacrifices to his outlandish god. You will still meet Romans who know for a fact that Elagabalus daily cut the throat of a young boy and bathed his sky-stone in fresh human blood.

The Emperor's popularity was in no way diminished, at least among those who had welcomed his advent to power. The soldiers upheld him because, whether he was or was not the grandson of the Divine Severus, he represented the Severan policy of privilege for the army at the expense of the townsmen. The peasants liked him, because he did not increase the taxes and sometimes supported them against townbred lawyers. The Roman mob was devoted to him, because he enjoyed the fun of being an Emperor and allowed the mob to share his amusements. The Senate, and the educated gentry in general, did not like him; but they would have disliked an Emperor of unblemished Stoic principles unless he were willing to reduce the Severan scale of military pay.

The Augusta could not see this. She had come to Rome as a

stranger when her sister was consort to the reigning Emperor; the arrangements she found then existing had seemed to her, a young girl, part of the immutable Roman constitution. The gentry had been loyal to Severus, grateful because he brought peace after a welter of civil wars. Why should they not be loyal to his successor, who carried on the same policy? She did not understand that the gentry saw the Severan privileges for the army as a temporary stop-gap, an emergency measure which should be abolished now that peace was secure.

She imagined that only decorous behaviour in public was needed to make the Emperor universally beloved. All the pressure of her strong personality bore down on her grandson to make him behave like the Divine Augustus, or at least like the Divine Marcus Aurelius. Her daughters seconded her efforts. Within limits, she was successful.

Throughout that first year of his reign the Emperor performed his public duties correctly and assiduously. He attended the Senate, and occasionally delivered a short speech to the assembled Fathers. The Augusta also attended these meetings, considering it a compliment to the importance of the Senate; for she was the Emperor's chief minister. But for a female to take part openly in the discussion of public business was a shocking breach of tradition. The Senators were more dismayed at the intrusion of a responsible minister.

Occupation was found for the Clarissima in a revival of the assembly of matrons. This was a venerable institution, once presided over by the consort of the Divine Augustus; the wives of Senators and curule magistrates met together to discuss problems of ritual in the various religious ceremonies which no man may lawfully witness, and the more absorbing subject of court etiquette. The Clarissima knew nothing of Roman ritual, but in matters of court etiquette she held decided views. The Augusta was heard to say that any fool could decide such problems, and that Soaemias was the very fool to do it; an unkind remark, but uncomfortably true. The Clarissima was busy and happy, too busy to interfere in more important affairs.

No work was found for the lady Mamea. Perhaps this was a mistake. She had a separate establishment within the palace, which she made a meeting-place for all the conventional hidebound gentry who would be sure to disapprove of the rule of Antoninus Elagabalus. The court in general expected that the lady Mamea would presently succumb to a fatal accident in her bath; that is the normal fate of a member of the imperial household who becomes a focus of opposition. Eutychianus hinted to me that he had suggested something of the kind; but the Emperor was determined that no harm should befall any member of his sacred kin. The strong clan-feeling of Syria had been bred into his bones, and he could not believe that a relative would ever plot against him.

Eutychianus was still the busiest and most trusted member of the government, under the general oversight of the Augusta. As Praetorian Praefect and Praefect of the City he controlled every branch of the administration. He was unmarried, and from time to time took his turn as one of the lovers of the Clarissima, which gave him a close tie with the imperial family. When it was announced that the Consuls chosen for next January were the Emperor himself and the Praefect Eutychianus everyone saw that the government was trying to do its conventional duty. The gentry are pleased if the Emperor occasionally undertakes a Consulship (though he must not do it too often and so block the road to promotion). That the Emperor and his chief minister would share the burden reflected glory on all other Consuls past and to come.

In the autumn of that year two old acquaintances looked me up at the palace. Demetrius and Hippias had come to Rome in partnership, bringing a string of horses for sale to the circus factions. I like to do a friend a good turn if it costs me nothing, and I was able to arrange that their best horses should be bought by the Emperor himself, at an appropriately imperial price. They were very good horses, imported Parthians, so I was not failing in my duty to the Emperor; though perhaps a purchaser of lesser rank would have got them cheaper. The partners asked me out to dinner, as soon as they understood that I did not want a share of their profit.

I enjoyed talking over the old days, less than three years past but already in memory a lifetime away. Then I had been a newcomer among the Praetorians, shy of my comrades and lonely in the foreign east. Now I was an important link between the army and the court. I was not exactly feared, for everyone knew the Emperor's mercy; but ambitious soldiers valued my friendship since a word from me might get them promoted even though an adverse report would not send them to the gallows.

It was best of all to learn that I had done good in the world. All three of us had worked in our different ways for the restoration of the true Antonine line, and our success had brought prosperity to the Empire.

'You wouldn't know Syria nowadays,' said Demetrius complacently. 'The taxes remain high, of course, but none of us will live to see them moderate. The point is that now they are collected with reasonable honesty, and that since the army marched west there have been no requisitions. My tenants have paid up their arrears, and there is talk of building a school if we have money to spare after the next harvest. Peasants with money to spare! Think of it!'

'It's the same in the cities,' Hippias chimed in. 'The townsfolk have money to buy imported eastern luxuries. There's no trouble now about muleteers going abroad and refusing to come back. On the contrary, orientals want to cross the river and settle within the Empire. Of course that's partly because of the internal troubles in Parthia. Our Emperor's had a bit of luck there. Things would be different if we had a Parthian army on the frontier.'

'Parthia is breaking up, that's true, and no one could have foreseen it,' said Demetrius judicially. 'You can call that a bit of luck if you like. But our Emperor has accepted his luck with great good sense. The legate in Syria was mad to conquer Mesopotamia. They tell me the Emperor ordered him to keep the peace. The Divine Severus, even the Divine Caracalla, would have tried to extend the Roman border to the east. They might have succeeded, at that, and ruined Syria in the process. We should thank the gods that we are blessed with an Emperor who loves peace.'

'War would interfere with his chariot-racing, I suppose,' said Hippias. 'All the same, he's no coward. He proved that at Immae. We are lucky that he doesn't want to prove it again. By the way, how is he getting on with his sky-stone? Do the Romans object to their new god?'

'So far the cult has caused no trouble,' I said cautiously. 'By the way, in public it is more tactful to refer to the Sun-god Elagabalus, not the sky-stone. The god has a new temple in the City, but quite a small one, besides a temple in the suburbs for the hot weather, which does not bother the Romans because they never visit the suburbs to see it.'

'It's nice to know that a fellow-Syrian is making a good job of ruling the world,' Demetrius said lazily. 'I suppose Syrians are in favour here? Do you think I would better myself if I resigned from managing my imperial domain and tried for a job in the treasury?'

'Not unless you can drive a racing chariot, or prove your kinship with the high priests of Emesa,' I answered at once. 'Charioteers and cousins are the only people who can count on imperial favour.'

'I shall go home as soon as my business is finished,' said Hippias. 'Rome is the centre of the world, and that's just what I don't like about it. I was born and bred a day's march from the frontier, and I'm not happy without a frontier handy. How frightening to talk to a policeman, knowing that his authority stretches for a thousand miles in every direction!'

'I think you are wise,' I said with a look that I tried to make significant. 'Imperial favour is all very well, but it does not last for ever.'

'We were planning to leave in the spring,' Hippias said quickly.

'Stay a year or two, if you like. But don't put down roots in Rome. One day I plan to retire to the northern provinces, the original home of my family.'

Perhaps it was disloyal even to hint that the Emperor was insecure. But these Syrians were my friends, and I wanted to warn them. Since they were Syrians, a hint was warning enough.

The Emperor seemed to me insecure because he was fretting at the prudent control of the Augusta. His marriage continually irked him; though Paula remained a virgin he had to see a good deal of her in the daytime, and that kept him away from his stable boys. He consoled himself by driving chariots, but there again the united efforts of all his advisers had stopped him from racing in public. Even the Divine Nero had never driven in a public race, and that he had sometimes put on a show before a large invited audience was one of the worst of the crimes still remembered against him.

In compensation the Emperor risked his neck by driving teams of strange animals. On the Vatican hill, across the river, a track was laid out where a runaway chariot would have plenty of room to pull up; it was not always private, but when the Emperor was to drive a cordon of Praetorians kept away the crowd. That is not to say the Emperor's exploits lacked spectators; he invited all his friends, members of the circus factions and the expert charioteers he had brought from Nicomedia. To make the track big enough a number of private houses were pulled down; but the owners got handsome compensation, and this particular arbitrary interference with the property of his subjects caused no complaint.

I was usually among the invited spectators, and my admiration for the Emperor's skill as a whip was genuine. He did things that no one would have believed could be done. In a special light chariot he drove a team of mastiffs, which was difficult but not dangerous. Then he drove a team of wild stags, such as are said to draw the bodies of German chieftains to burial. As a matter of fact that was easier than it looked. The stags only wanted to get away from the chariot, but they were so yoked that the harder they ran the faster the chariot pursued them. With any other driver there would have been the certainty of a spill, but the Emperor kept them all galloping in line until they stopped from sheer exhaustion.

A few days later he drove four riding-camels. In Syria I have seen camels draw the plough, but these riding-camels had never before been harnessed to anything. They fought one another, when they were not galloping very fast. Three times the Emperor was upset, but he persevered until he had completed a circuit of the track without mishap.

Before the next of these exhibitions a detail of city firemen were sent to pull down more houses. The track was the usual straight furlong, with a turning post at each end; but immensely broad, so that we wondered why all the extra space was needed. When the performances began we understood, and I have never heard more whole-hearted cheering. The gallant young Emperor appeared at the starting post in a special wide chariot, drawn by a team of four bull elephants. The huge beasts took to it kindly enough, but they were accustomed to walking in processions and doing anything their trainers commanded them to do. But when their driver had urged them into a gallop the chariot bucketed about, and of course it was quite impossible to control them. A spill would have been fatal, for the elephants would kick the chariot to pieces and tread on the driver; but the Emperor got them round the circuit, and then slowed them to a walk, without any trouble at all. I have never seen anything like it, as an exhibition of cold-blooded courage and mastery over dumb brutes.

These demonstrations were nominally private, because it would be ignoble for an Emperor to drive a chariot in public; but so many people saw them, including the soldiers who lined the course, that they very soon became the talk of Rome. Nobody objected. A fifteen-year-old Emperor was entitled to his private pastime, and this particular pastime could not harm his subjects. It was comparatively cheap, so the treasury did not suffer; and nobody was killed in the course of it, which is an unusual feature in an imperial hobby. In fact it was already the talk of all the taverns that the Emperor was almost too merciful for his great position. Since the reign began nobody had been executed on suspicion, no plots had been uncovered by secret agents. Even eminent Senators felt safe under his rule, though they could never bring themselves to approve it.

Some of the Emperor's private amusements had to be covered up a little more carefully. Unfortunately when he did these silly things he nearly always made me his accomplice. Once or twice he left the palace in disguise, perhaps to sell vegetables in the market, perhaps to get drunk in a low tavern by the river. He insisted that I should come along as his bodyguard, because ever since that unfortunate visit to the brothel in Nicomedia he thought I had a natural taste for low life.

Low life does not amuse me; and anyway the Emperor's attempts to mix incognito with the poor of Rome were pathetically unsuccessful. His fair hair and violet eyes made him an unmistakable figure. He was always recognised within ten minutes of the beginning of the escapade; though sensible loafers, who knew they were on to a good thing, would pretend to be deceived. The Emperor would sit happily on a barrel of wine, dressed in rags and paying with heavy gold coins for drinks all round; until someone grew tired of the farce and hailed him with the imperial salute. It was even worse when some joker began to repeat all the rumours about scandalous goings-on at the palace, pretending to tell this ragged stranger the latest gossip.

On these occasions the Emperor kept his temper, which is greatly to his credit. But he would blame me for giving away his disguise, though it would not have deceived an observant German. He said that my stiffness betrayed the centurion in civilian clothes, while he himself had exactly caught the manner of a market porter on the spree. Perhaps, but porters do not have so much gold to spend.

There were other entertainments, held in remote pavilions hidden in corners of the rambling palace. The Emperor danced more gracefully than was becoming in a gentleman, thanks to his training in the ritual of the sky-stone. Sometimes, late at night, he would dance a mime before a carefully selected audience; conduct which every Roman, whether soldier or civilian, rightly holds to be ignoble. One mime in particular he performed again and again: the well-known ballet of the Judgement of Paris.

The other performers were expert dancing-boys; I admit that the Emperor danced as well as his partners. Of course he took the part of Venus, and the climax of the ballet was his disrobing. Trumpets blared and cymbals banged as he dropped his gown; then he would strike an elegant attitude, ogling the audience long enough for us to see that he had been depilated from head to foot. On these occasions Gordius and Hierocles must appear to be overcome with admiration; though in fact both were a little sulky, because the Emperor had declared that they did not dance well enough to join him in the ballet.

Once you granted that the Emperor preferred boys to women, a fancy which nobody seriously condemns, it was all at bottom harmless enough. He was very beautiful and he danced very well; why should he not display his charms to his friends? He hurt nobody, and frightened nobody, and did not throw away the taxpayers' money. Few Emperors have been so little of a nuisance to their subjects. But this dancing and acting were undignified, and the spectators he invited proved that he had a liking for low company. In the eyes of the gentry lack of dignity and a liking for the wrong kind of friend are more serious crimes than the most bloody atrocities.

One imperial experiment gave me a nasty fright, though in the end no harm was done. When the annual festival of Cybele came round I was summoned to another of these secret evening parties. It was a most private entertainment, with no one present save the stable boys and myself, the only adult. After a fairly quiet and decorous supper the show provided turned out to be, as I had expected, the ritual dance of the priests of Cybele.

The full dance is performed only once a year, and then only if there is a suitable aspirant to the priesthood. The eunuch priests begin quietly, parading round an image of their goddess set up in the middle of the dancing floor. Then, as the music quickens, they throw off their sweeping robes. After a time they have worked themselves into a frenzy, capering stark naked with their ugly mutilations exposed. They gash their arms and legs with knives, shedding their blood in honour of the goddess; some of them fall to the ground, foaming at the mouth. The climax of the rite is the dance of the candidate, in which he reaches such a condition of divine frenzy that with his own knife he castrates himself, and so becomes a full member of the obscene brotherhood. Imagine my horror when, in addition to the two Asiatic candidates for whose reception the rite was held, the Emperor bounded on to the dancing floor!

He wore the dress of the candidates, the tall mitre hung with little bells and the wide-sleeved linen gown; he brandished the long curved knife. For a moment I wondered how I was to explain to the Augusta that I had allowed the Emperor to castrate himself before my eyes, and what she would do to me when she knew. Then reason reasserted itself. The attribute the Emperor valued above all others was his high priesthood of Elagabalus, and that could be held only by a whole man; on a lower level, though he had never loved a woman, he enjoyed toying with his pretty boys. Gordius and Hierocles were looking on, and they did not seem disturbed.

The Emperor was acting, as when he danced the part of Venus and for half an hour seemed to be the veritable goddess of Love. But he acted with great conviction. I wondered how he would manage the climax.

The two genuine candidates were allowed their moment of glory while the Emperor still whirled in the dance. First one and then the other cut himself, and fainted from the pain of the irreparable mutilation. Then the Emperor cast off his breech-clout and his blade flashed between his thighs. The effect was most convincing. Like an actor who must pretend to be killed on the stage, he had pricked a bladder of blood concealed below his waist; to make matters worse, though I stared hard I could not see his genital organs. Yet Hierocles was still grinning in admiration. I saw the gleam of metal under the artificial blood. I had never expected the Emperor to endure such discomfort for the sake of an illusion; he had submitted to the metal ring which is fixed to male slaves who must mingle with women without breeding.

In general the Emperor was a good actor. This was the only one of his performances which failed of its effect, and of course he had set himself an impossible task. Two vigorous young men had castrated themselves before our eyes, and we could not be moved by an acted imitation. Since he was the Emperor, we applauded with enthusiasm, but he was clever enough to sense that the mime, following the real thing, had left us unmoved. As usual, his disappointment did not make him lose his temper.

While the priests of Cybele were mopping up the mess he came over to sit on the end of my couch. 'A good idea, but it didn't work out,' he said cheerfully. 'Cybele owes me nothing, and I can't expect her to come down to me whenever I call. The Sun-god would never disappoint me, but then he is the hereditary patron of all my family. Oh well, one man can't control all the gods.'

'What were you trying to do, my lord? Surely you did not expect Cybele to inspire you to unman yourself?'

'Good old Duratius. The respectable Gallic nobleman always peeps out from under the tough Praetorian. You can't believe in any divine activity unless it leaves physical traces that you can see with your own eyes ... No, it was a bit more subtle and Syrian than that. The goddess enters into these priests when they dance for her; then she makes them do something very terrible. But I am the high priest of the Sun-god and, for what it's worth, Pontifex Maximus of Rome. I thought that perhaps such an exceptional person might be granted the ecstasy without its consequences. I danced. I emptied my soul for her to fill it. I fixed my mind on the idea that I was her servant and that she would command me. And nothing happened, nothing at all. At the height of my dance I saw Gordius, and thought how beautiful I must seem to him. That frivolous notion proved that the goddess was far away. So I cut the bladder, and here I am as complete as when I started. I wonder what would have happened if the goddess had truly possessed me?'

'For one thing, we should have had to look for a new Emperor,' I said crossly. 'My lord, you mustn't play with these things. The civilised world has been given to you, let us say by the god Elagabalus. You owe a duty to your subjects. The Roman army cannot be commanded by a eunuch. You yourself wouldn't really like being a eunuch. Enjoy what you have, which is a very great deal. Even you can't have everything.'

'No, I can't have everything,' he answered wistfully. 'But if only I could control my mind I might be able to *experience* everything. That's what I try to do. I want to be the Emperor, and the high priest of Elagabalus. But I want also to be a porter on holiday, and a poor man selling cabbages, and a virgin bride, and an ardent young husband, and a poor old harlot working when she's ill because the rent must be paid. I want to be *all* my subjects, a painted Briton and a black Ethiopian and a Cappadocian wrapped in yards and yards of linen trousers. I want to feel the whole civilised world beating in my heart. But I can't do it. I can't be a priest of Cybele. Her servants are driven by some mighty force, which you have seen at work tonight. It is a force I shall never experience.'

'You control your mind very well already, my lord,' said I, answering the only part of this harangue that I could understand. 'You know how the Romans expect you to behave in public, and that is how you behave even though it's against the grain. I suppose the only Emperor who could always control his mind was the Divine Marcus Aurelius. He put it on record for publication that he had known moments of happiness, but I don't think you would enjoy the kind of life he led. I wouldn't.'

'There's the voice of common sense. No wonder the Augusta approves of you, Duratius. But if I behave well in public I must have my relaxation in private. This is a private occasion, and Gordius is waiting for me. Tell these rascals that they have my permission to withdraw, and then go to bed yourself. Tomorrow you can watch me offer sacrifice to Capitoline Jove. Not a fold out of place in my toga, not a glimmer of intelligence in my eye, the model Roman magistrate. Until then, good-bye.'

During his first eighteen months in Rome the Emperor did in fact behave very well in public. There were stories about queer goings-on in the private apartments of the palace, and they happened to be true. But stories about queer goings-on in the palace are current under the most blameless Emperors; and everyone believes them whether they are true or false.

Elagabalus was dignified in the Senate and reverend in the temples, and always kind and merciful. Soldiers sometimes bullied the citizens, but in other respects the law was justly enforced; and no one has been able to control the soldiers since the Divine Severus taught them to know their strength. His rule deserved to be popular, and it was popular.

After his sixteenth birthday he found the constant advice of the Augusta more irksome. His public behaviour remained correct, but he spent more and more of his time at extremely incorrect private parties. What irked him most was that his grandmother tried to reform his sexual habits. Poor little Paula was still a virgin, neglected in a distant wing of the palace; though her nominal husband gave her a large household and an ample revenue, and saw to it that she was treated with the respect due to the consort of an Emperor.

The Augusta was still convinced that if only her grandson would sleep with a woman he would find it more enjoyable than his adventures with boys. She recognised that the shy Paula lacked charm, and tried to tempt him with more handsome bodies. When an enterprising dealer imported the most famous Alexandrian courtesan for sale in the Roman market the

Augusta bought her for a very large sum. Shortly afterwards the Emperor found this Cleonime in his bed. He turned her out at once, though he would not permit Gordius to beat her. Instead he gave orders that she should be well looked after, in some part of the palace where he would not often encounter her; and at his next party she had the job of holding up a large seven-wick lamp, standing naked on a pedestal like a statue. The Emperor made a little speech in praise of her beauty, and invited all his friends to admire it; but at his command a chain had been fastened round her loins, as a sign that henceforth no man might touch her.

The crisis that was to change the religious life of Rome broke unexpectedly. One afternoon during the second winter of our stay Eutychianus put his head round the door of the guardroom. We sprang to our feet, and then hesitated; by rights the guard should turn out for the Praetorian Praefect, but it was impossible to double smartly through the door while the officer we were to honour was himself blocking it.

'Stand easy, the guard,' he said pleasantly. 'I told the sentry I am invisible this afternoon, so you mustn't blame him. There you are, Duratius. I want a word with you, wait for me in my office. Not my office in the Camp, of course, but the cubbyhole I have squeezed out of the majordomo of this madhouse.'

Eutychianus had the right touch with Praetorians. He kept us up to the mark, but he never let us forget that we were superior to all civilians.

I was the first to reach the office, though soon it began to fill up. The Emperor arrived next, arm-in-arm with Hierocles; he remarked gaily that he was always incognito after lunch, and made me sit down on the hard wooden bench beside him.

Then there was a commotion as footmen brought in padded chairs for the Clarissima and the lady Mamea. Young Alexianus came with his mother, and stood deferentially in the background until the Emperor commanded him to share our bench.

When the Augusta swept in on the arm of the Praetorian

Praefect we all sprang to our feet. She sank into the Clarissima's chair; the Clarissima darted like lightning for the chair of the lady Mamea, who scowled with fury and sat down on the end of the bench. Eutychianus remained standing, evidently because he was about to address the council.

'My lord, tell that charioteer to get out before I throw him out,' he said genially. 'This is a private meeting of your most eminent supporters, and we have called in Duratius to give expert evidence about the feelings of the troops. But I don't think Hierocles can tell us anything we don't know already. Do you agree?'

'If this is a business meeting Hierocles must go,' answered the Emperor with a smile. 'He's ornamental, but not at all useful. Run away, my pet. But you had better produce really important business. I don't like being parted from my friends in the little time I have free from boring public ceremonies.'

'It's important enough,' said Eutychianus. 'The first dangerous conspiracy of the reign. I'm surprised it has been so slow in coming. A good many respectable Romans don't like us.'

The Clarissima gave a little shriek, either because she was really frightened or because she thought a shriek the appropriate comment.

'If the conspiracy has been uncovered it is no longer dangerous,' said the Augusta with a sniff. 'Tell us the facts, and stop trying to make us jump.'

'Very well. Here are the facts,' Eutychianus continued. 'A wealthy and respected Consular named Seius Carus has been tampering with the Alban Legions. A sound opening move. The Alban Legions are privileged above the ordinary frontier garrisons, but they are not quite the equals of the Praetorians. Therefore they may be expected to be jealous of us. They are men who would be willing to march on Rome and overthrow the government, and good troops who might defeat us. But Carus was too impatient. It's not three years since those soldiers murdered their commander to come over to the gallant Emperor Elagabalus, and they are still under the spell of our ruler's more than human charm and beauty. Most of the men took his money and then reported everything to the secret police. The revolt was planned to start this morning, but we had been warned. I have just learned that it was easily suppressed. A few desperate men took the Eagle from the regimental chapel, Carus and his friends mounted the tribunal to harangue them. Then loyal troops arrested the rebels. Those are all the facts I know. What are the Emperor's instructions?'

But as he asked for instructions he looked not at the Emperor but at the Augusta.

'Were all the rebels arrested? Were none killed?' asked the lady Mamea swiftly.

'All arrested, madam. They expected the troops to follow them, and were taken by surprise. Odd, in a way. If I were in Carus's shoes I would kill myself rather than face torture. Now that's the point on which I want instruction. These people wouldn't have started their plot unless they were sure of support from the Senate. If we torture them we shall drag out all kinds of admissions and half-promises, until we have incriminated every prominent Senator in Rome. On the other hand, while the troops are loyal no Senator will dare to move on his own. Shall we kill the guilty straight away, and not inquire too curiously into their backers?'

'We must find out all we can . . . ' began the Augusta slowly, but the Emperor interrupted his grandmother.

'You forget, Eutychianus. You have forgotten a promise I made to my sky-stone, when I first achieved the Purple. I have repeated it, too, in public, so honour as well as religion compels me to keep it. I have sworn that not one of my subjects shall be put to death save after a fair trial in open court. The mutineers will be tried by the army, Carus by the Senate. Since they were caught in the act it will be easy to prove them guilty. I want just enough evidence for that, and no more. No torture, no probing after hidden accomplices. We all know that the Senate would wish success to any rebellion against me. What of it? They can't hurt me. Leave them in peace.'

'That's merciful. I'm proud of you. What a noble example for Alexianus,' said the lady Mamea with a simper.

The Augusta uttered a little wail. 'I tried so hard to make them like us. I sat in the Senate, looking dignified even when my shoes hurt. Dear Soaemias talked and talked in that dreary assembly of matrons. I chose your consort from one of the best families in Rome. You climb up and down that steep Capitol and poke about in the messy insides of sacrificial victims, just because it's the right thing and expected of you. And after all that they still despise us as Syrians and foreigners.'

The Emperor sprang to his feet.

'That's enough, grandma. They despise us, and we despise them. Henceforth they shall feel my contempt. I'm sick of ruling like a true son of Romulus. That wasn't what gained me the Purple. I am Emperor because the soldiers love me, and I can manage without the love of the gentry. Instead they shall fear me. My oath holds, I shan't kill the scoundrels. But I shall make them grovel, and grovel in public. Perhaps this has come upon us because we neglected the sky-stone, who gave me my luck. From tomorrow the Sun-god Elagabalus shall rule in Rome. And his high priest will show these fusty pedants how their traditions are valued by the soldiers who rule the Empire, and by the Emperor who rules the soldiers.'

CHAPTER ELEVEN

The Emperor and the Gods

The Emperor was as good as his word. Even after this dangerous conspiracy there was no hunt for hidden traitors; the police were held in leash, and the only arrests were of open rebels. These were granted a public trial, and condemned on the evidence of disinterested eye-witnesses; so there was no need to torture them before they appeared in open court. The mutineers were convicted by court martial and immediately beheaded. Carus and the two Senators who had abetted him were tried by the Senate. These accomplices were respectable noblemen, Pomponius Bassus and Silius Messala; it seemed to me sinister that the lady Mamea should be a close friend of Bassus, but nobody else mentioned it and it was not my duty to draw attention to the curious fact. It is difficult to serve for long in the army without being drawn into spying, but during the whole of my service I managed to avoid it.

The three leading rebels were treated with great indulgence. After the opening speech for the prosecution, which showed them that there was no hope of acquittal, the Senate adjourned for lunch; the prisoners were permitted to kill themselves during the adjournment. Thus they died unconvicted and their property descended to their heirs, instead of being confiscated. In particular Annia Faustina, Bassus's widow, lived in great prosperity and continued her close friendship with the lady Mamea.

With the opening of the new year the Emperor put into effect his new policy. The unfortunate Paula was released from the palace; she went back to her parents an untouched virgin, and I don't know what became of her afterwards. The Emperor had given her an unpleasant time, but that was chiefly the fault of the Augusta. He had not harmed her. He never harmed any of his subjects.

Meanwhile the temple of Capitoline Jove had been put into order to receive a new tenant. On the great day of the move I was one of the escort of senior centurions who guarded the sky-stone with drawn swords. I had taken some trouble to get on that guard for I guessed, rightly, that soldiers forming the guard of honour would not be ordered to join in the ritual dancing.

The procession was modelled on a Triumph, with the sky-stone in the triumphal car. Priests from Emesa took the place of the army (there were nearly enough of them to make up a legion). The Senate and the curule magistrates marched in their accustomed places, as though they were escorting the Emperor after a victory. That left no place for the Emperor himself; naturally, since for more than 200 years a Triumph had been granted only to the reigning Emperor. My lord had devised his own duties in this new ritual. The triumphal car was drawn by the usual four white stallions, but the presence of that perky little sky-stone on a tall padded stool made the vehicle too holy for a human driver to share it. The Emperor controlled the horses from in front, leading them by the bridle. Since he refused to turn his back on his god he must walk backwards all the way. Gordius and Hierocles walked on either side of him, to support his elbows and warn him of stones in the road that might make him stumble; but only a really skilled driver like the Emperor Elagabalus could have controlled four fiery stallions from such an awkward posture.

The rite concluded with compulsory dancing for nearly everyone, as I had feared at the outset. With the other soldiers I was spared the indignity. I found it most enjoyable to watch grave Senators, and Consulars, and even the Flamen Dialis who hated it most of all, dancing in their robes of office to honour that obscene fragment of black stone. A great crowd drawn from the lower classes peered in through the open doors of the temple to mock their betters. Never, since the Divine Augustus first showed himself to be their master, had the magistrates of the Republic been so deeply and publicly humiliated.

Like every other responsible supporter of the government I had been very much afraid of the effect of this recognition of a new, foreign god. In fact it delighted the City mob, and outside Rome no one cared one way or the other. Some Romans still feel a fondness for the old rituals which have come down from the ancestors, but hardly anyone truly believes in the gods of Olympus; even the few who worried at the insult offered to Jupiter felt their worry outweighed by joy at the insult offered to the nobility.

The Emperor was intoxicated with exaltation when he saw his god supreme and unquestioned in Rome. Every morning he honoured the sky-stone with stately dances, and with hecatombs of birds collected from the ends of the earth. (It had been revealed to him that birds were the most appropriate offering to the sun.) But it was the rash interference of the Augusta that set him off on his next prank.

His grandmother had not yet lost hope of persuading him to marry and beget an heir. She did not believe that any young man could be indifferent to the charms of a really beautiful woman. The second-rate harlots of provincial Nicomedia had failed to rouse him, the shy and maidenly Paula would appeal only to a weary sophisticated taste; but she had the money, and the authority, to collect the most attractive concubines in the world, concubines whom no man could resist. Once he had learned to enjoy a woman he could be led on to enjoy a young lady, chosen by his elders as a suitable consort for an Emperor.

Only five days after the installation of the sky-stone a messenger summoned me to one of the Emperor's private supper-parties. It was late, and I was already going to bed; but the Emperor liked to surprise his guests by a sudden invitation.

My valet dressed me and I followed the messenger, expecting to be led through long passages to one of the outlying pavilions.

To my surprise, since it was the depth of winter, I found a litter waiting to take me to the imperial gardens on the Pincian. This pleasure ground is more of a private park than a garden, a great space of grass and tall trees and flowering shrubs, dotted with grottoes and little houses. The Divine Caracalla had kept his hundreds of concubines in it; for it is securely walled, with only two gates, and set on a hill where it cannot be overlooked.

More chariot-racing, I thought with a sigh of boredom. I had seen the Emperor drive elephants, and after that chariots strangely drawn could not amuse me.

The high-walled garden was a blaze of light, and all the stable boys were there in force. I was glad to see one of two of the younger gentry, nobles who had always been fond of debauchery and now considered it sound tactics to copy the Emperor; though when he had played at being respectable they had been even more respectable than he. A few adults would make the evening pass more pleasantly; there is nothing more deadly dull than being the only grown-up at a party of boys pretending to be men.

I found the Emperor warming himself at a brazier; for it was cold and he wore the dress of a charioteer, cloak and boots and cap and only a breech-clout in between. He had taken enough wine to make him speak rather loudly, but he was still firm on his legs. He greeted me boisterously.

'Duratius at last! Now we can begin. I suppose you were snuggled down into your virtuous bed, the only bed in the palace designed to hold one only ... I want your opinion of a new sport I have just invented. First I must explain that the Augusta provided the raw material. It's not the kind of thing I would spend my own money on. But since these creatures are here in the garden, eating their heads off, we may as well use them. Come along and look at the new race track.'

On a level terrace of grass was a barrier, like the spine that divides the track in the circus; but instead of a furlong it was barely a hundred yards in length. The turning posts at the two ends were slaves standing on pedestals, not an uncommon conceit on private race tracks. But I noted with surprise, for I had never before seen a female in these gardens, that the Emperor had chosen for the task his famous Alexandrian concubine, balanced at the other end by a hideous negress. Both were naked, but so many lamps flared at their feet that they did not feel the cold.

'Yoke up, yoke up,' called the Emperor, twirling a wooden clapper as though he were a starter at the circus. 'First Green driven by Gordius, second Green by Protogenes. First Blue driven by Hierocles, second Blue by Elagabalus. Place your bets.'

'The Blues pull the lighter weights. Has the race been fixed?' called a cheeky stable boy. Protogenes was another beefy and famous charioteer, like Gordius many pounds heavier than the young Emperor or the frail little Hierocles.

'The chariots have been fairly weighted,' answered the Emperor. 'See them on the weigh-bridge if you doubt me. Place your bets for an honest race.'

I laid a small bet on Green, taking advantage of the odds. The contest would be honest, if the Emperor said so; but the young noblemen, new to these parties, could not believe it.

Then someone opened the doors of a shed built under the terrace, and the four chariots emerged. Each was pulled by a single gardener, for they were in fact little handcarts fitted with a yoke in front. Solemnly the drivers mounted, and as they were pulled over the weigh-bridge we could see they were fairly matched.

So far there had been no hint of the teams, though on such a short track they could not be horses. Then there were cheers and catcalls and hoots of laughter, as sixteen naked women were brought out and yoked, four to each cart.

They were generously built women, in accordance with the Syrian taste of the Augusta. With their necks in the yoke they must bend nearly double, and their labouring buttocks looked enormous. They were frightened and cold, which made them move the more clumsily. Certainly on that evening they would not have tempted the most ardent rake.

'There you are, gentlemen,' called the Emperor. 'Four teams of unbroken fillies, a present to our private club from my generous grandmother. I'm not sure she intended them for racing. But she said they were given me as playthings, and I can't think of a better way to play with them.'

As a matter of fact the race was quite amusing. All the drivers were first-class charioteers; the three professionals, intimate friends of the Emperor since the beginning of his reign, were too vain of their skill to permit their lord to win without genuine competition. That was one of the reasons why he liked them. He expected flattery in words, since that is conventional court etiquette; but he could not enjoy a sport unless his opponents tried to beat him.

The charioteers followed the conventional tactics of the circus, the first team making the pace and trying to shut in the opposition, the second trying to come from behind in the last lap and snatch a close finish. There were desperate mix-ups at the turning posts, and a good deal of crossing in the straight; but the fillies were clumsy at answering to the bit, and they never got up enough speed to overturn a chariot when they collided. Long whips cracked and flickered over their sweating backs; but I had noticed before the start that the thongs were plaited from paper, so that though they may have stung they could do no real damage. That was typical of Elagabalus. Ridicule was his weapon against anyone who bothered him, but he was too kindly to inflict physical harm even on unwanted she-slaves.

The presents of the Augusta were always lavish. There were enough of these fillies to furnish another four teams, and each team turned out three times. Six races made an amusing evening, and my betting showed a slight profit; though the young nobles soon spotted that the Emperor was taking a fair chance, and no longer laid odds on Blue.

Then we all had a very good supper, reclining in the wintry garden with braziers all round us. While we ate we watched grooms rub down the teams; then they were given their evening feed, barley soaked in wine, served in a marble manger. Since they must eat standing, with their hands tied behind their backs, their antics were very comical.

The Emperor soon got tired of these chariot-races, for he found it boring to drive such slow-moving teams. But the light garden-carts seemed to him a more comfortable means of getting about than a litter. A number of them were adapted to be drawn by a pair of fillies, running upright with traces attached to the waist. Constant exercise made the girls fit and athletic, and exposure weathered them to a glossy chestnut. The carts never appeared on the public streets, for the Emperor did not wish to be stared at when he was not taking part in a public ceremony; but in his private garden they became the normal way of getting about. Barefoot girls could run over a lawn, where litter-bearers must walk slowly and horses would have cut up the turf. With practice the girls learned to obey the bit; or you could tell them where to take you and then sit back and look at the flowers. Soon everyone who had the *entrée* to the private garden grew accustomed to being conveyed in this manner. The sleek brown trotting girls became a part of the landscape; no one thought of them as desirable women, and it would have seemed as odd to put clothes on them as to dress up a horse.

Those concubines who could not run without waddling were housed in a distant pavilion, where they lived in comfort and embroidered vestments for the Sun-god. The Emperor would not ungraciously get rid of a present from his grandmother, but he could find no other use for them. When I suggested that they might be employed in the palace laundry I learned, with some surprise, that no such institution existed. The Emperor, and the ladies of the imperial household, never had their clothes washed; as soon as a garment was dirty it was thrown away and replaced.

Now that the Emperor had abandoned the struggle to live as a respectable member of Roman society, Roman society received him to its bosom. It is impossible for a gentleman to make a career in the army, since an officer with family influence is considered a danger to the state; a career in the civil service is too much like hard work to attract a pampered noble. There are the curule magistracies, of course, and the priestly colleges; but these honours are not serious occupations. Thus Rome is full of young men, sons and grandsons of tough military governors who retired rich. They have nothing to do but amuse themselves; some of their amusements were very like the Emperor's.

The Emperor took to dining out, and found that a dinner party was an excellent way of filling an empty day. It filled the whole day, because he was careful not to beggar his subjects by asking one man to furnish the whole lavish entertainment. The usual arrangement was that a single course was served in one house, and then the company drove in chariots to eat the next course under another roof. The gallop through the crowded streets was another attraction, though the Emperor made it clear that there must be no fatal accidents. He liked to frighten pedestrians, but he never ran over one. His hosts always provided dancing-girls, since they are the conventional accompaniment of a good party. The Emperor, who liked good dancing, would watch the performance with close attention and afterwards criticise it. But none of the girls ever took his fancy.

Once or twice I attended these parties, by imperial command. To move in cultured, wealthy, smart society had been the dream of my youth; the hope that one day I might enjoy the opportunity had driven me to mind my manners and keep up my reading during long years of service on the frontier. But the fulfilment of the dream came too late; I found that I was bored by the chatter of frivolous young men, who had never done anything useful and were ignorant of the world beyond the walls of Rome. I got out of the irksome duty by persuading the Emperor that it would be more polite to his hosts if he brought a full ceremonial escort rather than a single battered and elderly centurion as bodyguard. It was fun sometimes to see the chariots whirl by, dashing through the market at full gallop on their way from the fish to the roast; but it was better fun to watch this for a minute than to keep up my society manners for seven or eight hours at a stretch.

When he was not dining, or racing chariots, the Emperor occupied himself with the service of his sky-stone. It occurred to him one day to ask whether sky-stones were worshipped in other parts of his Empire. When he learned that there were quantities of them he commanded that they should be assembled in Rome, as courtiers and servants of the Sun-god. In the provinces some local authorities did not grasp what he was at, though they were anxious to please him; they sent him their most venerable statues, not understanding that human handi-work, no matter how sacred and miraculous, was of no value in his eyes in comparison with a shapeless lump of stone that had actually fallen from heaven.

In Rome the Vestals keep among the secret things in their ancient, round, thatched hut a sky-stone. The Emperor demanded that it be sent to the temple of Elagabalus the Sun-god. But Vestals are not in the habit of taking orders from anybody, even from an Emperor; they sent a very old and dusty jar, whose stopper was alleged to bear the seal of King Numa. No one was allowed to open this jar; but when shaken it did not rattle.

But from Laodicea they sent their famous Diana, an object so ancient that it had been worshipped by Orestes. The Emperor was a little put out that a goddess should intrude into his male sanctuary; he was comforted when the priests pointed out that Diana is an armed virgin, with no desire for masculine embraces. She was given an honourable post, on a pedestal by the inner door of the sanctuary; her duty was to threaten venturesome demons with her arrows.

The Flavian amphitheatre had been repaired, the Baths of the Divine Caracalla completed, and a new Bath constructed to honour the Antonine Emperors in general; all paid for out of the imperial privy purse. The Emperor was immensely popular with the mob, and well liked by the soldiers; while these supported him the enmity of the outraged Senate could do him no harm. But the treasury was beginning to worry about money. The Emperor himself cost less than any ruler since the Divine Augustus; for his stable boys were of such mean birth that they were content with free board and lodging, his jewellery had come to him by inheritance, and he was temperate in eating and drinking. But the service of the sky-stone was another matter.

Already the income of the temple at Emesa had been mortgaged for the next twenty years; though its land, dedicated to a god, could not be sold outright. The privy purse had been fortified by the estates of the pretenders who had tried their luck during the war against Macrinus; so that for the first year and a half of his reign the Emperor lived on his private revenue. But now, with expensive birds from foreign parts to be sacrificed daily in hecatombs, the Emperor had little of his own money left. The treasurer protested, in a stiff official letter, at the leniency shown to Carus and his accomplices; they had been very wealthy, and their estates should not have wastefully descended to their heirs.

The public revenue of the Empire goes straight to the military chest. In bad years even this is not enough for the soldiers' pay, and the Emperor is expected to make up the difference from his private fortune. I don't know why the government is always short of money; it was not so in the days of our grandparents. Perhaps the Divine Severus increased the pay of the soldiers to more than his dominions can produce. But if that is the case nothing can be done about it. Any Emperor who tries to reduce military pay is at once killed by his guards.

It was suggested that the Emperor should marry a rich wife.

No one could say who had first thought of it, but suddenly everyone spoke of it as the obvious solution to our troubles. The Augusta, of course, had never relaxed her efforts to make the Emperor a husband and father. Now her persuasion was reinforced by every responsible adviser.

In the end even Eutychianus took up the project. One morning he summoned me to the Camp, where I found a group of senior officers assembled in his quarters. He came straight to the point.

'Duratius, you are an intermediary between the army and the palace. The Emperor believes what you tell him about the sentiments of the soldiers. I want you to come with us when we advise the Emperor to take a wife. You will back us up by saying that the soldiers want him to marry.'

'If that's an order, my lord, of course I will. It won't be the literal truth, you understand. I talk to the soldiers a great deal, that's my job. None of them care whether the Emperor has a wife, or six wives, or none at all as at present.'

'That is of no consequence. The treasury wants him to marry, and the high command has decided to back the civil service. But that won't convince him. He must think the demand comes from the soldiers.'

As a trained soldier, I obeyed orders; but as an old soldier I used in addition my own judgement. When the deputation waited on the Emperor I supported the Praetorian Praefect. The Emperor thanked us for our advice, and promised to give his answer next day. That evening I hinted to one of the stable boys that I had said what I had been ordered to say, not what I myself believed to be true.

The Emperor was dining out in the City (a remarkable dinner in which all the food was blue, in compliment to a Blue victory in the circus; the cooks had great difficulty in devising a blue sauce for the venison, and next day the town talked of nothing else). He did not get back until very late, but then he sent for me.

Lately he had taken to sleeping in the Pincian gardens,

ostensibly so that his love for Hierocles should not shock the Senators, in fact to avoid visits from the Augusta in the middle of the night. I was taken there in a litter; but once I had arrived the Emperor put me in one of his famous two-girl carriages, and drove beside me in another. It was very private and peaceful in the dark, scented avenues; the sleepy girls jogged in silence, and our wheels made no sound on the grass.

'I got your message,' he said at once. 'I know the soldiers don't care whether I am married or single. But the Augusta gives me no peace, and now that the officers have joined in the cry I can't ignore it. So I have devised a wonderful plan, which will end this nonsense once and for all. Tomorrow I shall announce my betrothal. I wonder whether Eutychianus will approve of the bride I have chosen?'

After a moment's silence he shot a question at me. 'Who is the wife of the Sun?'

I could not think of an answer. 'Would it be the Moon?' I suggested timidly. 'In Gaul she is sometimes worshipped with the Sun.'

'A queer sort of wife,' said the Emperor in scorn, 'always gadding about when her husband is in bed. It's no wonder they have no children.'

'Then I don't know who is, my lord. All the other gods have wives, and most of them have children. Perhaps the Sun is an exception, the only great god who lives single.'

'You have hit it. The Sun is a bachelor, though once long ago he cohabited with the bare earth to produce mankind and the animals and every green living thing; for the Sun is the sole source of life. My sky-stone, for all that it is the phallus with which the world was made, is still the phallus of a bachelor. Now we shall change all that. Elagabalus the Sun-god has become the special protector of the Roman People, as Elagabalus the high priest has become their Emperor. So the Sun will marry the tutelary goddess of Rome, and the high priest will marry her priestess.'

'Can the sky-stone beget children?' I asked with a smile. But the Emperor was not in a mood for flippancy.

'It is not a thing to joke about,' he snapped. 'You are a veteran who has seen the wonders of the world, not a silly little city sniggerer whose universe is bounded by the Tiber. There was a time before man existed, every philosopher will tell you that. The first man must have had a father, and why shouldn't that father have been the Sun? I shall introduce a mighty goddess into the bed of Elagabalus the Sun-god; and if a god results I shall not be particularly surprised. Furthermore, that the sacred line of the priest-kings of Emesa may continue, I shall myself mate with a most sacred priestess. Most Emperors partake of divinity only after they are dead, but my successors will be something more than human while they are still on earth and reigning over the Republic.'

'I'm very sorry, my lord,' I said anxiously. He was kindly, but an angry Emperor is a very fearsome thing. 'I understood you were planning this marriage only to score off Eutychianus and the Augusta.'

'You are forgiven, my faithful Duratius. You are quite right. The plan was devised as a joke. But suddenly my god has inspired me, and now I am in deadly earnest. That's how inspiration comes, you know; while you drive about in a pleasant garden, not thinking of divine affairs. If you sit in a temple, fasting, the god sees you are trying to coerce him and won't answer. Come up, fillies,' he added with a tug at the reins and a flourish of his whip. 'I must get at my tablets while I still remember the details of this scheme the god has put into my head.'

Obediently the teams wheeled, and we glided back to the lights of the pavilion. It was a very pleasant way of getting about.

'It's a wonderful scheme, my lord, and the whole world will be glad to know you have consented to marry and continue the sacred line of the priest-kings,' I said as we bounced down a slope. 'But you haven't yet told me whom you have chosen to be the bride of the Sun-god, or which priestess you will honour by making her your consort.'

'You ought to know without being told. But then you are a barbarous Gaul, for all that your ancestors have been citizens for centuries. I said the tutelary goddess of Rome. That's Vesta, of course. And I shall wed a Vestal.'

In a moment we were dismounting in the lighted porch, and I had to compose my features. I longed for kindly darkness to hide my dismay. Of course Vesta is the tutelary goddess of Rome; everyone knows that. But the idea of the virgin goddess as a bride was shocking, and the idea of her priestess as the Emperor's consort seemed as terrible as if he had proposed to give a public demonstration of cannibalism.

In the pavilion the Emperor called for lights and wine, while his boy-friends gathered round to help him draft the decrees. The stable boys were Asiatics, who did not understand how a genuine Roman feels about Vesta; but even they were awed by the desperate proposal. The Emperor, on the other hand, was exalted. He was convinced that his god had spoken to him while he drove in the garden; only divine inspiration could have put such a plan into his mind. He roughed out a speech to the Senate, but he took more trouble over drafting the order of the marriage procession and the nuptial ceremony.

Ten days later the strangest procession in the long history of Rome defiled along the Sacred Way. First came the sky-stone, in his triumphal car drawn by four white stallions; but this time they were led by priests from Emesa, for the Emperor was otherwise engaged.

Behind the sky-stone, with his numerous train of Syrian priests, came the stone which is the most authentic embodiment of Vesta. I fixed my eyes on the ground as she went by, as did every other man in the crowd; for we knew that it is unlawful for any but women to see her. I heard later from a friend who knew a Vestal that she is indeed a shapeless lump of rock; though not, I believe, a sky-stone fallen from heaven but rather the summit of some holy mountain. She is the material body of Vesta, her dwelling when she is on earth; but the goddess spends much of her time in the upper world, so with any luck she was absent while her material body was profaned. At least that was the earnest prayer of every Roman who understood the facts.

The Clarissima had discovered this rock, which of course had not been within the earthenware jar delivered earlier to the temple of the Sun-god. Vestals are not dedicated for life, and a few of them marry after their service is finished. It happened that an ex-Vestal was a member of the Clarissima's assembly of matrons; in her excitement when she heard of the Emperor's proposal this woman talked indiscreetly, and once the Clarissima knew that the stone existed her threats did the rest. Being a fool as well as a foreigner, the Clarissima never knew how this action of hers had dismayed the Romans.

Vesta brought a great dowry to her lord, jewels of antique form, the offerings of 900 years, and chests of gold so heavy that two brawny slaves could scarcely carry one of them. That was the aspect of the affair which had finally persuaded Eutychianus and the officials of the treasury; the desecration might be unpopular, but it would bring in a great sum of urgently needed cash. Vesta herself was carried on a small plain litter made of untrimmed boughs, for everything connected with her is of set purpose primitive and simple. Her bearers were four of the Vestals, who are her only servants.

Behind Vesta came the Emperor, who wore the foreign robes of his high priesthood. Gordius drove him in a four-horse triumphal chariot, which made Gordius for ever after unpopular in Rome. With an odd lack of fitness for the occasion the Emperor had chosen as his escort the eunuch priests of Cybele; the Romans regard these creatures as at the same time comic and disgusting, and I heard hooting as they passed. Last of all came Aquilia Severa, the chosen Vestal, a relative of the house of the Divine Severus. She walked, veiled in bridal garments of the traditional colour and shape; but they were made of the loose homespun which the Vestals weave for themselves, her face was unpainted and she wore no jewellery. She was about ten years older than the Emperor, a lady of good birth who could endure the stares of the crowd with dignity; but I have seldom seen a less attractive bride.

I saw nothing more of the strange wedding; though like everyone else I heard about the dances, the exotic sacrifices, the incense, the Syrian vestments and Asiatic music which for three hours made up the marriage between Vesta, guardian of Rome, and Elagabalus the Sun-god of Emesa. In the course of the ceremony, though so unobtrusively that few noted the actual moment, Elagabalus the high priest married Severa the dedicated virgin. I could have been there, among the friends of the family who thronged what had been for centuries the temple of Capitoline Jupiter and was now the shrine of the little black sky-stone. The Augusta had pressed me to come. I made the excuse that it was my duty to mingle with the crowd and test the sentiments of the common people of Rome.

In fact I kept away because I was afraid, afraid of super-natural disaster. I did not expect Jupiter to avenge his eviction from his ancient home. No one nowadays fears Jupiter. The cult of the Olympians has become a part of good manners, with no sterner sanction; you are no more likely to be punished for an insult to Jupiter than for being rude in a drawing-room.

Vesta is different. She is part of the ancient and miraculous beginning of the City of Rome. Her little round thatched hut stands as it stood in the days of King Romulus, and she has no home anywhere else on earth. To me chastity still matters, as once, a long time ago, it mattered to the Romans of Rome. I have never in my life seduced a virtuous woman, and the mistresses I have taken from time to time knew from the outset that it was only a business arrangement; the wife I have married in my exile came to me a maiden. (I don't count rape in enemy country; you do that just because rape is wrong, and you want to do wrong to your enemies.) Vesta is the guardian of chaste family life. Now the Emperor had taken Vesta by force, to give her to his queer little bit of black stone from nowhere. If there is such a thing as luck, he was breaking the luck of Rome.

On a much lower plane, I thought he was also being unkind to Aquilia Severa. Vestals differ in their conduct, like any other group of human beings chosen at random. Their parents have vowed them to the goddess while they are too young to have minds of their own, and they know that the vow binds for thirty years only; some who began young have married after the vow was accomplished, and born legitimate children. But Severa had been for fifteen years a model Vestal, genuinely doing her duty. She had grown used to virginity, and it was generally believed that she would stay on after her thirty years were up and become the chief Vestal. I suppose it was just because she was a genuine Vestal that the Emperor had chosen her; and perhaps because of her remote connection with the family of the Divine Severus.

I could not avoid the festivities in the palace that evening; and indeed I did not wish to, for all the unlucky deeds had been done in the temple. There was a dinner of extraordinary magnificence, with literally hundreds of guests. In the huge banqueting hall part of the ceiling revolved, imitating the motions of the heavens; gouts of scent fell from it, mingled with rose-petals. The wainscoting of the walls, though patterned with coloured marbles and garnished with gems, had been arranged to slide by machinery as painted scenes slide in a theatre; for each of the seven courses the room completely changed in appearance. The food was magnificent and exotic, nightingales' brains, larks' tongues, elephants' trunk, ostrich and giraffe. The wine was Falernian more than a hundred years old, mixed with a very small proportion of water.

But everything was most sedate. The Augusta and the other ladies of the household were present; even little Alexianus came in for a few minutes to drink the formal toast. The only entertainment provided was the reading of a long epithalamium by its author, a fashionable poet whose name I have forgotten. Severa sat in a high chair at the head of the Emperor's couch.

He was most attentive, feeding her with dainties from his own plate. Unveiled, her cheeks flushed with wine, she looked more like a bride and less like a reluctant human sacrifice. She still seemed to me an odd choice for an Emperor who could choose from all the pretty girls in the world; but there was something attractive about her.

The stable boys were present, as usual. The Emperor suffered from the delusion that they were young men of exquisite sensibility, who would pine and fade away if they suspected that they were considered unfit for formal gatherings. But they had been placed all together at a group of tables in a corner, and I was not the only stalwart and influential courtier who had told them privately that they had better be quiet. They drank themselves to sleep without making any disturbance.

After the meal we drank for only an hour, listening in decorous boredom to the poet. Then the majordomo signalled us to rise as the Emperor prepared to leave his couch. To my surprise, for I had assumed that this second marriage would be a form like the connection with poor little Paula, the Emperor conducted his bride to the marriage chamber. That night it was whispered all over the palace that, for the first time in his life, our young ruler had climbed into bed with a female. By dawn every steward was planning a new use for the apartments of Hierocles and the other boy-friends.

The same evening I was summoned to the Pincian gardens, where the Emperor was trying out a draft of Arabian colts. I enjoyed the atmosphere of those gardens. They were crowded with slaves, and favourites from a very lowly station in life, and not one of them was afraid; a very rare condition in the pleasure-grounds of an Emperor. The colts were being galloped on a circular track; within it was a shorter track, where the well-trained carriage-girls could pull spectators fast enough to keep up with the horse-drawn chariots. We raced a little among ourselves; but not hard enough to distress our teams, for that would have angered the Emperor.

The charioteers were skilful, courageous, and considerate of their horses. It was fascinating to see how quickly the colts understood what was wanted from them. Soon they were pulling together without trying to kick one another, and stopping as they felt the bit. I noted that Hierocles was driving one of the chariots. He seemed not to have a care in the world.

When the horses had done enough the Emperor sent for me. He made me sit beside him on a marble bench, and ordered the stable boys to withdraw out of hearing. 'I want your advice, Duratius,' he began with his usual frankness, 'because you are the only normal man among my intimate friends. It would be no use consulting Gordius on a point of this kind. It's about my marriage. The Sun-god inspired me to marry, because it's obvious that any child born of a union between a Vestal and the high priest of Emesa will be something more than a mortal. Moreover, it's my duty to beget a son as soon as I can, to settle the succession. And besides all that I *want* a son, because fatherhood will be a new experience and my aim is to taste every experience open to mankind before I am called to join my predecessors among the gods. As you know, women don't attract me. But there's nothing wrong with Severa in particular, and last night I went to bed determined to do my best. Yet she is still a virgin. Now what do you advise?'

'I have never experienced your trouble, my lord,' I answered cautiously, 'and I am not a physician. But certainly you ought not to despair after a single night. All the same, it might be prudent to prepare your mind for a disappointment. A union between the priest-king of Emesa and a Vestal of Rome should, as you say, produce a god. But sometimes the great gods are jealous of too many newcomers. You yourself will join them when your reign is ended, as you have just reminded me. Perhaps they don't want to see Olympus swamped with your descendants. In short, if the lady Severa should continue barren blame the enmity of heaven, not any shortcomings in your own physical equipment.'

That was the best I could do on the spur of the moment; and not a bad effort when you consider my difficulties. There were so many truths that I dared not mention. The Emperor was manly enough with his boy-friends, according to the frank gossip of those low creatures; if something held him back from the terrible crime of deflowering a Vestal it might be holy awe, or even the direct intervention of the goddess. His fancy that the sky-stone had inspired him to perpetrate this wicked marriage was almost certainly mistaken, for the sky-stone was in general a kindly and virtuous god. But these were not suggestions that I could make to his face.

'You are not very helpful,' he said moodily. 'I thought a proper man would tell me exactly what to do. I shall try again, of course, but I can't try harder than I did last night. Perhaps Gordius and Hierocles were right after all. They told me the plan couldn't really have come from the Sun-god. Do you think I may have been bewitched?' he added, his face brightening as he clutched at this straw.

'Can a witch harm the high priest of Elagabalus?' I answered, anxious to scotch the idea. 'If you have been bewitched you must endure it. The police are not to be trusted when it's a question of discovering witches. Blackmail tempts them, or they work off old grudges. Remember your vow never to punish one of your subjects without due process of law.'

'No, I won't set the police to hunt witches. That vow of mine still binds. Besides, I hate cruelty, it makes me shudder just to imagine it. I shall persevere with my bride, and perhaps make discreet inquiries into how other men manage. I'm quite sure the Sun-god would never deceive me with a false inspiration. He wanted to marry Vesta, and that made it right for me to marry a Vestal. But there's always the chance that he may change his mind. In some ways he is strangely inconstant. After countless generations I am the first of his priest-kings whom he has chosen to be Emperor of the Roman People.'

I murmured agreement and the Emperor strolled off to chat with Gordius. He felt better after telling me his troubles, but he never cared to talk for long on one subject. I was very much relieved. He was evidently trying to find some dignified way to save his face if the marriage should prove intolerable.

During the next month curious stories of the Emperor's inquiries were current in the palace. I cannot vouch for their accuracy; he was beginning to think of me as a respectable elderly adviser, from whom some activities should be hidden. It was said that he sent police agents into the public baths, to pick out the men with the largest sexual organs; these were then brought to the palace, and commanded to demonstrate their prowess. Another story was that, to find out about the nature of women, the Emperor himself visited a bath reserved for females; he soothed the frightened matrons by claiming that he was in part female himself, and displayed his depilated body to prove it. This second story sounds more plausible than the first. In sexual matters the Emperor's curiosity was unbounded, and in spite of the girls who drew his garden carriages, he knew very little about the nature of women. But both may be slanders. At that time slander was busy.

After a month the high priest of the Sun-god announced officially to the Senate that Elagabalus had made a mistake. (Some Senators, unfamiliar with his phraseology, thought he was referring to himself, and nearly fainted at the idea of an Emperor publicly admitting a mistake.) The god did not get on with Vesta, who was too rough for his tender nature. Instead he would marry Astarte, whose Syrian ritual resembled his own.

That same afternoon Vesta was returned to her round thatched hut, with her sacred things and her jewellery; but her money had been spent on the army. With the goddess went the Vestal Aquilia Severa, still a virgin and therefore still competent for her old duties.

CHAPTER TWELVE

The Emperor Untrammelled

℃

The Emperor had held the Purple for more than three years, and was approaching his seventeenth birthday; an astonishing achievement when you consider it in cold blood. His self-confidence had increased, and he no longer looked to his grandmother for advice. But the ladies of the imperial household still enjoyed great influence, especially in the many branches of administration which bored the Emperor. The Augusta, in partnership with the famous lawyer Ulpianus, looked after the civil service. The Clarissima saw to it that a succession of handsome young officers held well-paid and unexacting posts in Rome. The lady Mamea interested herself in scholarship; she was the only member of the family who sought to please the opinion of conventional Rome, and in the Senate she had many devoted friends.

Alexianus, nearly thirteen years of age, was heir presumptive to the Purple. But to be heir to a healthy young man four years his senior was not so promising as it sounded; there was no reason to suppose that he would outlive his cousin. Outside the palace the public were inclined to forget Alexianus, though his mother saw to it that the court and particularly the Senate were frequently reminded of him.

The Emperor's main interest was chariot-racing. The Green faction was practically managed from the palace, though the Emperor was sportsman enough to allow the Blues a fair chance. Chariot-racing involved looking after the stable boys who had followed him from Nicomedia. His other hobby was making life unpleasant for pompous Senators; occasionally he was able to combine the two pastimes.

He promoted Gordius and Protogenes to the Senate, endowing them with the necessary income from his privy purse. Gordius was in addition Praefect of the Watch, in charge of the uniformed police of Rome; he was as competent as some other policemen I have known, but the nobility felt insulted when they had to obey his traffic regulations. One of the lesser stable boys, a fellow known as Claudius the Barber, was made Praefect of the Corn Supply, which he managed very well. Under his administration there was plenty of corn in Rome, though perhaps it cost the taxpayer more than was necessary.

By restoring Vesta to her hut and dismissing Aquilia Severa, the Emperor had regained his popularity with the middle classes. I myself could serve him with a more tranquil mind now that he was no longer under the displeasure of the gods. The soldiers regarded him with affection. He was doing to the Senators, mostly retired senior officers, what every ranker would like to do to senior officers.

He had never executed a Senator save after lawful trial; he had never even confiscated a Senator's wealth, or sent him into exile. All the same, he found ways to make life extremely unpleasant for these overbearing nobles.

The worship of the sky-stone continued, though now the Emperor rarely attended in person. The great annual festival of Elagabalus was a splendid opportunity to compel curule magistrates to dance publicly in his honour.

At the same time, the Emperor kept his friends among the younger gentry. Some of his private dinners seemed to take in the whole city of Rome. At one of them there were twenty-two courses, each eaten in a different private mansion; after each course a fresh troupe of dancing-girls entertained the guests, and everyone present was clothed in green silk.

People came gladly to these parties even though they might end in an undignified riot; because you never knew what you might draw in the Emperor's lottery. Little presents distributed by lot are an old tradition of Roman dinners, though I have never encountered the custom in the provinces. But instead of the usual bag of sweets or jar of wine, the Emperor's gifts were on an imperial scale. The climax of any feast at which he was host was the drawing of the lottery tickets.

I remember one great dinner at the palace, because I was roped in at the last minute to fill a vacant couch; that afternoon an invited guest had died of apoplexy, and it spoils a party if two men are set down at a table laid for three. As a rule I was not asked to these feasts, because I was even then too old and staid to fit in with a group of wild young men; but the Emperor still liked and trusted me, and often commanded me to attend his private race-meetings in the gardens.

With the invitation to dinner the Emperor sent my party clothes. The guests of honour were the leading charioteers of the Blue faction, and all the guests wore blue silk, provided free by the privy purse. But this was a small party of only thirty covers, so the cost of clothing us was not excessive.

We dined beside the swimming pool of the palace baths. The furnace had been damped and the room was not unpleasantly hot, though the smell of the scented water was a little overpowering. I resigned myself to getting wet before the end of the evening, since otherwise there would be no point in dining beside the pool. At least this great hall was covered with a solid ceiling, so there was no danger that rose-leaves falling from above would get into the food; the Emperor was too fond of that charming fancy, which will ruin the flavour of the best roast.

My place was a lowly one, a long way from the Emperor. My two table-companions were evidently old friends, who compared at length the charms of fashionable harlots, an expert conversation in which I could not join; at least it was a change from that endless discussion of pretty boys that you heard all over the palace. We began with very good oysters, and masses of them. You often get oysters at parties, but hosts are inclined to count them; I settled down to eat as many as I wanted, a rare treat.

While we ate we were entertained by a troupe of swimmers dressed in imitation seaweed to represent Tritons and Nereids. The Emperor's fancy revelled in complication, and I noted at a second glance that the bearded Tritons were girls and the long-haired Nereids boys. A similar conceit was evident among the waiters. Just when I had made up my mind that they were boys dressed as Athenian maidens I realised that some were girls after all; though it was almost impossible to tell the difference.

When we had finished our oysters the Emperor plunged into the pool; of course his guests must follow him. Since he had dived in naked we also took off our tunics, and I was relieved to observe that all the invited guests were definitely male – at least anatomically.

After a short swim among the Nereids we came back for the second course. Servants dried us with linen towels (no wool was used in the palace), and dressed us in tunics of a different shade of blue. While we ate a great marble basin was drawn in on wheels; and in it, swimming in sea water, a dolphin. The dolphin was tipped out on a marble slab where we could all watch him die; but to me it did not seem that he changed colour. We were advised to dally over our stuffed eggs in rich sauce, and then swim again; while the dolphin was cooked for the next course.

In the Aegean they consider dolphin a great delicacy, but it must be cooked fresh; the pickled fish sold in Rome is not nearly so good. This dolphin had been netted in the Propontis; a fast despatch boat had brought him alive to Rome.

Swimming, even in warm scented water, I found trying to my middle-aged stomach. When at last the dolphin was ready for the table I willingly changed plates with my neighbours, who had been served with an imitation steak made of wax. This I cut into small pieces and burned in a nearby lamp, where it stank horribly; we all knew that when the Emperor played this childish trick of serving imitation food the guest must empty his plate somehow. He would have been vexed if I had merely pushed it aside untouched. But it was also the custom that I might keep the silver plate on which the imitation had been served, as compensation for taking the joke in good part. My neighbour, a rich young rake, would rather dine well than take home a few pounds of silver.

During the roast (Libyan giraffe stuffed with mushrooms) my couch subsided to the floor. Under the blue silk it had been made of oiled canvas, inflated with air; at a signal from the Emperor a waiter had pricked it. I was unlucky to be the victim of two jokes during one dinner, but then the plate of wax dolphin had not been intended for me. What seems enormously funny to a sixteen-year-old does not always amuse a middle-aged veteran; but the Emperor gave so many of these parties that he could not be expected to invent fresh jokes for each one.

My memory of what happened after the roast has grown a little hazy; we were drinking the most marvellous wine. At some period in the evening Spintrians gave their usual performance; but what that was you may read in the Life of the Divine Tiberius by Suetonius, not in this memoir. Presently my companions drew me out about my travels, and I gave them a highly-coloured description of the grove of Daphne near Antioch, which cannot be matched even in cosmopolitan Rome. When we had finished eating, by this time quite sodden with repeated plunges into the pool, we were handed little cups of strong wine flavoured with pine-cones. This is supposed to make you sober, for a few minutes at least. I drank three of them, as did most of the guests, for we wanted our wits about us for the climax of the evening, the lottery.

There was a ticket for each guest, though that did not mean a real prize for everyone. The first ticket drawn represented literally a fortune, a strongbox full of gold pieces equal to half the Emperor's revenue for that day. I didn't get it. The other good prizes were costly but embarrassing: a live elephant, a choir of eunuchs, a team of four unbroken horses. One man drew a beautiful concubine, but he had to possess her then and there, before the whole company; the next got a withered old hag, and must pay the same forfeit. My ticket entitled me to a hamper containing one dead dog, which was comparatively easy to dispose of; the Emperor would not inquire how my pet was getting on in its new home, as he would to the winner of the elephant. There were cheers when a portly Senator drew Ixion's Wheel. Nobody liked Glabrio, who ought to have stuck with the faction of the respectable Senators; he dined with the Emperor because he thought himself younger than he was, and because he hoped to make money out of the lottery.

Ixion's Wheel was a novelty to me; though the others were familiar with it, for the Emperor rarely thought of a new joke. Someone explained to me that Ixion is one of the mortals eternally punished in Hades for crimes committed on earth, and that this Wheel simulated his punishment. It was a large water-wheel, brought in and erected on the edge of the pool. Glabrio was bound to it; then servants turned it so that at each revolution he got a ducking.

It was dawn before the Emperor dismissed us. By the end of the long night the drink had died in me, and I was beginning to feel the sober depression of the morning after. I was also feeling sorry for my poor young lord. He tried so hard to be a wicked debauchee, after the manner of Nero or Caligula; but it is difficult to earn a reputation for wickedness if you have sworn an oath never to give pain to an innocent subject.

The Emperor found an outlet for his high spirits in repeating these lotteries in public. At the circus he threw among the crowd little tokens marked with a number Ten. The lucky holder of a token might exchange it at the treasury for ten objects, and the joke was that he could not know what kind of object. He might get ten dead dogs, or ten purses of gold, perhaps ten strokes of the birch, perhaps ten camels. Animal prizes of any kind the winner was expected to keep as souvenirs of imperial favour.

The Emperor liked also to display his power over nature. In

the height of summer he caused waggon-loads of snow to be heaped up in his garden, ostensibly to see if it would make the place any cooler; but the real object was to have snow carried from the mountains to Rome so swiftly that it would not melt on the way. Once he turned out all the police and watchmen of Rome to gather a thousand pounds' weight of cobwebs; they did it, too, and made a most imposing pile. But when he offered a live phoenix as a prize in his lottery he found there were limits even to his power. The legate commanding in Arabia reported that he could not catch one; which was not surprising, since there is only one phoenix in the world, who renews himself by rising from the funeral pyre after he has died of old age.

The stable boy who won the phoenix thought himself well compensated by a thousand pounds' weight of gold instead. So much gold in private hands, untouched by the tax-gatherer, is as remarkable as any phoenix.

Unfortunately this gesture cost money, when the treasury was hard put to it to make ends meet. Collecting cobwebs or snow only made work for servants or soldiers whom the state must support anyway, and who may as well be kept busy at some absorbing task. But any gold that comes into the hands of the government ought to be used to pay the soldiers.

The Augusta warned the Emperor of the perils of extravagance, and he promised to abandon his lotteries. Instead he took up as hobbies kindness to animals and kindness to women, whom he regarded as comparable species. In the palace he sheltered animals of every kind, from mangy lions too old for the amphitheatre to unwanted cur-dogs. He decreed that these should eat what he ate, since nothing was too good for them. Dogs and lions managed fairly well, but the oxen he had rescued from over-work at the plough mostly died of indigestion.

The pensioned lions had the run of the palace. It was officially stated that well-fed beasts of prey will never attack man, and the Augusta reinforced this hopeful theory by having their teeth pulled out. In fact I never heard of an accident while these creatures roamed the corridors; but the story went round

Rome that some guests from an imperial supper, staggering home late at night, had bumped into a group of lions and died of fright.

The Emperor's concern for female welfare was a more serious project. Of course the only women who interested him were harlots; he could never subdue his curiosity about normal intercourse between the sexes. The police were ordered to draw up a list of every free courtesan in Rome, a task into which Gordius put all his energies. Free courtesans are those who live by themselves and manage their own affairs, as opposed to those who work in brothels and the private concubines of rich men.

When the list had been compiled the Emperor marked their dwellings on a big map of the City, and called in experienced staff officers to help him plan a route. After long effort they plotted one that would enable the Emperor, who drove faster than anyone else in Rome, to visit them all in one day. He took me with him in his chariot; because, he said, I did not get enough fresh air, cooped up in the palace guardroom all day.

The Emperor did not plan to visit these women on business. No man could have carried out such a programme in one day, and for him even one woman would be too many. But I was mildly surprised when he merely dashed up to each in turn (of course they were all waiting at home for him, in their most attractive undress) and presented her with a single gold piece – 'a present from Antoninus Elagabalus'.

He said afterwards that he had been inspecting their living conditions, an important duty shamefully neglected by the police. His gallop set up a record for chariots driven through heavy traffic which has never been equalled to this day.

Then he conceived the idea of meeting every loose woman in Rome, brothel workers and kept concubines as well as courtesans, the whole lot of them. Gordius pointed out that he could not visit them all unless he devoted the rest of his life to doing nothing else; and if they all came to him there was no hall in the palace big enough to hold them. Undeterred, the Emperor ordered them to be assembled in the circus, where he inspected them from the imperial box. I suppose he thought that if he looked at them long enough he might discover what made them attractive to normal men, and so himself become a normal man; or he may have hoped they would tell him their experiences, for on that subject he was madly curious. He was doubly disappointed. A whole circus full of lowclass harlots is a most dispiriting sight, calculated to make the wildest rake eager for marriage and respectability; and the women were much too frightened to speak to him when he asked them intimate questions. In the end, rather than go away without anything done, he was reduced to delivering a rousing harangue in which he exhorted them to perform their essential service with due regard to duty but to go on strike if their masters tried to cheat them of their pay. He then withdrew amid cheers.

The great investigation into harlotry became the talk of Rome. That was when I first heard it suggested that the Emperor was mad. Of course he was completely sane; but he had nothing important with which to occupy his time, he delighted in eccentric behaviour, and he knew that sexually he was unlike the majority of his subjects. It was unfortunate that he could not resign himself to the difference, and cease prying into a question he would never solve.

Then something happened that no one could have foreseen. Just about the time of his seventeenth birthday the Emperor fell in love with a woman. He could not have chosen anyone less suitable, if he had raked through that circus full of whores; but so it is that Cupid often strikes.

The lady of his choice was Annia Faustina. She was in fact a lady of good birth and excellent reputation, the kind of well-bred Roman matron any respectable Emperor might marry amid the applause of his subjects. But she happened to be the widow of Pomponius Bassus, who had been compelled to kill himself as an accomplice of Seius Carus; and she was in her middle forties, old enough to be his mother. In fact she was older than her closest friend, his aunt the lady Mamea.

It was just possible to discern the qualities that made her attractive to the Emperor. She was soft and pink-and-white and motherly, with a knack of putting young men at their ease, nothing could shock her, though her own conduct was always correct. She could talk by the hour about the gods, and was especially learned in the rituals of Syria. She knew the points of a horse, and could watch a race intelligently. What clinched it was that she had the courage, and the ambition, to wish to be Empress even if it meant marrying the Emperor Elagabalus.

When I first heard the rumour that a lady was visiting the Pincian gardens I refused to believe it. A few days later I myself was commanded there, and was thunderstruck to meet the lady Faustina driving sedately in a two-girl carriage. As a compliment the Emperor had lent her his best team; the girls, who were twins and a perfect pair, answered the bit without trouble and ran nearly as fast as real horses.

The Emperor's carriage pattered beside hers. He was gazing into her cow-like eyes as a dog gazes at a bone.

Six days later they were married. The courtiers began to adjust themselves to the new situation, like ants repairing their nest after it has been trodden on.

First to take advantage of the new state of affairs was the lady Mamea. Any unprejudiced observer could see that the new Empress was past childbearing; but the Emperor was not unprejudiced, and it was not difficult to persuade him that he might soon be a father. Since his son would be his heir that would settle the succession. But in the meantime, Mamea suggested, a Syrian with a proper respect for the ties of kinship ought to recognise his cousin Alexianus as Caesar and heir presumptive. The graceful compliment would mean nothing, but the denial of it might seem a slur on the best friend of the Empress, the lady Mamea. The whole imperial family united to press this proposal on the Emperor. Shortly afterwards the Senate and the magistrates were summoned to witness the public adoption of the Caesar Alexianus, who from that moment became in law the son of Antoninus Elagabalus. The father was seventeen years of age and the son thirteen; but in the past the Purple has been transmitted by less plausible adoptions.

The stable boys worried about their future. Hitherto they had done no harm to anybody, and the great point in their favour was that their maintenance cost the treasury very little. Every Emperor chooses favourites; in the nature of the case Senators will object to the low birth of these favourites; but if they are genuinely sprung from the dregs of the people, as were the stable boys, they will be content with soft living from day to day, knowing themselves unfit to govern provinces or command armies.

Now Gordius and Protogenes set themselves to make money while the sun still shone on them. As Praefect of the Watch Gordius could put the screw on all the bad characters of Rome, brothel-keepers, hired bullies, and the owners of low drinking-dens; though he was restrained from going too far by the knowledge that the Emperor liked people of this kind. The cost of loose living rose, but the rakes of Rome could well afford it.

Protogenes had less to work with, nothing but his voice in the Senate. He began quietly by speaking for various private interests; but there was not much money in that, since under our system of taxation a private interest can only flourish if it is completely unnoticed by the government. Soon he was black-mailing other Senators, threatening to accuse them of treason unless they paid him to keep his mouth shut. That is perhaps the most dastardly crime a public man can commit, and it made him hated even by the lower orders. He was not really a wicked man; but since our Emperor came to Rome there had not been a single delation, so he did not realise the full horror of his conduct.

Claudius the Barber was already on such a good thing, the control of the corn supply, that he grew rich without effort. He was hated by the peasantry, who saw their crops taken to feed idlers better off than themselves; but even an honest Praefect of the corn supply would be hated by the peasantry.

A new favourite, a cook named Zoticus, caused even more trouble. He was one of the finest men I have ever seen, tall with broad shoulders and a slim waist; he looked worthy of a place in the front rank of the Praetorians, and was in fact a chicken-livered scoundrel. He was a new arrival from the east, brought to Rome by a cousin among the stable boys, and he did not understand the fundamental kindliness of the Emperor. In the imperial bedchamber he had taken over some of the duties hitherto performed by Gordius; he was so high in favour that there were rumours of another marriage ceremony, though I myself doubted it. This rascal began to sell the Emperor's forgiveness to rich men who had never been in genuine danger. He would emerge from the bedchamber to whisper that the Emperor was looking for estates to confiscate, and promise to put in a good word for anyone who would reward him. Since the Emperor never wished to confiscate a great estate the good word put in by Zoticus never failed of its effect. But whenever he sold the Emperor's imaginary forgiveness some important noble went away hating the Emperor as an avaricious despot.

You will note that his first normal love affair had made no difference to the Emperor's private life. Faustina had her own apartments, next door to those of the lady Mamea; the Emperor visited her every day. But the Pincian gardens remained as well stocked with curious inmates as before, and his affection for Hierocles was unimpaired.

But if life in the palace was little altered there had been a profound change in the atmosphere of the City. The government was becoming unpopular, in the eyes of men who had the power to overthrow it. Talking with Praetorians in the guardroom I sensed the change. During the first three years of his reign the Emperor's pranks had been directed against people and institutions which no soldier likes, Senators and noblemen and the priestly colleges. Now peasants, cousins of the ordinary men in the ranks, were being badgered and oppressed by lowborn town loafers, stable boys who gained power because they yielded in an unmanly fashion to the Emperor's lust.

It was no longer considered funny that charioteers should make speeches in the Senate. The soldiers recalled that nearly every Senator had done duty on the frontier before he received his striped toga. Another grievance, oddly enough, was the Emperor's idea of comic relief in the amphitheatre. Soldiers complained that nowadays you could not take your girl there, for fear that the lewd performances would put ideas into her head.

I did my best to persuade the grumblers. I pointed out that the Senate was nothing special, and those Senators who thought it was must be enemies of the army. Every true legionary ought to believe that the Emperor is supreme and all his subjects equal to one another; that had been the programme of the legionaries who gave the Purple to the Divine Julius, nearly 300 years ago. The second objection was easily answered; any man who was rash enough to take his girl into a crowd deserved to lose her to someone more attractive.

But the discontent continued, and every grumbler repeated the same phrases until I suspected that in the Camp someone must be preaching subversion. It would be useless to warn the Emperor. He could not imagine that his faithful fellow-soldiers of Immae would ever turn against him, and he might suspect me of fostering the very grumbles I repeated. After some consideration I applied for a private interview with the Augusta.

I was no longer a member of the intimate court circle. I spent most of my time with the troops, and when the Emperor invited me to visit his gardens it was to show a trusted outsider what he had devised; not, as in the old days, to seek my help in planning the entertainment. I rarely met the ladies of the imperial family, except to salute them as they passed through the crowded halls of the palace. When the Augusta received me, I was surprised to see how she had changed.

In Nicomedia she had been the vigorous head of a family, which she was leading to success: bursting with energy, bubbling with new ideas, certain of victory. Now she looked as though she had never ridden a camel into the heart of a great battle, never done anything except loll on a cushion. Not that she had grown fat; her figure was still slight and she reclined gracefully. But her face seemed tired and fretful; as though she, who once had issued commands, must now nag and whine at events she could not control.

She listened quietly while I told my worries, and then asked me what remedy I could suggest. I proposed that the stable boys be kept within the palace, where they could attend to their duties in the imperial bedchamber. If they were removed from the Senate and the government offices the unrest would quickly subside.

'I expect you are right, Duratius,' she said when I had finished. 'At any rate it was good of you to warn me. But I cannot help you. The Emperor will not be crossed in anything. He no longer heeds my advice. The Empress is too wise to ask him to get rid of the stable boys; instead she encourages him to find them jobs which take them out of the palace. The only way to make him change his way of life is to approach the lady Mamea. She rules the Empress, and the Empress rules the Emperor. But don't think the family is divided. We are still the house of the priest-kings of Emesa, united against the outside world. Whatever shall come we are one family, and we regard you as one of us. Don't be afraid.'

I was afraid, but there was nothing more to be gained from the Augusta. She had hinted that I should lay my troubles before the lady Mamea: instead I called on Eutychianus at the Camp.

CHAPTER THIRTEEN

The Caesar and the Augusta

Since I went to the Camp in undress uniform the soldiers could see I was a centurion; most of them knew who I was and what I did. So I did not expect any frank revelations of their sentiments.

But there was no disguising from a veteran the uneasy feeling in the Camp. The men were sullen. Some N.C.O.s barked at them; others were too friendly, as though they feared their authority might snap if they put a strain on it. Nobody spoke to me, nobody smiled; though behind me I kept on hearing the whistling of a tune. It came always from behind, and was always the same tune. It was not hard to recognise it as the burden of some seditious song, especially appropriate when the Emperor's pet centurion came by.

Eutychianus was busy, of course; every Praetorian Praefect is always busy. But he made time to see me as soon as I sent in my name; he received me in his private office, with a guard on the door to scare away eavesdroppers.

When I began to explain my misgivings he cut me short. 'So you also have noticed it?' he said easily. 'But of course a man of your experience would spot it as quickly as any police agent. Don't think I am neglecting my duty. I recognise discontent – I expect a mutiny – I have a pretty good idea who is behind it. And I can do nothing.'

'What do you mean?' I began, but again he interrupted me.

'It's quite plain, when you look at the troops and read the police reports. Mamea is plotting to get rid of the Emperor, so that her brat shall succeed while he is still too young to rule. A woman cannot be Emperor, but she can be regent. In a year or two Alexianus will be old enough to manage without his mother. Mamea can't wait. I worked it out, and I know I'm right. So I went to the Emperor and advised him to kill his aunt, and his young cousin too though the boy may be innocent. It's wasteful to have a young heir *and* a young Emperor; the double household makes an unnecessary drain on the treasury. The Emperor answered that the ties of kinship are sacred to any Syrian, as they should be sacred to any honourable Roman. He won't believe that an aunt can plot against her nephew. Even if I convinced him he would still say that a nephew cannot execute his aunt. There you are.'

'Then what shall we do? Shall I murder Mamea without waiting for orders?'

'And be crucified for laying hands on a member of the imperial family? I would be grateful, but you would be a fool to try it. No, our only hope is to convince the Emperor. I shall take no action against the plotters. I may even give the impression that I approve of their activities. Luckily there are three or four cohorts who will follow me in anything. After a genuine outbreak the Emperor must be convinced. In the meantime I have given him a picked guard, commanded by the tribune Antiochianus. For the next ten days they will be in charge of the palace, and they can be counted on to defend it even against fellow-Praetorians.'

'Thank you, my lord. You have chosen the only course open to a loyal servant of the Emperor. In the palace I also will be on my guard. They won't be able to get rid of him by assassination; though the guard and I can't protect him if the Praetorians mutiny as a corps.'

'They won't do that, I assure you. I know what goes on in the Camp. Enough of them will obey me to keep me in control.'

I saluted and left, with apologies for interrupting such a busy official. I was now extremely frightened. Eutychianus had been emphatic that the bulk of the Praetorians would follow his orders, but he had not declared what orders he would give them. He had not protested his loyalty; he had indeed implied that he was loyal, but then he was speaking to a known adherent of the Emperor. I knew the subconscious feeling, common to so many conspirators, that it is honourable to deceive but dishonourable to tell a lie. I had felt like that myself as a reluctant soldier of Macrinus. When the time came the Praetorian Praefect might join the rebels. Then there would be no hope for the Emperor and his friends in the palace.

My only chance was to make the Emperor see reason. Eutychianus claimed to have warned him, but what exactly had he said at that private interview? It is so easy to pass on a rumour in a form that invites disbelief. Besides, Eutychianus was one of the grown-ups from whom the Emperor sought to escape. I was the companion of his secret pleasures. He would listen to me.

In theory I could always get a private audience, but all the same it was hard to see him. No one might intrude while he was with the Empress, and in the evenings he was down in the gardens, planning a special entertainment. For two days I hung about, waiting for word that he would receive me.

At last, on the afternoon before the great party (to which I had not been invited) he sent word that he was ready to hear me. I found him by the stables of the private race-track, surrounded by lengths of harness. He wore nothing but the breech-clout of a charioteer, and there were no attendants within call.

'Ah, Duratius,' he said pleasantly, acknowledging my salute. 'What's your grumble today? Nothing that can't be cured by a sack of gold, I hope. I can give you that, but I can't make you young and beautiful. Before you begin I want your advice on a practical problem. Tonight we are putting on a new kind of chariot race: mixed teams, two stags and two camels. I can't devise a harness for all four to pull together.'

I had to go into the question thoroughly before I could talk of anything else. The Emperor showed me a chariot with the mixed team yoked, and we hung various leather straps on them. It was half an hour before he would listen to me.

Even then I could not stir him. In the end he was ready to believe that his aunt and cousin were plotting to supplant him, but he thought none the worse of them for that. 'Of course it can't succeed,' he said airily. 'The Sun-god protects me, and I am the darling of the soldiers. I wonder what they plan to do with me afterwards? Exile in Antioch, probably. It might be a good idea to go there of my own free will, leaving poor little Alexianus to look after this troublesome city of Rome.'

'My lord, they will cut your throat. They cannot displace you and let you live. You must kill them before they kill you.'

'Cousins don't kill one another, at least not Syrian cousins. But Alexianus is being naughty all the same. Uppish, that's what he is. I've a good mind to let him feel my displeasure. I made him Caesar, and next January we shall be colleagues in the Consulship. What more does the child want? Well, what I gave I can take away. That's it. Duratius, you must be my messenger. If I send a stable boy to the Camp the soldiers will be rude to him, and there's no one else in the garden except slaves. Do you remember how you told me, long ago in Nicomedia, never to send a slave with orders for soldiers? Hurry along to the Camp, like a good fellow, and tell them that Alexianus is no longer Caesar. They must take down his statues, and his name must be omitted from standing orders. Be quick, if you think it's so urgent. Here, Diana and Pallas, take this gentleman to the west gate as fast as you can. You shall each have a lump of sugar if you run well.'

These last remarks were addressed to the team of girls who stood near, ready yoked to their light carriage. In the gardens the Emperor always kept a carriage by him, in case he should get tired of walking. The girls giggled with pleasure that he should remember their names; but with the bits in their mouths they could not answer. In a moment I was bouncing over the turf, with the team at full stretch.

It came into my mind that I had no written authority.

Supposing the soldiers should refuse to credit my instructions? But the Emperor would not carry writing materials in his breech-clout, and if I went back to him he might start some other topic and talk for hours. I would face that fence when I came to it.

From the gardens I walked as fast as I could to the Camp. It is as difficult to hurry in Rome as in a German swamp. Only the Emperor, and courtiers in his train, might break the law against driving wheeled carriages in daylight; litter-bearers never hurry, even if you threaten them with a flogging. The ancients walked everywhere, but in those days Rome was smaller.

Luckily Eutychianus was in his office, but I had to shout and argue before the sentry would admit me. Again I cursed the Emperor for not giving me any token of authority; a ring would have done. But when he dressed as a charioteer he wore no jewellery, because he took an actor's delight in playing a part thoroughly. Well, these rubs were among the penalties of serving a boyish ruler; if Elagabalus had always been prudent and circumspect I would not have loved him as I did.

At last I got into the office, and delivered the imperial command in a curt military tone. Immediately Eutychianus asked for my credentials, but when I admitted I had none he still believed me.

'It's tiresome,' he said. 'Someone is sure to raise the cry that this is a plot by the Clarissima to get rid of her nephew, and we can't prove him wrong. But the real trouble is worse than that. Even if the troops believe that the order comes from the Emperor they may not obey it. Someone has been persuading them that Alexianus is also a son of the Divine Caracalla. If that's not true he is still an Antoninus, with a claim on the allegiance of all followers of the Divine Severus. I wish we could explain to them that the life of Alexianus is in no danger. You and I know that the Emperor would never execute his cousin, but the soldiers assume that when a prince falls from favour he also loses his head. Still, the longer I think it over the more it will frighten me. Let's get it done. Orderly, tell them to sound the Assembly and get the whole corps on parade.'

Eutychianus was a good soldier, who kept his men up to the mark even in the soft living of Rome. When the trumpet sounded they fell in as quickly as though they were on active service. I stood among the orderlies at the back of the tribunal while the Praetorian Praefect issued the new standing orders.

The result was worse even than I had feared. Perhaps it would have been wiser to post the orders in writing, instead of giving them out to soldiers who stood in their ranks, fully armed. Those thousands of stalwart men, with swords on their thighs, could look round and see they were the masters of Rome. There were scattered cries of 'Long live Alexianus Caesar', and a general brandishing of weapons. When a cohort at the rear of the parade formed into column and began to march for the main gate I jumped down from the tribunal, seized an officer's horse from a frightened groom, and galloped out of the Camp before the sentries on the gate could join the mutiny and stop me.

My sword was in my hand, though I could not remember drawing it. The sight of an armed soldier galloping full tilt through the streets set off a panic that travelled faster than my horse. The clang of iron bolts as shops were closed spread outwards in waves of sound, and I wheeled my horse through deserted alleys. The Emperor was in his gardens, but his guard was at the palace. The mutineers also would make for the palace, unless they knew more about the Emperor's movements than they should. I rode for the main guardroom, where I was sure Antiochianus and his picked cohort would prove loyal.

I found the main guard already turned out on parade, alarmed by the disturbance in the City. As soon as I had told my news Antiochianus led them at the double to the Pincian gardens. We were in time, but only just; as we came in at the east end the mutineers reached the west gate. While marching on the palace they had caught a stray stable boy, and to save his life the wretch had told them where the Emperor was to be found.

The carriage-girls saved the situation. Every soldier had heard of them, but they had never been seen outside the gardens. As usual a group of carriages waited by each gate, for the convenience of arriving guests. The mutineers were so intrigued by the novelty that they forgot their object; with whoops of delight soldiers piled into the carriages and began to race one another before their cheering comrades. But the guard-cohort still obeyed its officers; in good order we doubled up to the Emperor, who was by the stables.

Then things began to go wrong. If the Emperor had himself led a charge we would have scattered the disorganised mutineers. But he thought first of saving his boy-friends. Briefly he commanded Antiochianus to 'restore order in the gardens', while he busied himself with hiding Gordius under a pile of forage. The tribune saluted and went back to his cohort.

Praetorians are always reluctant to fight fellow-Praetorians. Antiochianus had been commanded to restore order, not to kill the mutineers. Instead of leading a charge he walked forward alone, with a green branch in his hand, calling for a conference with their leader.

For half an hour we waited uneasily, while I grew more and more frightened. I had a sword but no shield. If the mutineers took me alive they would torture such a notorious imperial favourite. I must get myself killed at the beginning of the fighting, unless Antiochianus could fix up a compromise.

He fixed up a compromise. He came back to tell the Emperor that his soldiers would continue to serve him, if Alexianus kept his rank as Caesar and all the stable boys were dismissed. It is odd how a trifle can alter history. If the Emperor had been wearing the Purple, or even his robes as high priest, I think he would have kept his courage; but he was dressed in the breech-clout of an ignoble charioteer. I saw him glance down at his naked body before he agreed to the terms.

'Alexianus is of no importance, one way or the other,' he said, 'and I can manage without my old friends the stable boys. But I must keep the great love of my life. Tell them that Hierocles

231

will remain. If they don't like it they must kill me, for I cannot live without him.'

The rebels were delighted to learn they had got their way without a revolution; for in most ways Elagabalus the son of Caracalla was just the kind of Emperor they liked. There was some hesitation over Hierocles, until an old *optio* spoke up for him. 'Why shouldn't the Emperor keep his boy-friend?' he shouted. 'We have nothing against boy-friends in their proper place, which is bed. It's different if they try to be Senators, or to run the corn supply. Hierocles does no harm, and so long as he's the Emperor's concubine the taxpayer won't be rooked to support cohorts of imperial bastards.'

'Then everything is settled, fellow-soldiers,' said the Emperor. 'I am safe with you, and my guard may return to the palace. You understand, gentlemen, that all the amusements I have devised in these gardens must come to an end, now that I am parted from my dear stable boys? Would you care to join me in a final party, before the sun rises tomorrow to find all Romans virtuous?'

Cheering, the rebels set off in chase of the carriage-girls. The guard marched glumly away, seeing mutiny rewarded with a pleasant debauch while good soldiers stood to their posts. As I marched with them, I looked at the Emperor; he was standing proudly, his stomach tucked in and his chest thrown out, the most beautiful youth in the world. I saw that he was actually proud of what he had done. In his own eyes he had quelled a dangerous revolt by a single speech to the troops, in the manner of the Divine Julius. He was not a coward, in spite of appearances; but he was very foolish.

During that night's party the gardens were sacked. The pavilions were destroyed, the trees and bushes smashed, the exotic beasts killed or stolen; even the carriages were pulled to pieces by men eager to steal their ivory panels. Most of the carriage-girls were taken to the Camp, though a few preferred the brothels of the City. The stable boys fled to the palace, the next day fled further to Asia. No sensible man could disapprove, but all the same I was sorry. With those gardens something unique, a place beautiful and happy, had vanished from Rome.

As soon as I was free to leave the palace I went to a banker and transferred the rest of my savings to Britain, except for a hundred gold pieces which I carried in a belt under my corselet. For now I wore full armour and carried my shield wherever I went. An Emperor who has once given way to mutineers is on the way out. I was marked as his favourite, and unless I was very careful I would share his downfall.

The Emperor did not recognise his danger, and it seemed cruel to disillusion him. He still ruled the Roman world, so long as he did not interfere with the army; and no Emperor has dared to interfere with the army since the days of the Divine Severus. In fact, very soon after the mutiny he displayed his absolute power in striking fashion; but then anyone can bully the unfortunate Senate.

When the Emperor sent me to the Camp he had sent another messenger to Gordius, who thereupon rose in the Senate to announce that Alexianus had been deprived of all his honours. Of course the Senators have to ratify any imperial decree, even if, as in this case, it is introduced by a disreputable Senator. But the Fathers showed their feelings by receiving the announcement in silence, instead of with the usual cheers.

When the Emperor heard of this he was furious. That Senators should dare to show their disapproval seemed to him the ultimate insult. He proclaimed that meetings of the Senate were suspended until further notice, and, even more drastic, that all Senators must at once leave Rome.

Ten days later I was with the Emperor as he proceeded from the palace to the Camp. He had taken to visiting the Camp every day; I suppose he was looking out for handsome young men, now that he had been deprived of his stable boys. If there had been young recruits in the corps we might have had more trouble, but no one can be a Praetorian until he has done at least twelve years' service. I was his only bodyguard; it seemed pointless to employ Praetorians to guard him.

Near the Forum he suddenly called me to him.

'That man's a Senator,' he said sharply. 'I know him, fellow called Sabinus. Walking about Rome as bold as brass after I have commanded all Senators to go into exile! Kill him.'

'But your oath, my lord. He has not been tried and convicted,' I protested.

'Never mind my oath. I am the Emperor, and I may change my mind if I will. Besides, I know the will of the Sun-god, and he says I may lawfully kill any Senator who defies my orders. It's open rebellion. Kill him.'

I marched smartly up to Sabinus, who was peering into a bookshop. As I reached him I gave him a hearty shove, so that we both disappeared up a narrow alley. The man turned round in anger, and then recognised a soldier. At once he stretched out his neck, uttering a terse but graceful little speech about death being the last refuge from tyranny.

A feeling of hopelessness swept over me. Here was this Sabinus, who in his day had commanded legions and governed provinces; and just because he was now a Senator he made no effort to resist a single soldier, no effort to defend himself against a nearly powerless Emperor. His servants were within call; it was an even chance that the mob might take his side; dozens of respectable shopkeepers would be glad to hide him.

But a Senator wears a toga, and therefore he is undignified if he defends himself against a swordsman. No wonder the Republic decays, when the Senate is filled with philosophers resigned to death at the whim of their ruler.

'You ass,' I shouted in anger, 'if you stand there gawping I shall have to stick you. That's the Emperor's command. Why don't you run away? I might not be able to catch you.'

He took the hint. The Emperor had jumped out of his litter and was peering down the alley, so I had to make a show of running after him; but I failed to catch him. When I came back to the Forum the Emperor barked at me: 'Where's his head? I told you to kill the scoundrel.'

'I'm very sorry, my lord,' I answered with a blank face. 'I understood that you wanted me to chase him out of Rome. He's running now, and he won't stop this side of Antium. If I mistook your command I can only apologise. Perhaps I am growing deaf in my old age.'

'You're deaf and blind and obstinate, and always telling me things for my own good,' he stormed. Then he smiled, with all the winning charm of his amazing beauty. 'But you are on my side, I know that. So I'll still keep you for my bodyguard. Now can you get me to the Camp, or have you forgotten the way?'

Before the end of the year the Senators were commanded to return to Rome. All the machinery of government was needed for the inauguration of the new Consuls, the Emperor himself and his cousin the Caesar. To share a Consulship with the Emperor is the highest honour that can be granted to a subject; this inauguration would show the world that the imperial family was united, in spite of any rumour to the contrary.

But the family was not united. Though the Emperor had forgiven his cousin, the Clarissima had never forgiven her sister. During the Saturnalia, Soaemias got her son away by himself, and poured all her troubles into his ear. When the first of January came, the date for the inauguration of the Consuls, the Emperor refused to play his part.

Servants told us in the guardroom that he was discontented anyway, and in a mood to cause trouble to the grown-ups. He missed his stable boys; Hierocles, lonely and frightened and homesick, was not a cheerful concubine. He had grown tired of the Empress; he had realised at last, what any courtier could have told him from the start, that she was too old to bear him a son, even if he were capable of begetting one. He had always been bored by traditional Roman ceremonies, though he was willing to dance for hours in honour of his sky-stone.

Now he grumbled that all this business of Consuls, and

inauguration, and the auspices, was sheer nonsense; the Consuls were dummies, the flight of birds and the livers of sacrificial oxen meant nothing, Jupiter could neither help nor harm an Empire which was based on the swords of the legionaries. He was speaking the truth, of course. But then you might say that the Empire is sheer nonsense, and the Emperor too; neither makes very much sense, nor does anything useful in the world. But if the Empire is to continue Consuls must be inaugurated, and the omens read with appropriate ceremony; it is a most useful way of persuading the taxpayers to keep on trying.

He should have been at the Senate House soon after sunrise, for these antique rites begin early. Instead he sat in his bedchamber, decked out in his Consul's robes, muttering petulant blasphemies. The soldiers of his escort were waiting in the forecourt, uncomfortable in their ceremonial armour, and the horses of the triumphal chariot grew restive. At length the guard commander, Antiochianus again, sent me to find out the reason for the delay.

The Emperor sprawled in a comfortable armchair, with Hierocles crouched at his feet looking frightened. Eutychianus, the Augusta, and the lady Mamea were all arguing with him; but he would not budge. The Augusta had just tried reminding him that Alexianus Caesar was now waiting in the Senate House. How shaming if a thirteen-year-old could play his part worthily while the adult Emperor sulked at home! It might be worse than shaming if Alexianus were inaugurated Consul in the absence of his colleague. The Emperor answered with a flood of obscenities, picked up in the stable.

Eutychianus took me aside. 'If this goes on we may have to carry him by force to the Senate. Otherwise Alexianus will steal a march on us. Meanwhile that appalling ass the Clarissima confirms him in his stubbornness, just because she has quarrelled with her sister; and the lady Mamea adds fuel to the fire while pretending to make him see reason. What shall we do?' he asked with a despairing shrug.

'Have you tried the Empress?' I suggested.

'What's the use? He's tired of her. That filthy little Hierocles shares his bed every night.'

All the same, they sent for the Empress; and my suggestion worked, though I had made it only because I could think of nothing better. Faustina knelt before him, in mourning garments and with her hair loose. At once he agreed to behave himself.

We should have guessed it at the outset. The Emperor saw most of his advisers as 'the grown-ups', who had told him what he ought to do while he was still a child. Only with Faustina had he conducted himself as a man, only in her eyes did he wish to appear a sensible adult. When she asked something of him he had to give her a reasonable answer.

It was very late when we set off for the Senate House. During the ceremony young Alexianus behaved with perfect aplomb, while the Emperor sulked and grumbled like a baby. But worse was to follow. He flatly refused to go to the Capitol, and would not allow the Caesar to go alone. The sacrifice was offered by the urban praetor, as though there were no Consuls in Rome.

The winter was cold, after a bad harvest, and in Rome there was distress among the poor. Claudius the Barber used to provide abundant grain, at great cost to the treasury. The wholesalers knew he had the Emperor behind him, and things were so managed that everyone concerned with the corn supply made a very handsome profit indeed. But just after harvest the soldiers had sent Claudius back to Nicomedia. The respectable Senator who was now Praefect of the corn supply thought first of checking dishonesty; corn that should have come to Rome remained in the provinces.

It was a situation in which an energetic ruler might have regained all his popularity; if the Emperor has Rome behind him, and the Praetorians paid up to date, he can ignore suffering in the provinces. But our young Emperor refused to do anything useful. He had made up his mind that his advisers, and especially his family, had bullied him unkindly in the matter of the Consulship; in revenge he was going to make things difficult for *them*.

His gardens had been ravaged and his playmates dispersed; there was no money in the treasury and very little in the privy purse. He could no longer devise the magnificent orgies which had amused him when first he came to Rome. So now he gave ostensibly correct dinners, inviting the conventional number of eight guests; and these guests were the kind of eminent public servants who ought to be invited to dine with the Emperor. But when the time came for them to leave the palace they were no longer friendly to the government.

The simplest, and yet perhaps the most subtle, of his tricks was to fill his table with respectable gentlemen who had something in common, but something they were ashamed of. At one party all the guests were bald, and the dancing-girls who entertained them with sober traditional dances had shaven heads. Another dinner was given for eight senior officers, who did not notice until they were assembled that each had lost an eye. They were entertained by a harpist blind from birth, for the kind-hearted Emperor would not mutilate a slave even to further a practical joke. The most difficult party to collect was a gathering of eight veterans on crutches, who were entertained by a famous one-legged tightrope dancer.

At these parties the Emperor repeated his old joke of the inedible food. At each course one guest would be served with a plate of the stuff; but the imitations were no longer painted wax. Apples were carved out of crystal, peas were made of gold, beans of amber, lentils of rubies. The guest who got this imitation was allowed to take it home, which the Emperor considered ample recompense for being made to look ridiculous in public. But the elderly noblemen he invited and mocked had plenty of money, and did not consider a handful of jewels a fair exchange for their lost dignity.

The Emperor was energetic and full of ideas. But at seventeen he was still in love with the pranks that had amused him when he was fourteen; children will repeat a favourite game over and over, long after a grown man has tired of it, and in some ways this vigorous Emperor was still a child. Of course I was never invited to these new-style parties, because of my lowly rank. But even I, hearing of them from the palace servants, wished that occasionally the Emperor would give an ordinary sensible dinner, or at least think of a joke that was both new and funny.

The Augusta and the Praetorian Praefect were both worried at the growing weakness of the government. The soldiers, now that they had chased away the stable boys, saw themselves masters of the state; they were beginning to despise the Emperor, though so long as they enjoyed their pay and privileges they were content to serve him. The Senate of course hated him, and the mob was beginning to think him a tedious bore. But the Emperor now avoided the Augusta, and though he never refused Eutychianus, if he made a concrete demand, he would not follow his advice in matters of daily life. A brisk war on the frontier would have given everyone a new interest; but the Emperor, liking the comfort of his palace, would not lead his army to the Rhine.

The anniversary of the foundation of Rome is celebrated annually in March. The keepers of the record told us that this would be the 975th birthday of the City, which seemed to call for something extra in the way of commemoration. The Emperor was already planning the Secular Games he would hold in twenty-five years, to mark the millenary. This year the Games also were very fine, but the Emperor never really enjoyed watching gladiators kill one another; his chief interest was in the interlude performed in the dinner-hour. The bloodless interlude shown that year was the lewdest in the history of Rome. It was well known that the Emperor had designed it, and even I blushed as I watched it.

But the Emperor agreed with Eutychianus that the real celebration of the birthday of Rome, the festival of Mars in his own month of March, should be held in the Camp. The Emperor would offer the sacrifice, and afterwards distribute rewards among his faithful Praetorians, the most eminent servants of Mars. It would be a great ceremony, in the presence of the whole imperial family.

That meant in the presence of the Augusta, the Clarissima, the Empress and the lady Mamea. The trouble was that the Clarissima had not spoken to her sister since the military revolt last autumn. She believed (correctly) that Mamea had inspired the mutiny; and that the Empress had used what little influence she possessed to further the cause of her closest friend. At first she declared that there must be two ceremonies, if Alexianus Caesar need play any part at all. She, with the Emperor, would offer sacrifice and distribute a donative; after they had left the Camp the Caesar might do the same thing, though of course on a lesser scale.

Eutychianus would not agree. He pointed out that to leave Alexianus loose in the Camp without the Emperor would be asking for trouble; even if the boy behaved himself some of the soldiers might acclaim him. The Emperor must be beside him all the time, so that the soldiers could only cheer for the two Consuls, the joint heirs of the house of Antoninus Severus.

The ladies of the palace no longer confided in me, but servants told us in the guardroom all that passed in the private apartments (as I have already said, it was a court that did not seek secrecy). We heard that the Augusta had reasserted her authority. She had summoned her daughters and commanded them to make friends. They obeyed their mother; the Clarissima even spoke kindly to the Empress. The Emperor, as far as we could make out, remained unreconciled but indifferent. He was going to the Camp, because that was his duty and anyway he liked the company of soldiers; with him would come a great train, and if his cousin and his aunt chose to join it he had no serious objection.

On the day before the ceremony a clumsy ass of a soldier managed to tread on my foot as I was falling in for guard mounting. On parade I stood steady enough, for to any real veteran the ceremonial guard mounting in the palace forecourt is the most serious business of the day; but I suppose I limped a little during the Slow March. In the afternoon I was surprised to receive a summons from the Praetorian Praefect; when I reported at his little office in the palace he received me with a smile, and suggested that I should report sick.

'Let's look at the foot of yours,' he said kindly. 'Yes, I can see the mark of the hobnails. A military boot does a lot of damage. Now tomorrow we shall be standing at attention for hours and hours, while the Emperor sacrifices to Mars and makes a speech to his loyal troops. Even a sound man will be leg-weary by the end of it. Why don't you put on a bandage and stay comfortably in the guardroom? I know you are the Emperor's personal bodyguard, but after all he will be in the midst of his faithful Praetorians.'

'It's nothing, my lord,' I assured him. 'After twenty years' service I can stand on parade for an hour or two. It's going to be a trying day for the Emperor, with his cousin at his elbow all the time. The boy gets on his nerves. He will feel happier with me at his back; not that I am a better bodyguard than any other Praetorian, but he's used to me. Anyway, I like to see big military functions. That's one reason why I stayed on in the army.'

'I was advising you for your own good,' he answered, looking at me with an odd expression. 'But if you think you can be useful to the Emperor I suppose you must obey the call of duty.'

I went away puzzled. The Praetorian Praefect does not usually invite a centurion to go sick with a sore toe.

The great day began with a rather troublesome march from the palace to the Camp. The Emperor went in a triumphal four-horse chariot, and his cousin the Caesar rode a warhorse; but the ladies must be carried in litters and of course the escort must march. I walked immediately behind the Emperor's chariot, ahead of the cohort on escort duty; we all fretted lest we should arrive sweating and with dusty greaves, under the eyes of cool and immaculate Praetorians.

At the Camp there must have been more than 10,000 troops drawn up in close order, watchmen from the City as well as genuine Praetorians. The great parade ground was packed, until there was hardly room before the tribunal for the sacrificial oxen. The General Salute crashed out to greet the Emperor. Then there was an awkward pause while we waited for the ladies to alight from their litters and climb to the lofty platform. The etiquette on these occasions is that the Emperor shall be the last to mount the tribunal, so that the killing of the oxen can begin the moment he is in position.

The ceremony had been ill planned. I gathered from muttered comments that at the last minute the Augusta had altered the arrangements of the Praetorian Praefect. If there were to be ladies on the tribunal, in itself an innovation, they should have been carried to the Camp earlier, to wait for the Emperor; but the Augusta had insisted that they should figure in the procession. The horses of the triumphal chariot grew restive at the delay, and I could see that the Emperor was itching to snatch the reins from the nervous military driver. But while he waited he made a very fine figure, in gilded armour and a great many necklaces and bracelets; he was bareheaded save for the laurel wreath, with his beautiful golden hair floating free. The soldiers cheered from their hearts the gallant young hero of Immae.

When all the ladies were in position the Caesar dismounted. There followed a regrettable muddle, if indeed it came about by chance. As the Emperor got down from his chariot the Caesar stood by the lowest step. First he moved aside as though to wait for his cousin and lord to precede him; then, remembering the protocol of the Camp, he changed his mind. The result was that he marched up the steps a pace before the Emperor. I myself was a pace behind my lord, because as his personal bodyguard I must be near him wherever he went. As the Caesar ascended the tribunal he appeared to lead a following of two, and one of them his sovereign.

The Emperor shrugged his shoulders, dismissing the slight as an unimportant accident; but the Clarissima lost her temper in public. Turning on the lady Mamea, she gave her a resounding slap on the cheek. Then she was screaming abuse at the top of her voice.

'It's just like you, Mamea, with your sly cozening ways. Making your silly little brat take precedence of the Emperor! But all the same he's second, second, do you hear? My son is the heir of the Divine Caracalla, and yours is only important because he's the Emperor's cousin.'

'My son is as much Caracalla's heir as yours,' Mamea answered with spirit. 'Caracalla didn't father either of them, even though you boast of your imagined adultery. And my son is a noble Roman, not the bride of a charioteer.'

At this the Clarissima hit her again, and the Caesar stepped forward to protect his mother.

The soldiers shouted and cheered as though they were watching a fight in the amphitheatre. On the tribunal stood more than a dozen armed men, but so far none had moved to draw his sword. I jumped to get between the Emperor and the Caesar, while the Caesar jumped to get between his mother and his aunt. But my sword remained in its scabbard, and I folded my arms to show my peaceful intentions.

My movement caught the eye of the Augusta. 'You silly girls,' she shouted. 'Duratius was last on the tribunal. Does that make him Emperor? You are squabbling about nothing at all.' But she did not look angry, as I have seen her; on the contrary, she smiled as though she were amused by a comedy.

Still smiling, she moved to stand beside me, as if to intervene between her daughters. Then things happened quickly. For the third time the Clarissima raised her hand to strike, the Caesar fumbled for his sword, and I drew. (That trick of standing with folded arms can be very useful. You look peaceful, and yet your right hand is within a few inches of your sword.) As soon as the Caesar got his blade clear I would be justified in running him through; but he might still change his mind, and I hesitated.

Suddenly the Augusta was speaking to me, as quietly as

though we were alone on the tribunal. 'You keep out of this Duratius. You won us the battle of Immae, and you are not to throw away your life. Let things take their course. Whatever the outcome, a grandson of mine will rule in Rome.'

As she still spoke she drove her elbow hard into my stomach, which was the last thing I had expected. I stepped back, and found myself falling off the edge of the tribunal. As I landed on the hard ground someone wrapped a cloak round my head, and someone else gave me a tap on the skull.

I awoke in the dark. By the stink I was in a stable; very close a horse snorted and moved uneasily. My exploring fingers soon told me that I was lying on my back in a manger. I was naked, and there was a large lump on my head. My first fear was that I was in one of the cells of the amphitheatre, ready to be thrown to the lions. But in that case I would not be alone, and what was a horse doing beside me? I lay still, cautiously working my limbs to make sure they were in order.

Then the yellow glare of a lantern made my headache very much worse. A man was bending over me, and I recognised Eutychianus.

'I'm glad to see you coming round,' he said pleasantly. 'My men can hit hard enough but not too hard. Praetorians ought to manage that if anyone can. Anyway, I deduced from your public record that you would have an unusually thick skull. In an hour or two you will be perfectly fit. I shall leave this lantern with you. In the corner you will find your undress uniform, with your sword but no shield. The money-belt you so prudently carried is intact, with all its gold pieces. In it you will find your discharge from the army. You are honourably discharged, by special leave of the Emperor, so that you may take up a small estate in Britain which has come to you by inheritance. That fits in with your plans, I think? You can't keep that sort of thing a secret from the police. The horse is yours also, by the way. He's a good one. Soon after dawn I shall inspect my private stable as usual, and I shall expect to find it empty. If we should meet again, it will be my duty to see you crucified. Don't thank me; this was not my idea. One Praetorian more or less would not bother me. It was the Augusta who insisted you should be saved. She thinks you have a lucky face or something, and she maintains that she owes you a debt from the battlefield of Immae. But you will never see her to thank her, so don't let it bother you. Good-bye.'

'Wait a minute,' I called. 'If the Emperor needs me I can't run away to Britain. Or has he commanded me to disappear?'

'The Emperor now reigning cares nothing about you. He is Alexander Severus, late Alexianus Caesar, and heir to the house of Antoninus Severus. The late Emperor Elagabalus was killed in the Camp. I am sorry to say that at the last minute he lost his nerve. He and his mother were knocked on the head while they hid in a latrine. It's all for the best, really. The Augusta and I are agreed on that. Elagabalus had become impossible. We still have a young ruler who will continue the policy of the Divine Severus, putting the army first and paying the soldiers punctually. I remain Praetorian Praefect. The Augusta remains the grandmother of the Emperor. Even the lady Faustina is as well-off as before, a close friend of the Emperor's mother. No one suffered except Elagabalus and Soaemias, and there was no saving them after they had refused to be guided by the advisers who brought them to power. Now I really must be going. Oh, you will find a cold breakfast with your clothes.'

When the sun rose I was riding northward.

EPILOGUE

Today is my sixtieth birthday. This morning I came across a pile of papers, the memoirs I wrote so long ago that I can never publish. After all these years it is unlikely that the police will come after me. I ought to die peacefully in my British bed, far from Rome and the centre of affairs.

Even here news reaches us. Whenever an Emperor is murdered the garrison on the Wall must swear allegiance to his successor. I know what has happened, and the news is never cheering.

Young Alexander Severus held the Purple for thirteen years; I say 'held the Purple', for it is scarcely true that he reigned. He had to look on while the Praetorians murdered his Praetorian Praefect, the famous Ulpianus; nor did he dare to punish the murderers. Eventually he allowed the soldiers' pay to fall into arrears, and was himself murdered.

He was succeeded by Maximinus, the first man of barbarian birth to reign over the Romans. By this time the finances of the Republic were in such a desperate condition that he must confiscate all the temple endowments of the provincial cities to fill the military pay-chest. After three years he was murdered.

Now Gordianus rules, a boy as young as Elagabalus. In the east the Persians have displaced the Parthians, and their armies threaten Syria; on the Danube has appeared a new foe, the warlike nation of the Goths. There is still not enough money to pay the army.

But Eutychianus the Praetorian Praefect, the Augusta Maesa, the lady Mamea, and the Empress Faustina all died peacefully in their beds during the reign of Alexander Severus. So I suppose from their point of view the murder of Elagabalus was sound business.

My dear lord will never take his rightful place among the gods; indeed it is doubtful whether his shade is properly treated in the underworld that is the home of common mortals. With refined malice his murderers threw his body into the Tiber; it never received the ritual burial which is needful before the spirit can find rest. But even if demons surround him his beauty and charm will make them his servants.

HISTORICAL NOTE

Duratius is the only completely fictitious character in this story. It is assumed that he was born 12 June A.D. 182, and finished his Epilogue 12 June A.D. 242. During these sixty years the following Emperors were recognised in Rome, besides numerous pretenders in the provinces:

Commodus.

Pertinax.

Didius Julianus.

Septimius Severus.

Caracalla.

Macrinus.

Elagabalus.

Alexander Severus.

Maximinus.

Balbinus and Pupienus jointly.

Gordianus I and Gordianus II jointly.

Gordianus III, reigning in 242.

Of these Septimius Severus died in his bed. All the others were murdered by the soldiers, or killed in civil war.

All Orion/Phoenix titles are available at your local bookshop or from the following address:

Mail Order Department
Littlehampton Book Services
FREEPOST BR535
Worthing, West Sussex, BN13 3BR
telephone 01903 828503, *facsimile* 01903 828802
e-mail MailOrders@lbsltd.co.uk
(Please ensure that you include full postal address details)

Payment can be made either by credit/debit card (Visa, Mastercard, Access and Switch accepted) or by sending a £ Sterling cheque or postal order made payable to *Littlehampton Book Services*.
DO NOT SEND CASH OR CURRENCY

Please add the following to cover postage and packing

UK and BFPO:
£1.50 for the first book, and 50p for each additional book to a maximum of £3.50

Overseas and Eire:
£2.50 for the first book plus £1.00 for the second book and 50p for each additional book ordered

---

BLOCK CAPITALS PLEASE

name of cardholder ....

address of cardholder ....

....

....

....

postcode ....

delivery address
(*if different from cardholder*)

....

....

....

postcode ....

☐ I enclose my remittance for £ ....

☐ please debit my Mastercard/Visa/Access/Switch (delete as appropriate)

card number ☐☐☐☐☐☐☐☐☐☐☐☐☐☐☐☐☐☐

expiry date ☐☐☐☐   Switch issue no. ☐☐

signature ....

prices and availability are subject to change without notice